My Life as a Youtuber

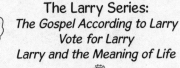

Praise for **My Life as a Book**:

* "Janet Tashjian, known for her young adult novels, offers a novel that's part *Diary of a Wimpy Kid*, part intriguing mystery.... Give this to kids who think they don't like reading. It might change their minds." —*Booklist*, starred review

Praise for **My Life as a Stuntboy**:

"Fans of the first will be utterly delighted by this sequel and anxious to see what Derek will turn up as next." —*The Bulletin*

Praise for **My Life as a Cartoonist**:

"This entertaining read leaves some provoking questions unanswered—usefully." —*Kirkus Reviews*

Praise for **My Life as a Joke**:

"At times laugh-out-loud funny ... its solid lesson, wrapped in high jinks, gives kids something to think about while they giggle." —*Booklist*

Praise for **My Life as a Gamer**:

"What did I think? I thought the book was wonderful." —Kam (from Goodreads)

Praise for **My Life as a Ninja**:

"Oh My God this book was so amazing!!!!!!!!!!!" —Caleb (from Goodreads)

Praise for **My Life as a Youtuber**:

"Perfect for the kids looking for other books like Wimpy Kid and Captain Underpants ... Your middle school library should have the whole series!" —Lisa (from Goodreads)

JANET TASHJIAN

My Life as a Youtuber

with cartoons by
JAKE TASHJIAN

SQUARE
FISH
Christy Ottaviano Books
Henry Holt and Company
New York

SQUARE
FISH

An imprint of Macmillan Publishing Group, LLC
120 Broadway, New York, NY 10271
mackids.com

Our books may be purchased in bulk for promotional,
educational, or business use. Please contact your local
bookseller or the Macmillan Corporate and Premium Sales
Department at (800) 221-7945 ext. 5442 or by email at
MacmillanSpecialMarkets@macmillan.com.

Library of Congress Control Number: 2017945044

ISBN 978-1-250-23367-7 (paperback)
ISBN 978-1-62779-893-8 (ebook)

Originally published in the United States by Christy
Ottaviano Books/Henry Holt and Company
First Square Fish edition, 2020
Book designed by Patrick Collins
Square Fish logo designed by Filomena Tuosto

10 9 8 7 6 5 4 3 2 1

AR: 5.5 / LEXILE: 870L

For Jessica Rose Felix

My Life as a Youtuber

BEST CLASS EVER

History. Language arts. Geography. Science.

To succeed in any of them, you have to be a pretty good reader—which unfortunately I'm not.

But our school is offering a new after-school elective this winter that doesn't require ANY reading. Plus, the subject is one of my absolute favorite things in the world.

elective

lottery

contain

YouTube!

Because every kid in school wanted to sign up, Mr. Demetri decided to have a lottery. I've never won a raffle in my life, so I was shocked when Ms. McCoddle posted the lucky few students who made the cut and Matt and I were on the list!

Umberto and Carly were on the waiting list—as if anyone's going to drop out of such an awesome elective. And when we find out the teacher is Tom Ennis—a local stand-up comic with his own popular YouTube channel—Matt and I can't contain our excitement. We race down the hallway screaming until Mr. Demetri tells us to knock it off.

"Tom Ennis is HILARIOUS," I tell Matt on our way to the cafeteria. "We're going to have a blast."

Our new teacher's YouTube channel is called LOL Illusions. He's gotten hundreds of thousands of subscribers by being a digital magician like Zach King. Every week he uploads a new video featuring an unbelievable trick. He's not a magician in the traditional sense; instead he's a wizard in post-production who edits his clips with special effects to make them look like magic.

In the 240 videos he's uploaded, he's turned a photo of a kitten into a real kitten in the palm of his hand, he's leaped into a speeding convertible without ever opening the door, he's jumped on his bed so hard he falls through and lands underneath it, and he's thrown a guitar into the dryer and shrank it into an ukulele.

ukulele

Tom's buddy Chris is usually in

the background too, texting on his phone and ignoring Tom as he pulls off these outrageous stunts. The joke is Chris never looks up quick enough to take a picture of the stunt and misses the magic trick every time. It's one of my favorite channels, one that I subscribed to immediately after watching Tom's first clip, where he "makes" dinner by reaching into a cookbook and pulling out a whole turkey.

"Stop rubbing it in," Umberto finally tells us. "I'd give anything to be in that class."

If I added up all the hours Matt, Carly, Umberto, and I have spent watching YouTube, the number would be bigger than all the hours we've logged at school since kindergarten, combined. (The total would be even larger if they'd let us use our phones during class.) But looking at YouTube from the point of view of a CREATOR versus a VIEWER is gigantic. The class starts tomorrow and I already know I'll be up all night, too excited to sleep.

gigantic

casserole

When I get home, Mom's in the kitchen putting a casserole in the oven. She must not have a full schedule at her veterinary practice today, because she's in her running clothes instead of her usual scrubs, which means she just got off her treadmill. I try to peek into the oven to see how many vegetables she's hiding in the casserole, but she closes the oven door and asks about my first day back at school after the holiday break.

I blurt out the news about the

ruckus

prehistoric

YouTube class with so much volume that Dad hurries downstairs.

"What's the ruckus?" he asks. "Are they giving out free puppies at school?"

"Even better." I repeat the story about my new class.

I'm not sure if it's to help celebrate or to show how cool he is, but Dad pulls his phone from his pocket and opens up his YouTube app. "This might be the funniest thing I've ever seen." He holds up the screen and plays a video of David coming back from the dentist. My father's laughing so hard I don't have the heart to tell him how prehistoric that clip is.

It's always hard to concentrate on my homework, but tonight it's especially difficult. Bodi curls underneath the kitchen table as I work, content to just sleep by my feet. Our capuchin, Frank, on the other hand, is jumping around so much, I begin to wonder if he can reach the coffee-pot from his crate.

We've been a foster family for Frank for almost two years, letting him acclimate to humans before going on to monkey college in Boston where he'll learn to help people with disabilities. Every time I think of Frank having to leave, I work myself into such a frenzy that one of my parents has to calm me down. Tonight I'm ALREADY in a frenzy, just thinking about how lucky I am to take part in tomorrow's elective.

acclimate

YouTube, here I come!

OUR VERY OWN
COMEDY NERD

When Mr. Owens monitored our comedy club elective last year, we looked at him as a necessary evil. With Tom Ennis, however, it's like having a rock star for a teacher. When the final bell rings, every other kid races out of school. But all twelve of us lucky students hurry into another classroom, eager to get started. Tom strolls in ten minutes

strolls

after school ends, wearing a GoPro camera with an elastic band around his head.

"Hey, kids, I hope you don't mind if I film our sessions."

Not only is he going to teach us—he's going to make us stars! We all sit a little taller in our seats, waiting for our close-ups.

"First of all," he begins, "I'm Tom. But Mr. Demitri INSISTS you guys call me Mr. Ennis, so we'll have to go with that."

He's wearing the skinniest jeans I've ever seen with a beat-up pair of Chuck Taylors. His hair is to his shoulders, with half of it pulled back in a small bun, held up by the band of his camera. His T-shirt is faded and says HAIRY MASTODON, which I'm guessing is a band. Given how

mastodon

larger-than-life he looks in his videos, I can't believe how normal he seems in person.

Mr. Ennis hands out sheets of paper for us to distribute. "These are release forms. If you don't sign them, you can't take the class."

distribute

I'm not sure what a release form is but I've watched enough TV to know you're not supposed to sign anything without reading it first. It hardly matters because there's no way I'm NOT taking this class. But leave it to Maria to raise her hand and ask Mr. Ennis to explain.

permission

"Signing a release means you give me permission to use video footage of you however I please," he answers.

Of COURSE I'm taking this class, but now I'm as confused as Maria is.

"So if I sign this," I ask, "you can take the footage you're shooting now, add a few filters, and turn me into an orangutan with bananas sticking out of my ears?"

orangutan

"If I want to, yes." Mr. Ennis takes out his cell and rapidly starts typing. "I'm writing that down. I love orangutans."

Matt turns and gives me a thumbs-up like I'm the class genius but I'm just secretly hoping our new teacher doesn't turn me into a cyber-primate for his own amusement.

primate

cross-legged

Mr. Ennis doesn't write on the whiteboard like a normal teacher. He's sitting cross-legged on the desk to face us instead. "The first thing you need to know about being a youtuber is that it's a full-time job, even when it's a part-time job. There are a million clips uploaded *every single minute of every single day*, and if you want your show to stand out, you need to be thinking about your show 24/7." He looks at us and grins. "So ... you think you're up for it?"

The answer from the class is a resounding YES.

"Good." He pulls a stick of gum out of his pocket. I get excited to see what kind of trick he might do with it, but he just shoves it into his mouth. It's still cool, and in all my years of school, I can't recall ever seeing a teacher chew gum in class.

recall

As Mr. Ennis continues to talk about "creative content," I catch myself focusing more on his headcam than his words. If Ms. McCoddle or any of my other teachers wore one of these, I'd be more distracted than usual and would NEVER retain anything they said.

We spend the rest of the class watching online videos, which is AMAZING. Mr. Ennis said he had to run clips by Mr. Demetri first to make sure they were appropriate to show in school so of course we beg him to show us the ones that Demetri didn't allow. I can tell that Mr. Ennis WANTS to show us but also wants to keep his job. Instead, he shows us a video of a girl instructing viewers how to blow-dry their hair like a movie star while her little brother pretends to be a zombie attacking her from behind.

instructing

"That's the mystery," he says. "Does the girl not know her brother's making fun of her or is she in on the joke and asked him to do it? There's no way for us to know—and that's half the fun."

I slowly turn to Matt, who's grinning as mischievously as I am. Neither of us needs to speak because we're both thinking the same thing:

We're starting our own YouTube channel!

EUREKA!

Even before Mr. Ennis's class, I was incubating ideas for a YouTube show.

incubating

"Don't get me wrong," Matt says as we grab a table in the cafeteria a few days later. "It sounds great, but having our own show is probably a ton of work."

"A lot of fun too. I'm with Derek on this." Umberto reaches across the table and gives me a fist bump.

practical

tutorial

macaroons

As usual, Carly is the most practical of the four of us. "I'm sure your teacher could point us to a good online tutorial. I think the four of us could create a GREAT YouTube channel." She offers us some macaroons from her bag. (Carly thankfully always brings enough dessert for all of us.)

I hate to bring up a sore spot while we're eating her food, but I ask Carly how the four of us are going to create a YouTube channel when Matt and I are the only ones taking the class.

She seems surprised; Umberto does too. "I just assumed since you guys were lucky enough to get in that you'd share the information with us."

Umberto then nods, looking as

expectant as Carly is. I turn to Matt, who plays with the cookie crumbs instead of helping me out.

expectant

"Of course we will," I finally answer. I reach for another cookie and wait for the awkward moment to pass. Matt finally jumps in.

"We could do a Let's Play channel," he says. "If that's not too complicated."

"You forget I've been taking computer classes for years," Umberto says. "I know how to do all KINDS of things, including an LP channel."

And just like that, lunchtime turns into a production meeting. Matt still thinks we should do a video game walk-through show, Umberto wants us to do challenges like eating handfuls of ground cinnamon until we choke (uh, no thanks), and Carly

cinnamon

possibilities

stipulation

snowboarding

thinks we should do epic sports fails. By the time lunch is over, we've come up with twenty-two possibilities for our new channel.

"There's one stipulation," Umberto tells Matt and me on our way to class. "You guys have GOT to stop talking about Mr. Ennis."

Umberto's right—Matt and I haven't shut up about our new teacher. We can't help it—we're on fire with new ideas.

Back in class, I'm a little freaked out by Ms. McCoddle's sunburn. I guess she went snowboarding at Big Bear this weekend so her face is red but the area around her eyes is white from wearing goggles. She keeps taking lotion from her purse to apply to her skin. Just looking at her makes me itchy.

When Matt and I had Ms.

McCoddle in kindergarten, we'd spend the first hour talking about what we did the night before. Now we barely sit down before Ms. McCoddle tells us to open our history books. "Today we begin the Industrial Revolution," Ms. McCoddle says.

industrial

It's cool hearing about one interesting invention after another, but my mind keeps drifting back to YouTube. What kind of screen name should we have? Will we get a lot of subscribers? What if we don't get any views?

invention

subscribers

Talking at lunch earlier, Carly didn't have to say it, but I knew what she was thinking. *Is this just another one of Derek's crazy ideas or will he have the follow-through to make it happen this time?* I can't say I blame her; it's something I wonder about too.

assembly

interchangeable

But as I half-listen to Ms. McCoddle discuss the assembly line, I get an idea. What if we ASSEMBLE something on our YouTube show? Not like a desk from IKEA but things that don't usually go together—like ham and marshmallows or chicken soup and Jell-O? Maybe Umberto's right and we should do a challenge channel.

Ms. McCoddle smiles when she finishes talking about Eli Whitney and interchangeable parts. "Derek, you're grinning from ear to ear—is all this talk of innovation making you happy?"

I mumble something about Eli Whitney being one of my favorite inventors of all time, but even as the words leave my mouth, all I can think about is making videos with my friends.

EXPERIMENT #1

Matt and Umberto don't need any convincing to come over after school to discuss our show. Carly's got an orthodontist appointment so she can't join us. That's actually good; we'll be able to get all our bad ideas out of the way while she's not here. Because Carly's worried that she'll have to get braces, I reassure her that everything will be fine, although I have absolutely no idea if she'll

orthodontist

refrain

need them or not. Matt tortures her by finding a website of people with terrible, gigantic braces, which almost makes Carly cry. In the end Matt feels bad, but not bad enough to refrain from sending a few of the pictures to her on Snapchat.

"Here's what I think we do," Matt says. He points to all the bottles and jars we've taken out of my refrigerator, now spread along the kitchen counter. "Let's find three of the most disgusting ingredients, mix them in the blender, then make ourselves drink it on camera."

"I still say eating handfuls of cinnamon and black pepper would be awesome." Umberto uses the deep voice he uses whenever he pretends he's an announcer at a monster-truck rally. "Master sneeze blast!"

I rub my hands together. "Time to mix up something vile."

vile

I take the cover off the blender and start dumping stuff in. Apple juice, maple syrup, canned clam chowder, a bagel, lettuce, and some blue cheese.

The three of us stare into the blender, looking down at the kaleidoscope of colors before turning it on. I take glasses out of the cabinet and divide the brownish mixture three ways.

kaleidoscope

"Whose idea was this, anyway?" Umberto asks.

"We should do this near the bathroom in case we have to puke," Matt adds.

We hold up our glasses in a mock toast then each take a sip before we gag. Only Matt finishes the drink and is declared the winner.

"I'm not sure if it's possible, but I think the bagel actually made it worse," I say.

"Not to mention the blue cheese," Matt adds with a belch.

"Um...Derek?" Umberto gestures to my phone set up on my dad's tripod. "Did you hit 'record'?"

tripod

We all look at the phone just sitting there.

"We're the worst youtubers ever," Matt says.

"So...take two?" I shrug as if this was all part of the original plan.

We obviously have a lot of work to do.

BUSTED

Matt, Umberto, and I spend more time disagreeing than agreeing on what to shoot, so I'm not surprised that we don't have anything even close to usable when I go through the footage. It might be easier to do a few practice runs on my own. Mom's Derek-might-be-getting-into-trouble antennae must alert her, however, because ten minutes after

usable

Weimaraner

my friends leave she enters the kitchen.

She's wearing her scrubs with the Weimaraner pattern and looking at the counter full of jars and bottles.

"I hate to ask, but feel I should," she begins.

I tell her my friends and I were trying to come up with an idea for a YouTube show. Mom can't take her eyes off the mess.

"I'm surprised Carly was in on this," Mom says.

I could tell her Carly wasn't here, but since my mother thinks Carly walks on water, I decide to leave out this piece of information.

Mom points to the phone perched on the tripod. "Were you recording this for posterity?"

posterity

I'm not really sure what that means, but it doesn't matter because we didn't record much of anything. I tell her what we were attempting to do but with no success.

She opens the fridge and tilts her head. After a moment, I realize she's waiting for me to start putting the food away.

"I think a challenge channel is a great idea," she says. "The techs in my office watch them on their phones all the time."

The last thing I want to do is create a show that PEOPLE WHO WORK WITH MY MOTHER watch. But on the other hand, that WOULD get me additional views.... I just let Mom babble as I continue inserting jars of condiments into the shelves on the refrigerator door.

inserting

"I bet a show about challenging yourself to be a better reader would really catch on," Mom continues.

I'm about to ask her if she's kidding but her slow smile tells me she is.

I've fought my parents on reading programs for years, finally coming up with one that works for me—drawing my vocabulary words in my sketchbooks to understand them better. I'm what's known as a visual learner, meaning I need to SEE things to learn them. I've done thousands of stick-figure drawings, which have definitely improved my reading skills. I know Mom well enough to realize she's not putting me down, just acknowledging all the hard work I've done since kindergarten.

acknowledging

Mom motions to the two jars in my hand. "Mustard or mayo? Paper or plastic? Truth or dare? Sometimes life just comes down to one thing or the other, right?"

Mom's semi-annoying observation gives me another idea. Instead of blending a ton of stuff together, what if my friends and I dare ourselves to complete challenges where BOTH options are disgusting? Would you rather have a booger sandwich or a dandruff shake? Would you rather go to school wearing your dad's pants or your mom's high heels? (Not that my mom wears high heels—she stands for many hours at work, so she usually wears clogs.)

disgusting

By the time the counter's cleared, I've thought of twenty revolting dares we can film immediately. I text my friends that it's time to make more videos.

revolting

With the camera on this time.

TAKE TWO

uploaded

Now that Mr. Ennis is our teacher, we watch every video on his channel a million more times. In the episode he uploaded yesterday, he plays Latin music to a tomato plant until it gives him a cup of salsa to eat with his chips.

Carly, Umberto, Matt, and I watch it several more times before we begin today's filming. Mr. Ennis's editing is so seamless, no matter how hard we look, we can't see any signs of his cuts.

seamless

"Are we ready to shoot?" Umberto asks. He's got two hours until his van driver, Bill, picks him up from my house.

Mom's relieved we're not recording anything food-related and gives us her consent to film anywhere in the house as long as we clean up. It seems like a fair deal, considering my friends and I are still unsure exactly what we'll be shooting.

consent

"I like the whole 'Would you rather have choice A or choice B?'" Carly says. "I just don't want the choices to be gross."

unsure

"They HAVE to be gross," Matt answers. "Otherwise what's the point?"

I agree and hold up the clipboard with the list I came up with.

"Would you rather wear your best friend's underwear or use their toothbrush?" I ask the group.

Carly scrunches up her face, clearly unhappy with the way this is going. "Clean or dirty underwear?" she finally asks.

Matt and Umberto look at her like she's crazy. "Dirty, of course," Umberto answers.

"That's easy," Matt continues. "Use your friend's toothbrush. I use my brother's when I can't find mine—doesn't bother me at all."

"Yeah, but does it bother HIM?" Umberto looks to me. "Underwear, inside out—done."

"Should we turn on the camera and try to catch some of this magic on film?" I ask.

"Nobody uses film anymore," Umberto says. "Even blockbuster movies are shot on digital now."

blockbuster

"I know that!" Yet another friend who's a zillion times smarter than I am. Carly opts out of the challenge and decides to record us instead. I've got my cell hooked up to Dad's tripod and after modifying the height, Carly tells us we're good to go.

modifying

"Three . . . . two . . . one . . . action!" she calls.

Matt, Umberto, and I stand there, unsure of where to start.

Finally, Matt nudges me and I talk into the camera. "Hello, everybody! Welcome to the WOULD YOU RATHER challenge with Derek, Matt, and Umberto. This is our first video and I'm really nervous!" Spittle actually comes out of my mouth as I talk.

spittle

forthright

apparently

Carly presses pause. "Should we try again?" she asks nicely.

Matt's a bit more forthright. "Derek, that was TERRIBLE! Are you trying to drown our viewers?"

"Then YOU go first," I answer. "We didn't even write anything down—I was winging it!"

"Should we make some cue cards?" Carly asks. "We can prop them up behind me on the couch so you can read them."

"I DON'T WANT TO READ CUE CARDS!" I shout at her. "I want to make a YOUTUBE VIDEO! IS THAT SO HARD?"

Carly picks up her bag and heads to the door. "Apparently, yes. See you at school."

I feel bad she's leaving, especially after our conversation this morning.

When I asked her at our lockers how it went at the orthodontist, she told me she has to get braces. Carly's one of the smartest, most fearless kids I know but she actually looked scared when we discussed it. Maybe I should've been a little nicer to her today.

fearless

I try to catch up with Carly but the only person in the driveway is Umberto's driver with the van.

Bill, Matt, and I help Umberto down the stairs in his wheelchair. Last time Umberto was here, Mom suggested getting a ramp that matches the one on the other side of the driveway for her patients. In all the times and different places Matt and I have lifted Umberto in his wheelchair, we've never dropped him. But I can't say I don't worry about it every time.

I go upstairs and drag Bodi out from his favorite spot—underneath my bed. Frank's in Mom's office, so Matt and I give up on our video and walk over to get him.

Nothing takes the edge off failure like hanging out with your pets.

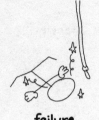

failure

A CHANGE FOR CARLY

Lots of kids in our class have braces; it's not like getting them is a big deal. But Carly must be especially sensitive to having a doctor poke around in her mouth because she's in full anxiety mode today.

sensitive

"The orthodontist says the first month might be painful." Carly looks ready to start crying outside science class.

anxiety

"It'll probably only hurt for a few weeks," I say. "Think of all the ice cream you'll be able to eat before you can chew again."

My comment obviously makes things worse because a tear forms in the corner of her eye.

"You're tough," I tell her. "Nothing ever gets you down!" I have to admit I'm a little surprised at how difficult this is for her.

confesses

"I'm a baby when it comes to pain," she confesses. "Getting braces is all I can think about now."

anguish

My first thought is that maybe Carly will be so distracted by her braces that she won't be able to do her homework and I can get a higher grade than her—for once. But even I know taking advantage of Carly's anguish isn't what a real friend would do.

"It'll be like lots of things," I tell her. "It'll stink in the beginning but then you'll get used to it and it won't stink so much."

She smiles at my weak attempt at explaining how the world works and the tear in her eye doesn't fall down her cheek.

"You'll still be pretty," I say. "Even with all that barbed wire in your mouth."

Turns out that tear was ready to trickle down after all.

I apologize ten times but Carly ducks into the girls' room, successfully avoiding me to go cry.

I can be such a moron sometimes.

apologize

avoiding

A SURPRISE

nosedive

The rest of the day isn't much better. I barely pass my English lit test, and Mr. Demetri took a nosedive into a mud puddle outside the gym and I missed it. (Matt DID get to see it and fell over laughing.)

YouTube class to the rescue! Not counting recess when I was little, I can't remember the last time I raced to anything at school.

"Welcome, welcome, welcome!" Mr. Ennis opens his arms wide like a ringmaster at a circus. I'm guessing he feels especially happy because the video of him making salsa already has a hundred thousand views.

ringmaster

I take my seat and notice the two empty spots where the Johnson twins usually sit.

"Melanie and Melissa won't be able to join us for the rest of the course," Mr. Ennis says. "I guess their dad's a bigwig in the computer industry and just got transferred to Palo Alto. Too bad—I thought they had a lot of potential."

bigwig

I stare at the empty desks. Two students on the class waiting list are going to be THRILLED. Matt and I nearly jump out of our own desks when Umberto and Carly enter the room.

"No way!" I shout.

Mr. Ennis just laughs; it's fun having a teacher who doesn't care when you yell.

When I last saw Carly she was crying, but now she's grinning ear to ear.

"Why didn't you tell me you got in?" I ask.

She shrugs like it's no big deal, when actually it's a gigantic deal. "I wanted to surprise you." Carly takes the seat closest to me.

grudge

I may have upset her a few hours ago, but one good thing about Carly—she never holds a grudge. With her and Umberto here, this class just went from amazing to off the charts!

"Today, we'll be laying the foundation for our own channels, so get out your phone or your notebook—however you take notes—and let's begin."

foundation

I pull out my sketchbook filled with hundreds of stick figures as well as notes for most of my classes.

"There are lots of steps you have to take to set up your own YouTube channel and the first thing you each have to do is come up with an original username," Mr. Ennis says. "There are millions of people already on YouTube so a lot of names have been taken."

When Matt pulls his desk over to mine, Mr. Ennis looks confused, then nods. "Everyone in this class is going to create their OWN channel. You may team up for projects in other classes but in this class, you'll be working alone."

Matt, Umberto, Carly, and I whip around to face each other. We've already put in so much work together!

Matt raises his hand. "How about if we WANT to work with someone else?"

Mr. Ennis laughs. "When I was your age, I hated working in pairs and groups. I was such a nerd, I always ended up doing all the work. Consider it a gift that you get to do your own thing."

harrumphs

setback

Matt harrumphs as he drags his desk back. Working alone is a definite setback but part of me is relieved. Some of Matt's ideas for our YouTube channel were good, but a few of them were definitely NOT my first choice. Bobbing for bologna instead of apples? Or challenging Bodi to a farting contest? Maybe getting to work by ourselves in this class will end up being okay after all. (Not that I tell the others; I put on a show and act as disappointed as they are.)

We all work on our own while Mr. Ennis scrolls through his phone, probably checking how many new views he has. Will any of us find the same kind of YouTube success he's found?

scrolls

I'm usually not much in the planning department—DUH!—but I've been giving my username a lot of thought.

"Okay," Mr. Ennis says. "Who wants to share?"

Matt's hand shoots up. "The UltiMATT Challenger!"

Mr. Ennis types into his phone so fast, it's like his fingers are caffeinated. "Already taken," Mr. Ennis answers.

"Super Girl," Carly volunteers.

"That's taken too."

Since there are a zillion people on YouTube, choosing an available username is harder than we thought. Half the class has to come up with different names.

"What about you, Derek?" Mr. Ennis asks.

slump

I slump in my seat, now unsure of what I've come up with. "Derek's Corner?"

"You asking me or telling me?" Mr. Ennis asks.

"Telling?"

Mr. Ennis laughs. "It's maybe a little—"

"Infantile?" Carly asks.

The rest of the class laughs and Carly shoots me a smile. I was worried the title might be a bit too *Sesame Street* and Carly just confirmed it. She's also doing something else—getting me back for making her cry this morning. Touché.

infantile

touché

Mr. Ennis takes a giant pack of stapled papers from his bag and starts to hand them out. "I planned to send you a PDF to save paper but your principal wanted me to hand out physical copies of what we'll be doing here too."

stapled

Tyler turns around in his seat to give me a handout as thick as that thing they used to call a telephone book.

"Turn to page one," Mr. Ennis says.

Everybody follows his instructions, but you can tell a few of us are puzzled because this is now beginning to sound like every other class in school.

"Before we get into what you guys will be doing on YouTube, we have to go over the things you *can't* do on YouTube."

I look down at the full-page list of restrictions.

restrictions

"It even goes onto the back?" Umberto asks.

Mr. Ennis nods. "Everything you make here has to be one-hundred-percent original, G-rated, and approved by your parents before it goes online."

Gulp. I wasn't expecting so many rules.

"YouTube does not play around

with material under copyright."
Mr. Ennis continues. "If you use a
popular song or clip from a movie or
TV show without permission, not
only will YouTube take it down, I'll
remove you from class."

copyright

Suddenly I'm nervous. "How can
anyone be creative with this much
structure?"

structure

Mr. Ennis takes a seat on his
desk. "You'd be surprised what you
can come up with. All the videos on
my channel obey the same guide-
lines I'm giving you. I also want to
make sure your expectations are
reasonable—I don't want anyone
thinking they're going to end up
an Internet sensation just because
they're taking an after-school class
in making YouTube videos."

I hate to pop Mr. Ennis's bubble,

pitfalls

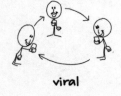

viral

but every single kid sitting here thinks just that!

For the next half hour, he talks about the pitfalls he and his friends faced when they first started on YouTube. "We had sports channels, epic-fail channels, LP channels, fake-instructional channels—believe me, we tried EVERYTHING. I hate to say it, but there's a huge amount of LUCK involved. I know people who work their butts off, putting out quality content, and they've never gotten any recognition, and friends who shoot something in two seconds that ends up going viral. There is absolutely no way to know."

Shouldn't Mr. Ennis be giving us a pep talk instead of telling us what a downer YouTube can be?

He then goes into what he

expects from us in this class. We have to work on the layout of our channel—complete with banners and a logo—set up playlists of our videos, create a short trailer for our homepage, get a custom URL, schedule our uploads—not to mention creating tons of original content.

layout

It sounds incredibly exciting but I don't know how I'm going to have time to eat or walk Bodi, never mind keep up with my other classes. I guess that's the price you pay for fame.

"Then there are your viewers," Mr. Ennis continues. "You need to turn viewers into..."

He waits for someone to respond, and we all us do.

"Subscribers," we announce.

"That's the name of the game!"

he says. "You need to engage with your viewers, answer their comments, maybe do a blog or newsletter, promote your channel on social media, share your videos outside of YouTube, study your analytics—in short, optimize your channel any way you can."

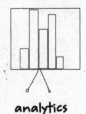

analytics

In SHORT? That sounds like *in long* to me.

optimize

"By next Friday everyone has to send me a basic outline of their channel, along with the rest of the details we talked about."

We all mumble, "Yes," and gather up our things.

"I can't believe how thick this handout is," I complain as we head to our lockers. "Even Ms. Miller doesn't give out this much work."

"We're making our own YouTube

channels," Umberto says. "Who cares how much work it is?"

Suddenly Matt starts laughing. The rest of us want to hear what's so funny.

"Derek's Corner?" Matt laughs. "Really? Sounds like story time at the library. You've got a LOT of work to do, my friend."

Back to square one—a place I'm pretty familiar with by now.

QUESTIONS, QUESTIONS

2000 EPISODES LATER

binge-watching

Mom is in the living room binge-watching a show on Netflix. She hits pause when she sees me.

"We need to schedule a call with Mary Granville from Helping Hands," Mom says. "Like it or not, we have to talk about giving back Frank."

She doesn't hit play, just waits for me to answer. I want to have a conversation about giving up Frank like I want to puncture my eardrum.

puncture

"Now?" I finally ask. "You're in the middle of a show."

"This can wait."

I pull out something I know she'll buy. "I have to do my homework."

She smiles. "Glad to see you're prioritizing," she says. "If it's not too late, we'll call her when you're done."

prioritizing

I stomp upstairs. I don't want to do homework. I don't want to talk to that lady. And most important, I don't want to give up Frank.

I take refuge with Bodi on my bed. Frank is a lot of fun but when it comes to comfort, there's nothing like lying next to your dog. My reverie is disturbed by texts from Matt, Umberto, and Carly all working on their YouTube assignments.

refuge

A message from Carly comes in. *Maybe we're just not cut out for YouTube.*

Umberto responds. *Oh, like a cat playing piano is? Or a rat carrying pizza? If ANIMALS can star in hit videos then we can too.*

Umberto's idea is GREAT. He's calling his channel Roll a Mile in My Shoes. It's a vlog where viewers will follow Umberto around while he goes to the store, to the beach, to the doctors. To people who can walk, that might seem like an ordinary itinerary but when you're in a wheelchair, there are lots of obstacles to overcome. Wearing a GoPro, Umberto will act as a tour guide for the viewer to see what it feels like to be in a wheelchair. Talk about virtual reality! We text Umberto our approvals.

Matt is torn between doing pranks or comedy skits. For once, Carly can't decide what to do, going back and

vlog

MONDAY- PARIS
TUESDAY- LONDON

itinerary

forth between an unboxing show or a news channel. Usually she's the first one with a game plan but given the limitless possibilities she's surprisingly stuck. But who am I to talk— I am too.

unboxing

I shove my phone into my pocket and bury my face in Bodi's fur. Instantly, my muscles relax.

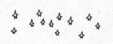

I don't know what I'd do without Bodi and Frank.

limitless

Hey ... wait a minute! BODI AND FRANK. Most of the popular videos on YouTube feature ANIMALS.

I'm going to make Bodi and Frank YouTube stars!

A NEW DIRECTION

badger

gold mine

Kittens, puppies, hamsters, an angry badger... they've all had millions of views. I've got a dog and a MONKEY—not to mention the thousands of other animals that go in and out of my mom's veterinary practice every year.

I'm sitting on a gold mine!

Matt goes nutty when he comes over that weekend.

"Your mom's a vet!" he says. "You can showcase a different animal every day. Does your mom have any sick hyenas? 'Cuz that would be AWESOME."

My mom, of course, would never in a billion years let me put any of her animal patients in my videos. I hate the thought of sneaking around her but we're talking about a future career here! Matt and I spend the next hour dunking chips into artichoke dip and brainstorming what kinds of videos I can shoot with Bodi and Frank.

artichoke

I've had Bodi since I was a toddler and he was a pup. He certainly is cute for a mutt. Frank, however, is a semi-trained capuchin who's very photogenic. Bodi is gentle and friendly; Frank is a downright ham.

photogenic

uncommon

Monkeys are a little more unpre-dictable than dogs, but they're also a lot funnier and uncommon too.

"How about if I record my voice and drop the audio in behind footage of Frank sitting at the table?" I ask. "It'll be like Frank is reading the news."

Matt shakes his head. "You have a MONKEY! Why do you want to put him at a table reading? He should be skateboarding or jumping off the roof!"

Matt and I have had the Frank-skateboarding discussion a million times. My mom would ground me for the rest of my life if she knew how many times Matt and I wanted to skateboard with my capuchin.

"Skateboarding's a no-go," I say. "But how about if we SHAVE him? A bald monkey would be hilarious."

"I thought the point was that your

mom DIDN'T find out," Matt says. "It would be fun to dye him with food coloring too but you'd still have the same problem."

Mom and I have talked about how people sometimes "paint" their pets with polka dots or stripes using paint that's not toxic, but Mom's not a fan of using an animal as an easel. Pet shaving and painting are definitely out.

toxic

"How about if he smashes stuff?" I suggest. "He can wear safety goggles and a lab coat and break things with a hammer? Then we play the video back in slow motion?"

"I'd DEFINITELY watch that," Matt answers. "Especially if he's smashing something messy."

"Like food?" I grab several handfuls of grapes from the bowl on the counter.

pulp

squashed

It takes Matt and me less than a minute to turn the fruit into a pile of green and red pulp.

"And that's just with our fists," Matt says. "Imagine what we could do with a mallet."

I scoop up the squashed grapes from the counter and throw them into the sink. "Wait—who's smashing things in the video? Me or Frank?"

Matt stops cleaning up and thinks. "Don't get me wrong—I'd love to watch you smash things. But you'd probably get more views with Frank, right?"

As much as I'd like to be the one on camera getting all the attention and having all the fun, a video with Frank would definitely get more views.

Looks like it's showtime for my capuchin.

BATHROOM BREAK

My dad's been traveling a lot for work so it's fun to have him home this week. He's a storyboard artist in the movie industry and he's been on location in Toronto for a film about a superhero acrobat. As he takes the lasagna out of the oven, he tells us stories about the shoot.

acrobat

"There was a lot of tomfoolery on the set. The director had her hands full." Dad puts the lasagna on the

tomfoolery

counter to cool. Judging by the amount of steam coming out of it, we'll be eating dinner at midnight.

While we wait, we Skype Grammy in Boston. Mom likes to talk to her once a week and I do too. But Grammy's hearing is starting to go, so the conversation ends up with the three of us in California screaming into a laptop to someone three thousand miles away. Grammy shares her plans for a luxury vacation she's taking with two of her friends. I'm happy for her but in a while find myself staring at the lasagna and wondering if I'm going to have time to film Frank.

After we eat, I race to clean up the table then take Frank out of his crate. I'm hoping that Skyping Grammy doesn't make Mom realize

luxury

that we still haven't scheduled that call with the woman from Frank's foundation. I clip Frank into his harness and take him upstairs.

harness

I gave a lot of thought to the smashing idea but eventually decided against it. Number one, I don't feel like cleaning up the mess every time I make a new video for my channel. Number two, it'll be pretty hard to hide the fact that I'm using Frank in my videos with all that smashing. In the end, I chose a much simpler idea: MONKEY IN A BATHTUB.

Sure, lots of other youtubers jump into bathtubs of Silly String, jelly, paint, slime, shaving cream—anything messy—but on my channel, a MONKEY's going to do it!

I prop my cell on the counter and crank up the music so my parents

extraordinary

can't hear what I'm up to. But given my mom's an alien from another planet with extraordinary antennae for trouble, she's immediately at the door.

"Are you taking a bath?" she asks. "Without being asked?"

I tell her I'm sweaty from PE and making myself sick with the smell.

"That's a first," she says. "I hope you're not thinking about taking Frank in the tub with you."

Is there anything mothers DON'T know? I tell her I'm not taking a bath with Frank, which is technically true because I don't plan on being in the tub with him. I wait for her to leave then undo Frank's harness and continue with my plan.

While I empty every bottle of Mom's bath stuff into the water,

Frank burrows into the dirty laundry in the hamper. I let him play for a bit while I finish setting up my phone.

burrows

When I'm ready, I scoop up Frank and suspend him over the tub.

suspend

"This is going to be fun," I say. "You LOVE to swim."

It's true that Frank usually loves the water but maybe because this is full of bubbles and smells like a forest, he's not sold on the idea. He gnashes his teeth the way he does when he's threatened or afraid.

gnashes

You don't need a mom who's a veterinarian to figure out submerging a capuchin into a bubble bath probably isn't the smartest of plans, but having stupid ideas has never stopped me before.

submerging

"Come on, Frank—the water's

fine!" I check the camera to make sure it's filming.

"You better not be up to any monkey business in there," my mother calls from the hall. "No pun intended."

I roll my eyes and let Frank scramble up my arm and onto my shoulder. If I'm going to make Frank a YouTube star, I'm going to have to film when my parents aren't home. I pull the plug on the tub and the water starts to drain. Luckily for me, tomorrow is Thursday Night, Date Night.

I'll just have to convince the babysitter that I ALWAYS film my monkey doing crazy stuff on Thursday nights.

SOMETHING NEW

Even Matt thinks my new plan is impractical—and that's saying something.

"There's no way that can work— especially if Brianna's at your house," he says.

impractical

Matt doesn't need to remind me of the time we told my babysitter we baked her a cake, when what we really did was pack several sponges into a pan and spread them with frosting to make it LOOK like a cake. Brianna was NOT happy when she took a bite of our chocolate surprise. (My parents weren't too happy when they found out either.)

"You can film Frank at my house while your parents are out," Matt suggests. "Tell them you're sleeping over."

I shake my head. "Number one, it's a school night and they won't let me. Number two, Frank wasn't too happy about taking a dip."

polished

Matt holds out his phone and shows me the footage he shot last night for his new LP show. It looks polished, with his face in the corner of the screen, commenting on Steve's movements in his Minecraft video.

"It's not original, but I had fun," he says. "I'm still looking at other ideas too."

As Matt debates various options, I watch Carly approach us from the other end of the hall. Something's different about her, but I can't tell what it is. Then it hits me; Carly ALWAYS smiles—at pretty much everyone. Now her lips are pursed and her eyes are looking downward, which can only mean one thing.

pursed

She got her braces.

Before I can tell Matt not to joke around, Carly comes over.

"Don't say a word," she says. "My teeth really hurt and I'm not in the mood for wisecracks."

Matt smirks and starts to open his mouth until he sees the look on

Carly's face, which is so intimidating he immediately shuts it.

She turns to me and slowly opens her mouth, exposing more metal and rubber bands than I've seen in one place, outside of the vintage Erector set Grammy gave me several years ago. I COULD make a joke; however, Carly looks so awful, I don't have the heart.

vintage

"I'm sorry it hurts so much," I say. "The pain should go away soon, right?"

Carly shrugs. "One of my teeth is impacted, so it might be uncomfortable for a while."

impacted

"I wonder how those braces will photograph on your new YouTube channel?" Matt asks.

Carly looks like she's about to shove Matt into his locker. Instead she takes the high road and just leaves.

"That was mean," I tell him. "Why make her feel worse than she already does?"

"She's always so perfect," Matt answers. "It's about time she has something we can make fun of."

When we get to math, Carly's seat is still empty. She finally comes in just as the bell rings and I can tell she's been crying again. I shoot Matt a look to make sure he doesn't make fun of her anymore.

Even if Carly WEREN'T one of our best friends, it's not cool to hit someone when they're down.

SKETCHING WITH DAD

It's a good thing I hadn't planned on shooting my video while my parents were on their weekly date because one of Mom's longtime patients—a dog named Kitty—just got hit by a car and Mom is operating to save his life. Dad understands and they postpone their date a week to celebrate an early Valentine's Day. Now Dad's making us breakfast for

postpone

dinner and helping me with my homework.

"Remember when you'd only eat pancakes when they had Mickey Mouse ears?" he asks.

"Yeah, when I was two," I answer.

"You have a selective memory," he laughs. "I hate to tell you, but you demanded mousey-cakes until you were in third grade."

demanded

"I did not!" I can't help but laugh when he slides two mousey-cakes onto my plate. I'd never admit it in a thousand years, but pancakes DO taste better this way.

When my math worksheet is done, Dad asks about the YouTube class. I tell him I'm still not sure what I'm going to do for my channel. I DON'T tell him I was having a problem on set with my actor.

"Your mother and I were convinced you were trying to film Frank last night," he says. "You realize that wouldn't be a good idea, right? He's not a performer for your amusement."

I try and tell him I would NEVER do that, but Dad's not buying it. I finally give up and tell him I'm stuck.

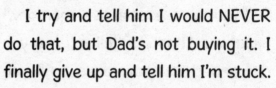

unscripted

"Some of those YouTube channels are spontaneous and unscripted," he says. "But some are very planned out. You might want to think about storyboarding your show first."

I smile because Dad thinks storyboarding is the answer to EVERYTHING. Over the years he's tried to get me to storyboard my homework, presentations, even Mom's surprise party. I don't mind drawing all my vocabulary words, but now I'm supposed to illustrate my YouTube show as well?

"Just something to consider," he says. "You're a lot like me and I always think better with a pencil in my hand." As if to demonstrate, he grabs his sketchbook off the counter and starts drawing.

demonstrate

I love watching my dad sketch; he's lightning-fast, and even with a rough draft, you can always tell who or what he's drawing.

He holds up a drawing of me with a mouthful of pancakes.

"I'll give it a try," I say. At this point I'll take all the help I can get.

I spend the next hour sketching alongside my dad, which is my definition of a pretty great night. We talk about the movie set he's been on and his friend Doug who runs a prop company and just celebrated his fiftieth birthday. It's great to talk about Dad's life for a change instead of dissecting mine all the time.

When Mom comes in later, we both can tell by the look on her face that the surgery didn't end well.

Dad gets up from the table and gives her a hug. "You tried your best," he says.

mourning

She nods in agreement but I can tell she's mourning the loss of her patient. Dad pours them two cups of tea from the kettle while Mom sits beside me to look through my drawings.

kettle

She points to one of the pictures. "You didn't tell me Carly got braces!"

Until my mom said that, I hadn't even realized I'd been drawing pictures of Carly.

BRING IN THE
PROPS

Dad's storyboarding technique actually helped a lot. After all these years, you'd think I'd realize the best way for me not only to learn something, but to THINK about it, is with a pencil in hand. Illustrating thoughts for my new YouTube channel thrust me into a whole new level of ideas. (I won't use the pheasant jumping out of a helicopter—even if it did make

thrust

pheasant

me laugh out loud while I was drawing it.)

I've been spending 99 percent of
my time thinking about Mr. Ennis's
class, but I still have my other classes
to worry about. (Not that I ever
really WORRY about any of them.)
I finish my assignment for science,
then blast through my math problems as fast as I can. After an hour,
I'm finally ready to tackle my YouTube
work.

established

We're almost three weeks into
the curriculum and I still haven't
established what I'm doing for my
channel. I decide to do some research,
which basically means watching
videos.

I check out challenge videos,
instructional videos, prank videos, DIY
videos, educational videos, and lots

of wannabe rappers. Nine o'clock. Ten o'clock. Eleven. Twelve. Mom checks on me and I pretend to be asleep, but as soon as she closes the door, I dive back under the covers with my phone to watch another clip.

The next day at breakfast I'm so exhausted, I can barely keep my head off the table. (Mom's made her mixture of nuts, oats, and dates that she thinks Dad and I like but we just tolerate.)

mixture

The good news is, I know what I'm going to do for my show. IF Dad will help me.

"Remember when you told me about your friend who runs the prop company?" I ask.

"Of course I remember—it was last night."

I don't tell him that I watched so

many videos between then and now that it seems like a century has passed. "Do you think he'd let me borrow a few props to use on my YouTube channel?"

Dad takes a sip of coffee and thinks for a moment. "They're shooting a big Western now so you couldn't have those. But I'm sure Doug could lend you some props that weren't being used."

If I had more energy, I'd jump out of my seat. After my talk with Dad last night, I realized that as much as I'd like to use Frank in my videos, I'd be in for a heap of trouble if I did. If I have to star in my own show, having killer props will definitely set me apart from the crowd.

"BUT," Dad continues, "movie props are costly—you'd have to treat

costly

them with the utmost care. I'm seeing Doug tomorrow—you want to come?"

I thank Dad profusely then shove my books into my pack and grab a lift to school.

Hopefully some movie magic will rub off one of those props and onto me.

SO MUCH STUFF

fraternity

divorce

On Saturday, Dad takes me with him to meet Doug who has all the props. He and my dad have been friends since college, where they were both members of the same fraternity. Doug's been married three times and is going through another divorce, so Dad warned me not to ask Doug any personal questions—as if I was going to. All I want is to get my hands on some cool movie props.

When we get there, Doug's examining a shipment of the most lifelike skulls I've ever seen.

shipment

"That's because they're REAL." Doug takes one of the skulls from the top of the box and hands it to me.

"Just because we're in the movie business doesn't mean we don't use the genuine article when we can get it," Doug continues.

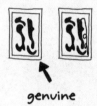

genuine

I've dissected frogs in Ms. Miller's class before but this is the first time I've held someone else's head. I hadn't planned on today being so hands-on—literally!

"Don't get any ideas for your video." Dad points to the label on the box. "Those are from a museum."

I carefully hand the skull back to Doug.

"From what your dad told me, you're not really sure what you're looking for. Why don't you stroll through the aisles and see if anything inspires you?"

It's an offer no kid could refuse. We're still at Doug's desk but already I can see rows of aliens, costumes, toys, bikes—it's like someone's garage, overflowing with a million things to rummage through. My mom LOVES yard sales; if this stuff was for sale, she certainly would've come with us instead of running errands.

errands

Doug asks me if I want some water or juice but I can't wait to start poring through these shelves. He gives me a giant cart—even bigger than the ones at Home Depot—and tells me that Jerry, one of his interns, will accompany me. Jerry barely looks up from texting but I don't complain, because I know that even with a chaperone, this is a tremendous opportunity.

chaperone

I'm not interested in any of the dishes or glassware but I'm impressed with how they've sorted everything by color, size, and shape. Every object is neatly labeled; now I understand why so many people work here.

I don't really care about the aisles and aisles of clothes either but the hats are a different story. Rows and rows of bowlers, fedoras, army helmets, aviator hats—I wish I'd known about this place back when I used to run around in costumes all the time.

fedoras

I take a turban off the shelf and ask Jerry if it's okay to try it on.

Jerry barely looks up as he nods.

I can't find a mirror so I use a nearby medieval helmet to see my reflection. Maybe I can tell fortunes on my YouTube channel!

"You're not thinking about dressing up like a fortune-teller, are you?" Jerry asks. "It's been done a thousand times."

I tell him OF COURSE I wasn't thinking of that and place the turban back on the shelf. Why does this guy have to be so negative?

Dad and Doug catch up to me in the room with all the nautical props. (After the intern's comment on my fortune-teller idea, I don't even THINK about doing a submarine show.)

nautical

"You need some help brainstorm-ing?" Dad asks. "This place can be a little overwhelming."

I assure him that I can definitely come up with something on my own.

Dad points to his wrist where his watch used to be even though he uses his phone to tell time now. "You've got another half hour," he says. "After that, we let these good people get back to work."

snobbish

I'm not sure if this snobbish intern falls into the "good people" category, but I realize Doug is helping us and I don't want to take advantage of the favor. I tell Dad I'll meet him at Doug's office soon.

As I wheel my empty cart into the next aisle, I can't help but let out a yell. Jerry looks up from his phone and nods.

taxidermy

interviewing

"The taxidermy section always freaks people out," he says. "Especially the lion. We call him Walter."

I reach out to touch the gigantic creature. Of course, I know it's not alive but the creature is posed like it's ready to pounce and it takes a few moments for me to adjust.

"I think Walter might be too big for your school project," Jerry says. "Although it would make for a funny talk show interviewing a lion sitting on a couch in a TV studio."

Number one, it's more than a "school project." Number two, please stop coming up with ideas for MY YouTube channel. Number three, I am not going through rooms and rooms of props so I can have a stupid TALK SHOW! I don't share any of this with Jerry, just focus on all the animals, one more realistic than the next. (I compare the stuffed pheasant to the one I drew jumping out of a helicopter recently. My version was pretty good, if I do say so myself.) I also take a million pictures, which I immediately post to Instagram and Snapchat.

Believe it or not, something more impressive than the lion makes me grind the cart to a halt. A petite woman is carrying a humongous set of barbells, tossing them around like they weigh as much as a feather duster.

humongous

bodybuilder

"Is she a famous bodybuilder or something?" I ask Jerry.

Jerry looks up from his phone. "Sophia? She can barely open a jar. Those are fake weights."

Jerry must be getting bored with babysitting me because he shoves

lightweight

his phone in his pocket and leads me over to the shelf.

"Everything here is made to look heavy but is really lightweight—the barbells, the medicine balls, the beer kegs, even the rocks. They use these in movies all the time."

Before he finishes talking, I'm loading items onto the cart. I can lift a boulder over my head! I throw an anvil into the air—and catch it! If Doug lets me borrow all this stuff, I'm going to have the best show on YouTube; there are so many ways I'll be able to use these!

The cart is really full. It takes me a while to maneuver it to the front of the warehouse. Doug nods in approval when he sees my choices.

"Ahhh, the magic of moviemaking." He picks up a giant boulder and hoists it over his head. "You should have some fun with these."

While Jerry makes a precise list of every item I'm taking, Dad makes his own list—of how I have to be 100 percent responsible for each prop, how each of them would cost a lot of money to replace, how Doug is doing me a favor, blah blah blah. It's usually the kind of speech I tune out but because I'm so eager to start making content, I listen and agree to everything Dad says.

On the way home, he continues in suggestion mode by recommending that I storyboard the show before I start shooting. This time, I don't even pretend to listen because I'm thinking about setting up my camera the second we arrive.

precise

responsible

PRE-PRODUCTION

fiddling

placement

It takes a lot of fiddling around but after several tries, I finally figure out the best placement of the camera. Then I dig out a fake mustache from the Halloween box in the garage and slick my hair back to create the look for my new on-screen weight lifter— THE TANK. The joke is that in real life, I'm a skinny kid with barely any muscles, but with these fake weights it'll look like I'm lifting three hundred pounds. I test out a few different accents but decide to just use a lower version of my regular voice. A gray hooded sweatshirt, gym shorts, and sneakers round out my character's outfit. As I rehearse in my room, Bodi's not sure what's going on and eventually crawls underneath my bed to get away from all the action.

rehearse

The beige walls of my room make a boring background so I ask Mom if there are any old bedsheets I can paint to make a backdrop. She rummages through the hall closet and gives me a sheet from when I was little, covered with clouds and turtles. When I tell her I need a plain sheet, she finds a peach one for me to use. Peach isn't the ideal color for a bodybuilder but when you're scrounging for props, you can't be

backdrop

scrounging

fussy. She helps me hold the sheet up while I tape it to the wall to paint it.

"You need a drop cloth," she says, "so you don't get paint everywhere."

It takes a while to get the room ready and even longer to paint the words and background. I don't care if this is WAY more work than just talking into a webcam—I'm determined to have one of the best videos in class.

determined

Teachers and parents have always told me how creative and imaginative I am, however those qualities are unfortunately difficult to measure in school. I do well in a few subjects, but since so many of them involve reading, it's often hard for me to keep up with the rest of the pack. I can look at a globe and easily tell latitude from

latitude

longitude, yet seeing those words in a textbook is a different thing altogether. This YouTube class is a way for me to shine, so I take my time making sure everything is perfect.

longitude

After spending hours on pre-production (that's what they call it in the business) I'm ready to shoot. The actual filming takes less than an hour, but when you add it all up, this is much more time than I usually spend on homework. I'm relieved when I play back the video and laugh out loud at how ludicrous I seem. With some minor edits, I can tell by looking at the first pass that I've got a winner.

Even though I'm exhausted, I toss and turn all night, excited to show off my work tomorrow.

VIEWING PARTY

eclipse

demons

At school the next day, all Ms. Miller can talk about is the upcoming eclipse. I guess in ancient times, people used to freak out when the moon suddenly disappeared and thought demons were involved. She makes us write down what time it will occur so we can see it, but as soon as she says it's at 3:00 in the morning, I just move my pen across my notebook as if I'm writing it down but don't. There are plenty of things worth waking up for in the middle of the night, and watching the moon play hide-and-seek isn't one of them.

Umberto skids over to me in the hall. "Wait till you see my vlog," he says. "It came out GREAT."

I do a double take—Umberto's now sporting a GoPro camera on his head like Mr. Ennis. I wave to the camera and make a bunch of stupid faces until he tells me the camera's not on.

As we head to class, Umberto skids to another halt when we spot Mr. Ennis. His long blond hair is gone, leaving nothing but a shiny bald head—and his headband with a camera.

scalp

vanquished

SCRAM

unwelcome

He runs his hand over his scalp. "It was a spur-of-the-moment decision. I'm still getting used to it."

Umberto and I try not to stare; when Matt joins us, he bursts out laughing.

"You look like Lord Voldemort!" Matt says.

"Then prepare to be vanquished!" Mr. Ennis smiles before he goes inside but the look in his eyes tells me even though he's joking around, Matt's comment was an unwelcome one.

"You realize you just insulted the guy who's grading us," I remind him.

"My video's primo," Matt answers. "I could run him over with my skateboard and still get an A."

"Highly doubtful," Umberto says.

In the room, the class asks another

fifty questions about Mr. Ennis's hair before we finally get down to screening our videos.

Mr. Ennis had us upload our clips to his Dropbox so he's got them all cued up to project onto the screen. Carly sneaks in later, apologizing that she had to hand in an assignment for another class. Carly is the school queen of extra credit.

The first video we watch belongs to Dave. In it, he's sitting at his kitchen table reviewing a new Netflix show. His comments are actually interesting, but every other word is *ummm*, which gets kind of annoying. He goes on and on about how terrible the Netflix show is. Is it weird to say that his horrible review makes me want to watch it?

"Wow," Mr. Ennis says when the

scathing

clip is done. "That was one scathing review."

"The show stinks," Dave says.

Mr. Ennis asks Dave what else he plans to review and if he's going to concentrate on a specific genre.

"I just want to find the worst shows and trash them," Dave says.

"It's easy to be critical of others but more challenging to create original content," Mr. Ennis says. "Why not try to be more creative with your show?" Mr. Ennis points to the soda can and bag of chips in front of Dave in the video. "You trying to get some kind of product-placement deal?"

monetize

"I want to monetize everything I can," Dave answers.

Mr. Ennis laughs. "Only a small percentage of the millions of people on YouTube make any money. Believe me, I should know." He hits play on the next video, which is Matt's.

"Strap yourselves in for a wild ride," Matt says.

I wait for the video to GET wild, but it's pretty much Matt sitting at his laptop doing a run-through of an old Crash Bandicoot game.

run-through

Matt turns around to watch the glazed eyes of his audience. "Come on, guys," he says. "It's really hard to get to that level!"

glazed

I proudly cheer on-screen Matt as he clears another level in the game, although my fake enthusiasm can't hide the fact that Matt's content is the worst thing anyone can say about a YouTube channel—it's BORING.

Mr. Ennis is kind with his feedback, giving Matt tips on how to spice things up a bit.

"But it was good, right?" Matt asks.

Mr. Ennis rubs his head for the hundredth time. "Sure."

Matt slinks down in his chair. I hadn't anticipated such a tough crowd either.

The rest of the videos are a lot like the ones we already watch on YouTube. Abby did an instructional video on French-braiding your hair. Barry made a meme generator with animal backgrounds that was hilarious. Candace shows us her advice channel dealing with a new stepmother, but she's so nervous onscreen, she looks more like someone who NEEDS advice than someone who should give it.

generator

Umberto blows everyone away with his footage of trying to cross the street in his wheelchair when someone carelessly parked their car in front of the sidewalk ramp.

carelessly

Since being friends with Umberto, I've often put myself in his place as he maneuvers through the world, but I'm not sure the rest of the population thinks about all the obstacles someone with a physical disability has to go through every day. His video is a keeper for sure; Mr. Ennis even fist-bumps him before moving on.

population

I suddenly wonder if Mr. Ennis is taping our videos with the camera on his head as he's watching them. He wouldn't make a magic video out of our rough cuts, would he? Or edit them with boos and people throwing garbage at the screen? Between the bald head and the camera, he looks like an overgrown Minion and I decide not to worry about it.

Next up is Tyler, who's doing a YouTube Poop channel. His clip is a mash-up of *Gravity Falls*, old black-and-white vampire movies, and a gazelle getting torn apart by a lion to the sound of SpongeBob's famous laugh. It's random and gruesome and weird. Everyone loves it, especially Matt, who's a huge fan of YTP.

gazelle

gruesome

"Okay, Carly," Mr. Ennis says next. "Let's see what you've got."

Carly gives him a thumbs-up. She's been very secretive about her YouTube channel, sharing only that she decided to do a vlog.

secretive

Maybe I DO have a chance to be number one now.

When the clip begins, I'm surprised

at how simple the setting is. My banner and props make her no-effort
background look dull. Since Carly
usually decorates everything from
lunch bags to lockers, it's strange
she decided to go so plain.

"I just got braces," she says into
the camera. "And I HATE them."
She clenches her fists in frustration as she talks on-screen. "I am
CONSTANTLY running my tongue
over my teeth like there's some for-
eign object on them—because there
is! I can't believe I'm going to have
this contraption on my teeth for
almost two years!" She hurls herself
on her bed and throws a tantrum
like a little kid.

This is so stupid, I think. *Why are
you talking about your braces?*

But when I look over at my

clenches

classmates, they're leaning forward in their seats, laughing.

"That's how I feel with mine," Natalie says from the back of the room.

"Me too." Tyler gives a huge smile exposing his own metallic mouth.

Mr. Ennis has to pause the clip. "Okay, guys, let's wait until the end for comments."

caramels

Back on-screen, Carly continues. "I hate not being able to eat caramels! They're my favorite food in the world."

She starts fake crying and throws herself on the bed again. She looks as cute and smart as she does every day but I just don't get it—who's going to subscribe to THIS?

When the clip is finished, the

applause is greater than what the other videos got—even Umberto's, which was awesome.

Mr. Ennis turns to me. "You're up next, Derek."

I don't understand why I'm so nervous. I'm more scared now than I was in that play with Carly last year. I tell myself I worked hard and people are going to love it.

I hope.

WHO'S THE DUMBBELL NOW?

"Helllooooo, it's me: the strongest guy in the world. Stronger than John Cena! Stronger than the Rock! I am THE TANK!"

On-screen, I'm lifting a giant barbell over my head. In the classroom, I'm not paying attention to the video as much as studying the reaction of the class.

reaction

No one's laughing.

"You're probably wondering how I'm lifting something so heavy," I begin.

"No, I'm not," Tyler says.

Mr. Ennis puts his finger to his lips, motioning for us to be quiet. "Let the video speak for itself," he says.

motioning

Back on-screen I juggle three oversized bowling balls as I talk. When I turn to Matt, he gives me a thumbs-up. (He's always been amazed by my juggling skills.)

oversized

"Welcome to my new workout show: Bodybuilding with THE TANK. The first thing we're going to do is some stretching."

On-screen, I bend down to touch my toes.

stretching

"You should've totally added a farting sound there," Matt says.

critiquing

Everyone laughs, even Mr. Ennis. I can't believe my best friend is critiquing my video!

I'm about to respond but Mr. Ennis points to the screen, where I'm lifting an anvil over my head. I squint and struggle under the weight, which in reality is only a pound.

"You can do it," I tell my viewers. "Grab some weights and work out."

The class is quieter than after Mr. Demetri gives bad news on the PA system.

"Tune in next time for more exercises with THE TANK!"

Mr. Ennis pauses the clip then puts his hands over his head, as if gathering his thoughts.

Before he can say anything, I jump in. "It's an instructional video like you said we could do. But it's also funny." I turn to the rest of the class. "Don't you guys want to know how I lifted such heavy stuff?"

"They're props, right?" Carly asks. "Not real barbells."

"Yes, but they look like real anvils, bowling balls, and weights, don't they?"

Carly seems confused. "But they're not—or you wouldn't have been able to lift them over your head."

"That's why it's funny!" I turn to Matt and Umberto, hoping one of them will take my side.

"I thought they were real," Matt says. "It was incredible."

incredible

Even I can tell Matt's lying.

"Here's what concerns me," Mr. Ennis says. "You never know who's going to click on your videos. Someone could watch this video, think it's a real exercise show, try to copy you, and get hurt. We talked about making responsible videos in our first class—I'm not sure this one is."

Why is everyone missing the point?

"The background is great," Umberto says. "Really nice lettering."

"Nice lettering?! I worked hard on that video!"

"We can see you put a lot of time into getting expensive props and building a professional set," Mr. Ennis says. "I'm just not sure a potentially harmful exercise show is the way to go."

Why did I think that just because I'm kind of creative my work would automatically be good? After years of being at the back of the pack, I had the tiniest sliver of hope that I'd

harmful

sliver

be able to ace this class. Will there ever be anything I'm good at in this world? Because school certainly isn't one of them. I thought even I couldn't mess up a YouTube video, but I guess I was wrong.

Riding back home, the only thing Matt and I can talk about is class.

"The good news is that we BOTH have to reshoot," I say.

reshoot

"We're two of the funniest kids in school," Matt says. "How did we end up with the lamest videos?"

I tell Matt his video wasn't lame—just a little boring.

"Same thing," he argues. "But yours was definitely lame."

I skid my skateboard to a full stop.

"How is lifting three hundred pounds lame?"

Matt doesn't stop, just yells as he passes me on his board. "It looked fake."

Which is worse—boring or fake? All I know is that I don't want to be either.

I jump on my board and catch up to him. "Of *course* it looked fake—it WAS fake."

"I know that," Matt says. "You couldn't lift that much weight if your life depended on it."

"That was the JOKE!"

"I thought jokes were supposed to be funny." This time Matt's the one who pulls over on his board. "I'm as surprised as you are that Carly's video was the class favorite, but you have to admit, it was real."

"I wish someone had told me that's what we should be going for."

Matt tugs at his hair which he's growing out. "There are a million directions to go in, with no way to know what's going to work. Your video could've been the one everyone loved—it just wasn't."

I've been wondering something since we left Mr. Ennis's class. "But what if OTHER people like my video?" I ask. "Just because no one in class did doesn't mean that EVERYONE will think it's lame."

Matt agrees. "There could be some kid in Argentina who thinks it's the funniest thing he's ever seen."

snort

I laugh so hard I snort. "One kid in Argentina? That's the only viewer I get?"

"Don't feel bad," Matt says. "My only viewer is probably some

medication

grandmother in Kansas who found my channel by mistake."

"She was trying to buy some medication online, made a typo, and accidentally found your channel."

"The thing is," Matt says, "she leaves really thoughtful comments. She's improved my game tremendously."

Matt and I continue to make our silly stories even more ridiculous, and just like that we both feel better. We still have work to do, but we're entertaining ourselves and making each other laugh—which is what our videos were supposed to do.

TODAY IS WHAT?

Dad's not too happy that I don't want to use his friend's props any-more. He tells me Doug gave us a lot of time and that I should make another attempt to use them before bringing them back after just a few days. Unfortunately, I'm determined to come up with something fresher and more original than the Tank. As we load the barbells and bowling

attempt

balls into his car to bring back to Doug, Dad loosens up a little and we pretend we're being crushed by all their weight as we lift them. It's stupid and funny and neither of us can stop laughing. I wish my class-mates had thought my stunts were half as funny as Dad does.

evident

When I get to school the next day, it becomes evident that some-thing out of the ordinary is going on. Maria and Perry are both wearing dresses, and they NEVER wear dresses. Teddy's hair is actually combed and Matt is wearing a BLAZER. And there's only ONE day a year that Matt gets dressed up.

blazer

Class picture day.

Matt gestures to my striped shorts and T-shirt. "What's with the outfit? Did you forget again?"

"You know I forget half the stuff

McCoddle tells us in class." My mother's going to KILL me. Just like last year.

Umberto slides up in his wheel-chair, looking as dapper as Matt. "Maybe everyone will think you're just one of the cool kids who doesn't care how they look in the yearbook." He and Matt exchange glances, then burst out laughing. "Nah."

dapper

The only person who looks unhappier than I am is Carly. She's got on a plaid skirt with leggings and a black T-shirt and looks kind of cute. But the expression on her face is pure anxiety.

Then I realize why. Her braces.

"I could have postponed getting these a few weeks until after picture day! Why didn't I look at my calendar?" she complains.

Carly stops ranting as soon as she

sees what I'm wearing. "Oh no—did you forget again?"

"Kind of."

A slow smile creeps across Carly's face. "That makes me feel the tiniest bit better."

Matt pulls the collar of his shirt. "Let's get it over with so I can take this stupid jacket off."

photography

The lady from the photography studio is set up in the gym. She looks pretty old, hunched over and with thick glasses. She must be trying to disguise the fact that she's ancient, because her hair is dyed jet-black with an inch of gray roots showing where her hair is parted. She's barking instructions to an assistant as she points with an arthritic finger to each kid in line. The bent fingers remind me of

hunched

arthritic

Grammy, who has arthritis too, but I've never seen a scowl like this on her.

scowl

Matt couldn't look more uncomfortable if he tried.

"At least I'll be relaxed in MY picture," I say. "Not pulling at my clothes like you."

He looks like he's about to smack me then suddenly starts laughing. He points to my surfing T-shirt with the migrating birds. "Your shirt is green."

migrating

"So?"

He points to the large green screen set up underneath the basketball net. "You can't wear anything green in front of a green screen!"

He's laughing so hard, Tyler and Umberto stop talking to listen in. I get it; Matt's just trying to take the focus off himself. But does he have to make fun of me to do it?

"I guess you didn't read the e-mail," Umberto says. "There are six different backgrounds to choose from. They insert them after they shoot us in front of the green screen. Don't you remember from last year?"

"Like that's the kind of information I remember!" I'm starting to really get annoyed with my friends.

"Hey!" Tyler yells. "Derek's wearing a green shirt!"

The news spreads down the line faster than if we were all playing telephone. Suddenly I'm glad I'm wearing green—it'll hide how sick I'm starting to feel.

Carly moves up the line until she's

beside me. "It's okay," she says. "No one cares about these stupid pictures anyway."

Sure, Carly's trying to make me feel better but all this attention is making me think I'm REALLY going to get sick—with my luck, just as this cranky lady snaps the photo.

cranky

Carly, unfortunately, is now the target of my pent-up irritation. "Thanks for the update," I respond. "I hope the photographer's lights don't bounce off your braces. It might look like you've got lasers shooting out of your mouth."

Matt's talking to Maria but runs over when he hears me. "Does this mean we can finally make fun of Carly's braces? I've been saving up a million insults!"

Before I can answer, Umberto

does. "No, we are NOT making fun of Carly's braces."

Carly whips around to face me. "Are you sure? Because it certainly sounds that way to me."

I feel bad that I'm the one who started this whole thing and just want this line to finally move so I can get out of here.

"I'm sorry," I tell Carly. "You look great for your photo—really cute."

chants

"Ohhhhhhhh," Tyler chants behind me. "Derek likes Carly! Derek likes Carly!"

He stops when Carly glares at him, crosses her arms, and faces down Matt and me.

$$2 + 2 = 5$$

inaccurate

"If you think you're going to send me running to the bathroom to cry again, you're wrong, inaccurate, erroneous, mistaken, misguided— you want me to keep going?"

Matt and I stare at the parquet floor and shake our heads. It stinks having a friend who's a billion times smarter than you are—especially when she's angry.

parquet

Even though I ask her to stay, Carly goes back to her place in line with Natalie.

Umberto lets out a low whistle. "That girl is a thesaurus! She thrashed you—and for good reason, too."

thesaurus

If I had a dollar for every moronic thing I've ever said to Carly, I'd be able to buy a plane ticket TO FLY ME ANYWHERE BUT HERE. I'm actually relieved she stood up for herself; I'd feel horrible if her picture came out bad because of me.

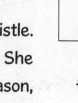

thrashed

It doesn't take long before I'm first in line. I comb my hair with my hand and hope for the best.

"YOU!" the woman yells. "Stand on the X. Now!"

I do as I'm told and hurry to the spot on the floor marked with two pieces of duct tape. Behind me is a large screen of green fabric, pulled tight. Three large studio lamps have been lighting up this spot for hours; I hope this woman takes the picture before I start sweating through my shirt.

"The instructions said NOT to wear green," she says.

I mumble something about forgetting, even though I never read the email.

"It's your funeral," she says.

"My funeral?! Isn't that a bit extreme?"

And just as my face is scrunched up and puzzled, she clicks the camera.

"Hey!" I say. "That's not fair! You have to take another one!"

"One per student. Next!" The woman points to a large table with several sample photos. "Pick a backdrop—not that it'll matter with that shirt."

Why did they hire this lady? Why can't we have some cool, NICE photographer instead of a tyrant?

The backdrop choices are totally boring—swirly gray and brown, bricks, a grassy field, a wall of books.

swirly

At this point it doesn't matter what I chose. I select the wall of books as a joke—that no one else will get since I'm never showing this picture to anyone.

AN ANNUAL EVENT

incident

This weekend is the annual street fair that everyone at school's been talking about for days. All I can think about, however, is Tuesday's incident with Carly. Over the years we've had plenty of arguments, and in the end, we always end up okay. This time she hasn't responded to any of my texts, which has me worried. I even called her last night—and

I never make voluntary phone calls—but it went straight to voice mail.

voluntary

I hate that feeling you get when things are off with one of your friends. It's like you're wearing a shirt that doesn't fit. You feel tight and uncomfortable all day, no matter what else is going on. I've been looking forward to the fair but hope I can still enjoy it with this weird feeling inside.

The street fair doesn't start until eleven, so I've got time to hang out before walking over with my parents. Both my parents are good cooks but neither of them can compare to having lunch at a food truck. There'll be grilled cheese trucks, lobster trucks, taco trucks, ice cream sandwich trucks, Korean BBQ trucks—how are you supposed to choose?

I know I should eat a small breakfast but I wolf down two bowls of Cinnamon Toast Crunch while watching TV with Bodi and Frank.

"SMC?" My dad sticks his head into the living room. SMC is our acronym for Saturday Morning Cartoons—something Dad and I came up with when I was little. I enjoyed cartoons back then—DUH!—but still haven't outgrown them. I don't plan to, either. Maybe it's because paying attention in school all week is so difficult, but by the time Saturday comes around, sitting on the couch with my monkey, dog, and a giant bowl of cereal is the perfect antidote to all that work.

Mom's new thing is slathering coconut oil all over her hair so her

TOO MUCH
INFORMATION
↓
TMI

acronym

outgrown

antidote

head's wrapped up in a towel when she sits down with her coffee. Hydrating your hair seems pretty unnecessary to me. I don't have to do anything to mine and it gets oily on its own.

hydrating

"I talked to the director of the capuchin foundation about Frank," she says.

As if he knows he's being discussed, Frank moves from his place on the couch to Mom's lap.

"Can't we talk about this later?" I ask. "There's nothing worse than hearing bad news while you're watching cartoons."

Mom sips coffee then smiles. "It's actually *not* bad news. Their training classes are so full that she gave us an extension. Frank can live with us for another six months."

extension

Hearing this makes the strait-jacket of anxiety I'm wearing loosen up the tiniest bit. I jump up from the couch, grab Frank, and swing him around like we're dancing. "That's great!"

"Better than thirty food trucks?" Mom asks.

"Better than a hundred food trucks!"

agonizing

Over the past few weeks, every time I started to think about Frank leaving, I pushed the thought out of my mind. I know Frank has to go someday but I've gotten so attached to him, it's going to be agonizing to say goodbye. Six months may not be forever, but it's better than losing Frank now.

"You've done a good job working with Frank since he's been with us,"

Mom says. "You two have really bonded."

bonded

Frank definitely does have some kind of sixth sense, because he looks up at me with this expression so full of emotion it almost looks human.

Mom grabs her phone from the pocket of her robe and snaps a picture. "That's a keeper."

She holds the phone up for me to see. Frank and I look like a film poster for a cross-species buddy movie.

When Mom checks the time, she tells me we'll be leaving for the street fair in an hour.

I suddenly wonder where Bodi is and it doesn't take me long to spot his two paws peeking out from underneath the curtains. I scoop him up in

convoluted

my arms and settle back on the couch for some more SMC with the two greatest animals in the world.

The whole way to the fair, Dad tells this convoluted story about one of the women in the costume department who got transferred to a different job because she kept shrinking the actor's clothes when she washed them.

He's acting out all the people in the story with different voices and sound effects, but as we walk toward Wilshire the only two things I can think about are if Carly will text me back and finding a new idea for my YouTube channel that doesn't include barbells. Maybe there'll be a performer or vendor here who'll ignite my creativity.

The line at the Korean BBQ food

vendor

ignite

truck snakes around the entire parking lot. The lines at the chowder truck, the taco truck, and the Philly cheesesteak trucks are almost as long. NOOOOO!

"Want to get a salad with me?" Mom points to the veggie food truck with only three people in line.

"I'M NOT GETTING A SALAD AT A FOOD TRUCK!" I shout so loud that a mother with two kids in a stroller turns and gives me a dirty look. So does Mom.

"Come on, let's get some sliders," Dad says. "That line is long but manageable."

manageable

We each use our phones while we wait. (Carly still hasn't texted.) When it's our turn, Dad orders turkey patties with cheese and I get the bacon and mushroom sliders. The baby burgers don't take too long to come out; even so, by the time we find Mom, she's already finished eating.

There are lots of people here from the neighborhood and several of Mom's patients. It's nice to see them, but I'm on the hunt for inspiration and end up walking ahead of my parents.

inspiration

Moon bounce? Too young.

Face painting? Too messy—AND too young.

Adopt-a-dog? Already have one.

When I double back to see what my parents are up to, I find Mom at a booth learning how to make soap with herbs and olive oil. She ends up buying several kits to make her own lemon and lavender soap, which is probably good since I used up all her bath stuff trying to film Frank.

lavender

Dad just shakes his head. "She's

never going to use those—you know that, right?"

I laugh, knowing how enthusiastic Mom gets about arts and crafts projects, forgetting she doesn't have a lot of extra time to do them in.

Dad tries on a few T-shirts and buys one with a minnow swimming against the tide. I don't really get it, but he seems happy so I am too.

minnow

"You want to get something?" he asks. "There's a vintage Pac-Man there."

Usually I'd take advantage of some cool free stuff but my attention is fixed on a guy in the next booth putting handfuls of earthworms into a bucket. He sees me looking at him and motions me over.

"Did you know you can start a compost heap with worms in your backyard?" he asks. "They'll eat your

compost

fertilizer

food scraps—even coffee grounds! The garbage passes through their bodies, making a rich fertilizer you can use in your garden."

Mom peers over her reading glasses into the bucket. "I wonder if Carly's mom knows about this."

Carly's mom's a landscaper and their garden is full of the biggest birds of paradise I've ever seen. Maybe Carly's mom uses GIANT pooping worms.

Mom asks the guy more questions until Dad drags her away. "Making your own soap AND composting?" he asks. "Are we quitting our jobs now?"

Mom ignores him, moving on to the leather sandals in the next booth.

sampling

Dad LOVES sampling food—it takes forever to get him out of Costco, where he tries bite-sized pieces of everything from cheese to salmon. Today is no different. Spoonfuls of blueberry honey, multigrain bread on a toothpick, and sausage in a little paper cup—Dad's not fussy when it comes to trying new foods.

salmon

"Try this hot sauce," he tells me. "It's got ten different chilies—it'll blow a hole in the back of your skull."

Mom shakes her head and walks away; she's not a fan of spicy foods like Dad and me who'll put hot sauce on just about anything.

Dad hands me a piece of bread doused with a sauce called Taste Bud Explosion 10.

"It makes our Taste Bud Explosion 9 seem like baby formula," the vendor tells us.

The sauce has barely hit my mouth when I start sweating. The vendor doesn't blink, just hands me a glass of water. If I were a cartoon, there'd be steam coming out of my ears with fire engine sound effects. I still can't talk but give my dad a big thumbs-up.

He takes out his wallet and reaches for two bottles of the hot sauce. "It'll kick our chicken chili to a whole new level."

But I'm not thinking about chicken or chili or even nachos. I just figured out the premise of my new YouTube show!

premise

YET ANOTHER IDEA

My parents have been adamant about me not using Frank in my YouTube videos, but considering the class reaction to the Tank, I don't have a choice but to go back to using my capuchin. I'm facing some fierce competition—not just from the other kids in Mr. Ennis's class, but from the billions of people already on YouTube. Anybody with a monkey

adamant

disobey

gratefully

at his or her disposal would use it, right?

Even if I'm going to disobey my parents, I know better than to give hot sauce to a monkey. Of course that doesn't stop me from putting a tiny drop of the new hot sauce on my finger and letting Frank lick it off when we get home. He seems to like it—even tries to grab the bottle out of my hand—but if I'm going to shoot lots of videos, I'll need a substitute for Taste Bud Explosion 10.

Gratefully, Mom's meeting a friend and Dad's catching up on work so the chances of them cutting into my fun are slim. I rummage through the back of the fridge where all the half-eaten jars of curry and pickles are until I find a bottle of hot sauce from the last street fair or farmers' market Dad went to. I empty the contents into the sink, rinse the bottle, and refill it with ketchup, a harmless condiment that will look exactly like hot sauce in the video.

Frank must know something's up because he's already clambering to get out of my arms. As soon as I douse one of his monkey biscuits in ketchup, Frank grabs it out of my hand and gobbles it down. I squirt some ketchup on the outside of the bottle to keep him interested.

Capuchins are pretty good at foraging, so my idea is to hide the bottle of hot sauce and have Frank root around the house to find it. In post-production, I'll speed up the footage, add cartoon sound effects,

clambering

foraging

as well as a theme song to make the video even funnier. So question number one: Where should I hide the hot sauce first?

Inside the fridge, the vegetable bin is full, so I bury the bottle underneath the lettuce, zucchini, and carrots. Frank's on my shoulders, bouncing in anticipation. I make him wait a few more minutes as I set up my cell on the tripod.

zucchini

When I'm finally ready, I prop open the door of the refrigerator so Frank can have full access—and I can have light to film. He doesn't wait for me to turn on the camera, just starts shoveling out the vegetables until he finds the bottle. I constantly try to get Frank to look into the camera but he's pretty focused on finding his snack.

focused

By the time he's finished, the floor of the kitchen looks like a produce stand. Frank's gotten ahold of the fake hot sauce and is guzzling it down and squirting it on the vegetables. I scoop all the veggies back into the bin so my parents won't find out.

guzzling

Before I put Frank back in his crate, I snap a picture of him holding the bottle of hot sauce and text it to Carly. She might still be angry with me, but she's always had a soft spot for Frank.

My phone immediately dings with a new text.

It's from Carly. A *picture of you with hot sauce is NOT an apology.*

I type back. *That was Frank, not me. Besides I apologized WITHOUT hot sauce too.*

I watch the three dots bouncing on the screen as she types her reply.

Come on, come on!

Are you sure? Looked more like you than Frank. Then the school emoji and a wave goodbye.

Yes! I am forgiven!

Cleaning up the kitchen after that is a breeze.

forgiven

READY, SET, GO!

I can't wait to show Mr. Ennis and the rest of the class my new video. Unfortunately, I've got a full day of school to get through before that.

There's a test in social studies on Islam; I tried to study for it but spent too much time with hot sauce and ketchup instead. I know three out of the twenty questions and end up guessing the rest. Mr. Maroni tells us we'll be starting the section on

Islam

Buddhism next week—maybe I'll have better luck with that religion.

Buddhism

When it's finally time for Mr. Ennis's class, Matt and I race down the hall until Ms. Cardoza in the media center gives us the evil eye. I almost slam into Carly, which is weird for a moment—are we still good?—until she hands me a stick of red licorice and tells me to stop clogging the halls. Yup, things are back to normal.

licorice

In the past week, Tyler made more than ten YTP videos—all of them wacky and ridiculous. He always kept a low profile so I'm kind of surprised his work is head and shoulders above everyone else's. I guess all the time he's spent watching YTP has paid off when it comes to making clips of his own.

Umberto's video is also funny—but unpleasant to watch at the same time. In the clip, he's at a restaurant on the Promenade with his brother, getting ready to have lunch. When the waitress comes over, she only talks to Eduardo, asking him what Umberto will have too.

unpleasant

I've been in those embarrassing situations with Umberto before—when people talk to Matt or me instead of Umberto as if he's just his disability and not one of the smartest, funniest kids on the planet. It's not that strangers should KNOW he is; they just should give him a chance. This time, Umberto kindly—but firmly—lets the waitress know that HE'LL be having the chicken tacos without the cabbage but with lots of sour

cabbage

cream. When the clip ends, Umberto gets even more applause than Tyler.

Throughout the class, I keep glancing over at Mr. Ennis, who looks as mischievous as I do before Brianna comes over to babysit. He's got something up his sleeve but I can't figure out what it is. (A pizza party after class would be AWESOME.)

As Mr. Ennis cues up Carly's video, she leans over in her chair. "Don't freak out," she whispers.

Alarm bells go off in my head. "What am I going to freak out about? I don't freak out."

"Yes, you do!" Carly points to the screen where her video is starting.

I guess she's still doing that tiresome show about her braces because she's sitting in her room talking on webcam again.

tiresome

"Talk about bad timing," on-screen Carly begins. "I got my braces the week before class picture day! I felt ridiculous! Should I smile with my teeth and flaunt my braces? Or smile with my mouth closed which feels totally unnatural?" She then runs through several kinds of smiles for the camera—some of them are funny, some are cute, and a few are downright scary.

flaunt

unnatural

When I look over at Matt to see what he thinks, he's staring at me and making a cut-your-throat motion with his hand. I mouth, "What?" since I have no idea what he's talking about. He just shakes his head and looks back at the screen.

"So I've got swollen gums, I feel ugly, and the photographer is mean— and as if THAT'S not enough—two of my best friends start making fun of me while we're in line! You heard me—two of my best friends!"

I look around the room, hoping everyone doesn't know who she's talking about, but pretty much everyone does and is staring at Matt and me. Carly just shrugs as if she's not the one who made the video.

Throwing herself on her bed and pretending to cry must be a running gag on Carly's channel because she does it again now. At the end of the class, she gets as much applause as Umberto and Tyler.

"Well," Mr. Ennis says. "Any comments?"

I don't even bother raising my hand. "You said we were fine," I tell Carly. "Why'd you have to make that video?"

Carly looks at me with an expression that's not mad, just serious. "I think a better question is, why'd you have to insult me in the first place?"

It's a good point but it doesn't answer my question. "I know all our channels are still set to private, but you wouldn't post that if they were public, would you?"

Before she can answer, Mr. Ennis jumps in and asks the rest of the class if THEY think Carly should post it.

"Totally!" Natalie says.

"Absolutely," Tyler adds.

Umberto looks torn but joins in anyway. "I think sometimes the uncomfortable videos are the ones that hit the hardest."

Mr. Ennis says it's time to

move on to the next video, but before he does, he asks Carly what she'd do.

She doesn't hesitate. "I'd totally post it."

Great—make me look like a thoughtless moron just as our teacher is about to screen my new video. Thanks, Carly.

thoughtless

But I don't need to worry—Monkey Love Hot Sauce is a hit. I'm glad I decided to speed up the video and add sound effects; it makes Frank's search for hot sauce even more frantic and silly. Mr. Ennis laughs out loud which puts a cherry on top of the class reaction.

"That was great, Derek," he says. "See what you can accomplish even with all those rules and parental supervision? Your parents did sign off on this, right?"

I can't tell Mr. Ennis that I was the one who scribbled Mom's signature on the parental permission form, so I just nod and tell him they liked the video too.

scribbled

"Frank's a star," Tyler says. "Please say you're using him in all your videos."

Getting one good video has taken much more time and energy than I'd planned on. But after all those practice attempts, I finally came up with something that works. As I tell Tyler I'm definitely using Frank again, all I can think about is how I'm going to hide my shooting schedule from my parents.

Next up is Matt's video, which has been shrouded in mystery. All

shrouded

he's told me is that he gave up the LP idea in favor of something different.

Before Mr. Ennis hits play Matt turns to the class and tells us he decided to do an unboxing video.

WHAT?!

If you'd asked me to bet on what type of YouTube channel Matt would create, unboxing would be at the very bottom of the list. Most of the unboxing channels consist of a woman with fancy nail polish opening toys while her disembodied voice talks to you like you're a two-year-old. Please don't say Matt's going to do THAT. Unboxing a new smartphone or even a bag of Doritos is more like Matt. I'm confused—and curious— to see what he's come up with.

On-screen, Matt is dressed like a

disembodied

caveman; I recognize the outfit he's wearing as his mom's sheepskin rug. His face is dirty and he's sitting in the woods—which I also recognize as a trail we've hiked in the Santa Monica Mountains. Did he use a tripod or did someone else tape it? Does he have another best friend now? I decide to stop worrying and just watch the clip.

His caveman character holds an old cardboard box painted gray, fastened with a piece of jute. Matt put a lot of work into his video too; I guess coming up in the rear of the class taught both of us a lesson last week.

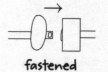

fastened

jute

"Welcome to Shopping with Neanderthals. Today, we're going to see what's in this package I just picked up at my local StoneMart."

Several kids laugh, including me.

Caveman Matt unties the string and slowly opens the box. As he does, he's swatting imaginary flies.

swatting

"Ohhhhhh, look at this." Matt slowly lifts a large rock out of the box and holds it up. "This one's a beauty. Nice shape, good grip. I'm going to be able to clobber lots of other cavemen with this bad boy." He weighs the rock in his hand. "They really made some improvements over last year's model; even the packaging is better."

packaging

He signs off with a grunt and we all applaud. Matt beams, happy that he came up with something funny and original. He tells us his brother Jamie helped him, which eases my fear about a new best friend.

After all the videos are shown, Mr. Ennis tells us he has a surprise. NOW can we have some pizza?

"As of today, you can all move your YouTube settings from private to public so everyone can finally enjoy these beauties."

Wait—everyone in the WORLD is going to see Carly talking about how mean Matt and I were?

"From here on in," Mr. Ennis says, "you'll be promoting your channels and uploading new videos. And remember: It's not just about views and subscribers—it's about creating videos you can be proud of."

As much as Mr. Ennis says it's not about numbers, I don't have to ask my classmates what they'll be aiming for because I already know the answer—views. Umberto, Matt,

Carly, and I originally thought we'd all be making videos together. Now I have to compete with not only everyone in the class, but my best friends.

BAIT AND SWITCH

Several kids in our class already have lots of videos "in the can," which means shot and ready to go. I, on the other hand, have to film all the new Monkey Love Hot Sauce videos from scratch.

As I lie in bed Saturday night, my mind is abuzz with everything I have to do. Film the videos, edit them, upload them, promote them, answer

abuzz

comments...then start all over again. Is this what it feels like to be a grown-up—a constant stream of stuff you need to accomplish? If it is, I'm not in any hurry to sign up.

Even though today is Sunday, Dad has a meeting and Mom's next door interviewing for a new receptionist, so I'm clear to start filming the next episode of my channel. But first I need to come up with a theme song!

It's been a while since I used GarageBand, so it takes me over an hour to make a song I'm happy with, one that feels panicky and fueled by hot-sauce energy. I turn on the laptop's internal mic and record the theme song to my new channel.

Monkey love hot sauce!
Monkey love hot sauce!

It's so hot, I love it a lot!
Monkey love hot sauce!

It's ridiculous and stupid—in other words, perfect for YouTube.

I don't know how long Mom's going to be working, so I have to hurry if I'm going to film Frank. Where should he go kooky for hot sauce today? The TV room? The trash?

kooky

Within the next few hours, Frank scours my mother's jewelry box, the recycling bin, as well as a basket of laundry, and the washing machine. The only difficulty Frank had was with one of Mom's bangles. He was in such a frenzy to get his hands on the hot sauce that he ended up with the bracelet caught around the lower part of his face. It made for hilarious footage but he started

scours

bangles

165 ★

tangled

freaking out, so I had to stop being cameraman/director and help him. A few of my mother's chains and necklaces got pretty tangled, so I put them back in the bottom of the jewelry box where she won't find them for a while.

By the time I get Frank in his crate, he's exhausted and passes out on his blanket. Then I look for Bodi. I can't give him equal time tonight, but I need to at least give him some. I settle him next to me on the couch as I download the footage from my phone to my laptop.

The footage came out GREAT and I'm excited to get to the editing phase, until I realize I've forgotten something. Since I can't show my parents Monkey Love Hot Sauce, I'm going to need a decoy channel to

decoy

show them what I'm doing for class. I not only have to make Frank's show, I need to make another whole fake channel. What's THAT show going to be?

I look around the room and bat around ideas. Derek eats? Boring. Derek eats candy? Been done. Derek watches TV? Too passive.

passive

Mom's got a few boxes near the front door of things going to Goodwill. She asked me a few days ago if she could get rid of some of my old toys and I said fine. I open up the boxes until I find the one full of action figures.

I really don't feel like working but there's no way around the task at hand. I set up the camera again and dump the box of action figures onto the kitchen table.

"Hi! Welcome to Action Figure Mashup," I say to the camera. "I'm Derek, your host, and we're going to create some NEW action figures out of my OLD action figures."

I don't have time for a lot of takes so I make sure to speak as clearly as possible. "First, we're going to take off Bart Simpson's head and put it on Gumby." I yank off Bart's yellow head and shove it onto Gumby's stretchy green body. "Ta-da!" I hold my new creature up to the camera. "Say hello to Bartby."

stretchy

I sign off then check the quality of the video as Mom enters the kitchen with a stack of folders. She pours herself a glass of wine and asks how filming went. I lean over and show her the footage I just shot.

She takes a sip of wine. "Do you

think it might skew a little young? You haven't played with those toys in years—you might get a lot of four-year-old viewers."

skew

I tell her I don't care WHAT age my viewers are, as long as I have some. But her comment makes me wish I could share my REAL show with her.

"See what your teacher says," she adds. "But I think you might be able to challenge yourself a little more."

She takes her glass and work upstairs and tells me it's time for bed.

She has no idea I'll be up for hours.

THE HEADLESS
HORSEMAN

remarks

In school the next day, everyone who takes Mr. Ennis's class is talking about how many views their videos have received, as well as some of the funny comments. Tyler's YTP site has lots of absurd remarks, which only makes sense. Umberto's are very positive, which makes sense too.

The real surprise is Carly's

channel; while the rest of us have single-digit viewers, Carly received more than thirty comments in twenty-four hours, even a few from people who DON'T wear braces. I check my channel between classes and at lunch, but only have seven views—all of them probably mine when I was testing it last night.

"The day you've all been waiting for," Ms. McCoddle says before she dismisses us. "Your class pictures are back."

Just what I need—MORE bad news.

There's lots of excitement as she hands the pictures out; I just hope that lady who took them was better with a camera than she was with people.

Ms. McCoddle stands in front of

wavering

cranes

decapitated

my desk, wavering. "I'm not really sure what happened here. Maybe you should sign up for the reshoot day next week."

She hands me the see-through envelope. I DON'T want to see it, but like an accident on the other side of the freeway, I can't help but look.

My head is suspended against a wall of books. Just. My. Head.

Matt cranes his neck toward my seat. "Dude! It looks like you were decapitated."

It doesn't take long before everyone is on their feet, mocking my head floating amid a backdrop of books.

I'm not sure if my parents will laugh or be annoyed that I didn't pay attention to the photographer's dress instructions. Either way, they'll insist I do a reshoot.

I grab my pen and write NO GREEN SHIRT on the back of my hand. Hopefully I'll remember to read it this time.

NUMBER
CRUNCHING

portrait

Both Mom and Dad think the class photo is hilarious; Mom even insists on buying it AND scheduling a makeup. She removes an old family portrait from the shelf above the TV and slips my disembodied-head picture into it. After all these years, I still can't tell when Mom will find something funny or not.

I end up working all night EVERY

night for the next week. Finding new ways for Frank to be obsessed with hot sauce, staging, filming, editing, adding sound effects, uploading, creating playlists, tagging them, tweaking the tags, responding to people who leave comments—who knew being on YouTube was so much WORK?

tweaking

Carly's vlog continues to get tons of comments; she's got the most viewers and subscribers of all of us, by far. It's actually infuriating because her videos take a few minutes to shoot, even less to edit, with hardly any pre-production. How can she put in the least amount of work and get the best results? I should realize by now that my accomplishments will NEVER compare to Carly's. Ever.

infuriating

Tyler continues to create bizarre YTP videos that have no point to them, which of course IS the point. Matt's channel is kind of a one-joke bit, but since he uploads a new video every week, he's gotten a few hundred subscribers. For someone who goofs off as much as Matt does, he is surprisingly focused. He hasn't said anything, but it makes me wonder if he might end up going into filmmaking for real.

accessibility

We all knew Umberto's videos would reach a wide audience; there are other people doing accessibility shows on YouTube but none are as funny—or by someone as young— as Umberto's. I can't decide which of his videos is my favorite. I love the one where he's trying to order a smoothie but can't see over the counter because he's in his chair and the guy working there can't tell where Umberto's voice is coming from. I also like the one when his shirt gets caught in the mechanism of his wheelchair and he brings pedestrian traffic to a halt as he tries to remove it. I've been in the world with Umberto enough to know that he'll never run out of new material.

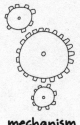

mechanism

pedestrian

Monkey Love Hot Sauce is doing okay; I've had lots of great comments and proudly have 165 subscribers. But I barely sleep, barely stay awake through classes, and, most important, I'm so busy MAKING YouTube videos that I no longer have time to WATCH YouTube videos. Unless you count my own.

Is it weird to watch your own

videos to increase your views? Are the other kids in this class doing the same thing? Or am I the only loser in the bunch? These are the questions I'm too embarrassed to ask the others, even my best friends.

mystified

My parents seem mystified by what they think is my YouTube channel.

"So are you going to take these mash-up action figures and DO something with them? Some *Robot Chicken* kind of thing?" Dad points to the pile of figures on the kitchen table. He picks up half Batman/half Pikachu and walks him toward me.

Sure, Dad, great idea. Why don't I create a THIRD show?

Mom just shrugs at the pile of misfit toys. I can tell she's not impressed. I just want them both to go to bed so I can shoot more secret videos of Frank.

I DID have time to watch Mr. Ennis's new video a few days ago. In this one, his friend Chris joined him in the weekly digital magic show. Chris has set up a Slip 'N Slide in the yard and Mr. Ennis walks by in a tuxedo. Chris blasts Mr. Ennis with the garden hose and suddenly the tuxedo becomes a tuxedo-printed wetsuit. Mr. Ennis slides down the Slip 'N Slide and lands perfectly dry in his regular tuxedo again.

tuxedo

Carly's newest videos follow her same vlog format and you can see that the positive response she's received has made her even more confident. In one, she talks about having lunch with her cousins, then looking in the mirror later and

lunch meat

gingerbread

seeing her braces are covered in everything from lunch meat to gingerbread and how embarrassed she was.

"None of my cousins told me my mouth looked like the inside of a garbage disposal," she says on-screen. "Not one!" As usual, she throws herself onto her bed and fake cries. She ends the segment by saying she's putting up an AMA video next week. Mr. Ennis says Ask Me Anything videos can be fun but cautions Carly to make sure all the questions are appropriate before she answers them.

I'll be the first one to admit that I didn't get Carly's vlog in the beginning. But the more I see it, the more I understand why others are attracted to it.

People mostly watch videos for entertainment and to learn how to do something, but over the past few weeks, I've seen there are also other reasons. To connect with people or to feel like you're a member of a group. Without planning to, Carly created a forum for other kids to share their thoughts, feelings, and stories about having to deal with braces. And it's paying off.

forum

"Do you think we were wrong to just go for laughs?" Matt asks.

We're at my house where he's helping me set the stage for Frank to forage through the tub of old sports equipment looking for hot sauce. So far, I've spent half of my birthday-money savings on ketchup, which Frank has devoured.

equipment

"I just wish I'd done something

easier," Matt continues. "I have to get into my caveman costume, put on makeup, find something new to unbox, beg Jamie to drive me to the trail, then film me....I hate to say it, but it's not as much fun as I thought it would be."

"You had me fooled," I say. "I thought you loved it."

"I did," Matt says. "But my channel's been up for weeks. That's practically forever in YouTube time. I thought I'd be a star by now, like Logan and Jake Paul or Jacob Sartorius—girls screaming, hit records, the whole thing."

"What bothers me," I confess, "is that it makes you realize how you're just a drop in the bucket—one of a zillion people posting videos every day. No one's sitting around waiting for us to post something, that's for sure."

"Do you think anyone in our class will get BIG?" he asks. "Superstar big?"

"I doubt it. The chances are minuscule for that kind of fame." I hide the bottle of hot sauce in the bin. "You're not thinking about SINGING online, are you? Because you have a terrible voice."

minuscule

"It's not about the singing," he says. "It's about the fans."

When Mom appears in the garage, I block the tub of gear and the hot sauce. The whole reason we did this today was because she wasn't supposed to be home until later.

She asks what we're up to.

"Just going through stuff." I hold

up my old baseball mitt, which is so small I couldn't fit into it if I tried. "Remember this, Matt?"

"We played a lot of baseball with that mitt," Matt agrees.

nostalgia

"I hate to interrupt the nostalgia party," Mom says. "Just wanted you to know I canceled my appointment and I'll be working here if you kids need anything."

She leaves—along with my plans for filming Monkey Love Hot Sauce today.

ANALYZE THIS

"It's important to try and understand why some videos work and
others don't," Mr. Ennis says in class.
"Let's talk about Carly's latest video
on her playlist and try to analyze
why it already has 212,530 views."

WHAT? I had no idea Carly was
bringing in those kinds of numbers.
If I had numbers like that, I'd make
sure the whole school knew.

He hits play as we watch Carly tell a story about talking to her mom when one of the rubber bands on her braces snapped.

"You'll never guess where it landed," she says. "In my mother's mouth! I mean, she's my mother, but still! Suppose it had been someone from school? OMG—suppose it was someone I had a crush on!"

Does Carly have a crush on someone I don't know about?

Mr. Ennis hits pause and asks us for feedback.

vulnerable

Natalie raises her hand. "Carly isn't afraid to be vulnerable. If you have braces, you can really relate to her frustration."

"She's cool and funny," Tyler adds. "I bet half of her subscribers don't even HAVE braces."

Is Tyler the one she has a crush on?

Mr. Ennis asks Carly if she's tried to figure out who her subscribers are.

calculations

"Sixty percent of them are girls," Carly says. "And in my rough calculations, approximately seventy percent of both boys and girls who leave comments wear braces."

Is she kidding? Who does this kind of research on their viewers?

"One girl—at least I think it's a girl, but you never know—is so cute, writing her own braces anecdotes in the comment section every single day. I actually look forward to Power73's thoughts."

Mr. Ennis is impressed with how much work Carly's put in to analyzing her data. "Today we're ALL going to look at our numbers." He pats his

demographic

estimating

stomach like he just ate. "Guess what the number one demographic is for my channel, LOL Illusions?"

We all make different guesses, with most of us estimating Mr. Ennis's audience to be made up of kids and teenagers like us.

He shakes his head. "The biggest group of viewers I have are women over eighty. I have a huge following in the assisted-living community."

"No way!" several of us shout.

He laughs and shrugs. "You're right—it's kids your age. But wouldn't it be great to reach seniors too?"

He tells us to go to our YouTube channels and head to the Creator Studio. We follow his instructions and click *Analytics* in the menu on the left.

"You can also check your videos individually by clicking the Analytics button under each video."

A few kids in the class—Carly and Natalie—seem familiar with these pages but for the rest of us, this information is a revelation. How many people liked and disliked each video, how old they are, what kind of device they watched it on, how long they watched it, if they shared it, even how many times they watched it.

revelation

device

Mr. Ennis walks around the room as we study who our viewers are. He stops when he gets to my desk and points at the graph I'm staring at.

"For example," he says, "this shows that Derek had two hundred and twenty-three views on his new

shabby

12957	35961	96419
97869	12439	67198
89818	92321	47982

column

Monkey Love Hot Sauce clip from last night."

I puff up my chest a bit. Not too shabby!

"But what this column shows is that two hundred and twenty-one of them were from the same person." He looks at me and laughs. "I'm guessing that's maybe a grandparent who misses you?"

I can't let my classmates know I spent all last night clicking on my own videos to raise the number of views for today's class! I laugh and say my grandmother watches everything I post multiple times.

Mr. Ennis continues to study the chart then moves to another area in the menu. "Well, unless your grandmother is a twelve-year-old boy in Los Angeles with a smartphone, your enthusiastic viewer doesn't seem to be her."

Umberto and Matt start laughing hysterically.

"You're tweaking the stats by watching your own videos?" Umberto says.

Everyone laughs, including Mr. Ennis. I can feel my checks flush bright red.

"Okay, that's enough humiliation for Derek for one day," he finally says.

It turns out Mr. Ennis is wrong because Matt, Carly, and Umberto remind me of it endlessly for the rest of the week.

Many, many times.

endlessly

COMMENTS

maximize

ratchet

We're all very aware that because Mr. Ennis's class is a weekly after-school elective, it runs for a shorter period of time than our other subjects. When I realize there are only three classes left, however, I go pedal-to-the-metal to maximize my number of subscribers. Matt, on the other hand, tries to ratchet up his views. Even though Mr. Ennis keeps telling us that views and subscribers are only one way to track YouTube success, my classmates and I spend a lot of time debating which is better—to have a lot of subscribers or to have a lot of views. In the end, I guess they're BOTH pretty important. Not that it matters much in terms of the competition, with Carly and Tyler so far ahead of the rest of us.

From studying the comments, I discover that lots of people really like my Monkey Love Hot Sauce theme song. A few people think I shouldn't be using a capuchin in my videos in case he gets hurt. (Frank getting stuck inside Mom's bangle drew several negative comments from people who were worried about his safety.) But on the whole, most people seem to really like my channel.

In class the other day, Mr. Ennis talked about the pressure to always come up with something new, having to best yourself and make every video better than the last. "At first, I was just pulling things out of pictures and books," he said. "Next thing you know, I'm climbing out of a mailman's pocket to surprise my mom on Mother's Day and jumping through subway cars without opening the doors." First and foremost he talked about making sure what you do is safe. I always try to be safe with Frank—no matter what people might suggest in the comments.

All this thinking about Frank makes me miss him, so I head to the kitchen to take him out of his crate.

foremost

Mom's cleaning up after dinner then sits down at the table with us.

She reaches over to pat Frank's head. "I thought Frank looked like he's been putting on weight, so I took him to the office to weigh him. He's gained three pounds in the past month—that's a lot for a capuchin this size."

I suddenly wonder about the caloric content of ketchup.

Frank leaves my arms and jumps into Mom's.

"You're not feeding Frank extra snacks, are you?" she asks me. "The woman at the foundation wants him to stay on a pretty specific diet."

I tell her I feed him the chopped-up veggies and fruits we're sup-posed to, along with his monkey pellets.

pellets

She holds Frank in front of her and talks to him in her baby voice. As a vet, she's professional 99 percent of the time, but once in a while the kid inside her pops out and she lets herself be amazed by how cute all these animals are.

"Who's putting on a little weight? Who is?" she coos to Frank.

Between Frank's unpredicted weight gain and Mr. Ennis's class coming to an end next week, it looks like I'll only be able to film one more Frank video.

It's got to be a showstopper.

showstopper

RACE AGAINST TIME

My parents are next door at the Blakes', which should hopefully give me enough time to film.

After my conversation with Mom about Frank's weight yesterday, I decide to use something else besides ketchup and monkey biscuits to get him to go nutty over the bottle of hot sauce.

I take out the jar of mealworms

mealworms

delicate

piñata

from the cupboard where we keep Frank's and Bodi's food. But what should I put them in? Eureka! I place the dead worms in the mesh bag Mom uses for delicate clothes. Thankfully, the holes in the mesh are small enough to keep the worms inside. I hang the bag of worms and hot sauce from the dashboard of Mom's treadmill like a piñata that Frank will try to grab. Frank is really going to have to work for his hot sauce today.

"Okay, buddy," I tell him. "This is going to be fun."

Frank's as excited as I am and leaps onto the base of the treadmill. He immediately starts jumping to reach the bag. I lean over him to the dashboard and put the treadmill on its lowest setting. Frank doesn't miss a beat, just takes tiny steps and begins to run.

This time I don't use the tripod so I am able to move around and get some action shots that I'll edit into a fast-paced scene. Frank is doing great! He continues to hop up during his jog, striving to get those worms. Would it be bad to let a few of them loose on the treadmill?

striving

I open the bag and take out some mealworms, filming myself as I do it. I dangle them in front of Frank who starts running even faster, trying to grab the snack. As he's about to, the worms fall out of my hand and roll into the guts of the treadmill.

A few dead worms can't break a big piece of machinery, can they?

I scrunch up my face, waiting for

grinding

the treadmill to come to a grinding halt, but it continues to move. To make sure it doesn't get stuck, I raise the speed a little. Frank runs even faster so I increase the speed a little more.

The next noise I hear is the outside door, telling me my parents are home. I shut off the treadmill, grab Frank, and duck into my room.

I forgot the bag of mealworms and hot sauce!

From the sound of their voices, my parents are at the bottom of the stairs so I race back to the treadmill and untie the bag.

untie

Come on, come on!

snatch

I don't have time to snatch the several mealworms that fall on the rug as I race out of there.

Seconds later, Dad opens the door

to my room. "You get all your work done tonight?"

I tell him I did.

"Why are you so out of breath? Exercising?"

He gives me a thumbs-up when I tell him yes.

Mom sticks her head in and tells me the Blakes say hello. When she sees Frank, she tells me to put him back in his crate. I tuck the bag of hot sauce and mealworms underneath my shirt and take Frank to the kitchen.

Frank seems exhausted from all that running so I sit at the kitchen table and hold him.

"You did a GREAT job," I whisper. "Now it's time for your reward."

I empty what's left of the bag of worms on the table and watch Frank scramble to eat them. If I'd thought about it longer, I would've taken my phone with me to get this on film.

"You deserve every one of those." I rub the top of his head then put him in the crate.

Upstairs, my parents are still in the hall. Mom's balancing in the doorway, taking off her shoes. "I couldn't wait to get these off." She turns to Dad. "Some yoga before bed?"

Dad agrees and takes off his shoes too. They say goodnight and head to their room.

squishing

The thought of mealworms squishing between my parents' toes during downward dog makes me want to gag.

I hope they're using yoga mats.

YES!!!!!

The treadmill clip of Monkey Love Hot Sauce brings me over nine thousand views in the first twenty-four hours! Watching the number of views grow every few minutes makes me happier than the day we first got Frank.

Suddenly my number of views puts me in Umberto and Tyler's league. With only one class left, the chances of us knocking Carly out of first place are slim, but second place is still something to aim for.

A few of the comments are negative—"you're abusing that poor animal!"—but most people say they like it. The popularity of this clip must be carrying over to the others on my playlist because ALL my videos increased overnight; my subscribers are way up too.

quarterback

At school, I feel like a quarterback who just made the winning touchdown.

touchdown

"Dude!" Matt says. "That video is killer!"

"The sound effects and song really make it," Umberto says. "I laughed the whole way through."

So many pieces of music that I wanted to use were copyright-protected; Mr. Ennis talked about only using royalty-free music many times, so I knew he'd go nutty if I illegally downloaded a piece of music instead of buying it. In the end, I found a great piece of free music that sounds like the circus and really works.

When we get to class, Mr. Ennis and Carly are huddled at his desk. Wait—are they planning a surprise to celebrate my smash hit?

huddled

Mr. Ennis waits for us to take our seats. He must not have liked being bald because his scalp is now covered in stubble where his hair is growing out.

stubble

"We've got some big news." He bows toward Carly and asks if she wants to tell us.

Carly stands in front of the room and takes a deep breath. "Remember how I told you that I had one viewer who wrote to me every day? Power73? Well, it turns out her mom is a producer on *Ellen*."

Natalie and Bridget actually scream.

"And they're doing a segment on youtuber kids and they want me to come on the show!"

The rest of the class goes ballistic along with Natalie and Bridget. Ellen has a HUGE fanbase for her show as well as online viewers. Being on her show will launch Carly's vlog into the stratosphere!

stratosphere

I'm happy for Carly—that's GIGANTIC news—but can't we take ONE SECOND to acknowledge my big accomplishment? Am I doomed to follow in Carly's footsteps forever? Still, seeing how thrilled she is makes me realize I'm being petty

petty

and so I let out a hoot to celebrate Carly's windfall.

windfall

"There will be six of us and they're looking for one more kid to replace the Fine Brothers who had to cancel. Since I live locally, they asked if I had any recommendations on such short notice."

I'm Carly's best friend! This is a slam dunk!

Carly runs her tongue along the front of her teeth, a new habit since getting her braces. "I wanted to talk to Mr. Ennis first because I don't want to hurt anyone's feelings." She opens her arms to encompass everyone in the room. "I love all your work but I only get to pick one."

encompass

I'm gonna dance with Ellen! I'm gonna dance with Ellen!

"Umberto, do you want to join me on the *Ellen* show?"

Wait, what?

Umberto lets out a Tarzan yell. "Absolutely!"

Carly addresses the rest of the room, but she's mostly looking at me. "I think Umberto's vlog is really important and can make a lot of people aware of what people with disabilities go through every day. Millions of people watch Ellen's show—Umberto's videos can really have an impact."

impact

I obviously can't argue with Carly's thinking—it makes complete sense to choose Umberto. However...

"Maybe you can talk about some of OUR channels too while you're on," I suggest.

Mr. Ennis interrupts before Carly

can answer. "The focus will be on their two channels," he says. "But two out of six kids are from this school? That's incredible! You should all be proud of yourselves! It's also important to note that their channels weren't chosen because they had millions of views but because they connected with people." He turns to Carly and praises her again.

praises

Matt leans over and whispers to me. "Aren't you used to swimming in Carly's wake by now? I am."

He's right. But at least this time, Umberto will get some well-deserved recognition too.

recognition

After class, I'm halfway down the hall when Carly catches up to me. "I LOVE your channel," she says. "You know that. It was a really hard decision."

"I know it was."

She spins around to face me. "As funny as your channel is, I just couldn't waste the chance to make a difference."

Carly stands in front of me, waiting. I know she wants a smile and it only takes a few seconds before I give her one.

"I'm proud of you," I tell her. "You did the right thing."

She squeezes my arm and runs down the hall.

"When are you filming *Ellen*?" I call after her.

"Tomorrow!!" she yells back.

There are actually worse places to be than swimming in Carly's wake.

NO!

My mom's going to FLIP when I tell her. She loves Carly and she loves Ellen so it's going to be twice the good news.

But when I step inside the kitchen, both my parents are waiting for me. Dad looks as mad as I've ever seen him; Mom looks incredibly disappointed.

On the kitchen table is Mom's laptop.

fishy

comprehend

It's open to Monkey Love Hot Sauce.

"I knew there was something fishy about your action figure mash-up channel," Mom finally begins. "I just couldn't comprehend why you were doing it and now I know why."

"Was that some kind of decoy so we wouldn't find your REAL videos?" Dad asks. "The ones you made with Frank that we told you over and over NOT to create?"

"You better start talking, and I mean NOW," Mom says.

"No one liked the videos I made of me," I finally stammer. "We live with a monkey! I had to use Frank!"

Dad tilts his head. "Even after we told you repeatedly not to?"

"There is not enough punishment to go around for this one," Mom says. "Not only did you betray our trust, you put Frank in dangerous situations."

"It wasn't hot sauce," I cry. "It was ketchup!"

"Frank is on a restricted diet! Do you know how much sugar is in a spoonful of ketchup?" Mom asks. "More sugar than a chocolate chip cookie! Frank could have diabetes now." Mom takes a deep breath, winding up for more.

Dad takes a seat on one of the kitchen stools. "I took you to Doug's, he let you borrow props, we signed off on every one of your decoy videos. We've been very supportive from day one. But you were deceitful with us, and it's hugely disappointing."

deceitful

"I didn't want to lie," I answer. "But I HAD to. The competition is

STEEP. Frank may be a few pounds heavier, but he's FINE. I'll take any punishment you want to give me for lying—and I'm really sorry you feel betrayed—but, everything's okay! Frank didn't get hurt!"

It's a solid pitch, even if my voice did sound like I was a little desperate toward the end.

desperate

"Derek, how do you think we found out about these videos?" Mom asks.

It's something I've been wondering since I walked in the door.

Mom answers her own question. "Mary Granville told me."

"Is she one of the techs in your office?"

Mom turns to Dad with an expression of disbelief before turning back to me. "Mary runs the foundation where we got Frank."

"Oh, the lady who said we could keep him—I remember."

"Yes, the lady who said we could keep him when she thought we were taking good care of him. Now she's the lady who thinks we're endangering him so she's hopping on a plane to take Frank back. She'll be here first thing Monday morning."

WHAT HAVE I DONE?!

endangering

A HIGH PRICE
TO PAY

defunct

The videos on my Monkey Love Hot Sauce channel have now reached 15,750 views. I have over 2,000 new subscribers. What my subscribers don't know is that they've subscribed to a channel that is now defunct.

My parents make me take everything off YouTube, even the decoy action-figure channel I'd set up just for them. They make me send an email to Mary at the capuchin foundation to apologize. Her response is immediate—she will still be here Monday morning.

Everyone in the entire school is excited about Umberto and Carly talking about their YouTube channels on *Ellen*, but it's difficult to get caught up in all the excitement when I only have a few days left with Frank.

Matt takes the news hard—he loves Frank almost as much as I do. I make the decision not to tell Carly and Umberto until after the *Ellen* taping so they're not upset during the show. Matt think's that's a mature thing to do, but mature is the last thing I'm feeling right now.

Mom and Dad go back and forth with the appropriate punishment.

privileges

sandwiched

Take away my phone? My laptop? Ground me? Take away my skateboard? To me it doesn't matter what they choose because all those things are nothing compared to losing Frank. (Yes, even phone privileges.)

When I get home from school the next day, I immediately take Frank out of his crate and hold him. Bodi won't leave our side, as if he knows something's about to happen, the way animals can sense a change in the weather. I pull them both toward me until I'm sandwiched between them on the couch.

I know I'll have to explain everything to Mr. Ennis, but right now the furthest thing from my mind is making videos. But who am I kidding? The videos weren't at fault—I was.

I guess Mr. Ennis was right when he talked about the pressure of creating the latest and greatest videos, having to top yourself each and every time out of the gate. Without realizing it, I got caught up in views and subscribers and beating the other kids in class. Maybe if I'd done something simple like Carly or helpful like Umberto or downright absurd like Tyler, I wouldn't be losing one of my best friends.

Dad comes in and plops down beside me. He holds out his arm for Frank, who climbs up it to sit on Dad's shoulders. "You're not the only one who's going to miss Frank," Dad says. "We ALL love this guy. It's going to be strange not having him around the house anymore."

I'd been so wrapped up in my own feelings that I hadn't thought about how this would affect my parents. Or Bodi.

"I'm really, really sorry," I say for the zillionth time.

"I know you are." He leans across the table, grabs his sketchbook, and starts drawing. Frank inside the window of an airplane. Frank reuniting with his capuchin friends back in Boston.

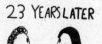

reuniting

"Does drawing Frank help make the pain go away?" I ask.

"I don't know," Dad answers. "I always think art helps, don't you?"

A slow smile spreads across my face.

Dad just gave me the BEST IDEA EVER.

pry

I reach up and pry Frank from my father's back. "Come on, buddy. We've got some work to do."

A BETTER VIDEO

In hindsight, I should've done this from the beginning. But if your name is Derek Fallon, you usually take the long, windy road to success instead of the short, simpler one.

hindsight

This time, I'm doing a vlog—but not for YouTube—for the lucky person who'll end up with Frank as a companion.

I start in the kitchen where I go

mangoes

through Frank's favorite foods—mangoes, bananas, sweet potatoes, and turnips. "But you have to make sure to chop everything really small to fit into Frank's hands," I say into the camera. "And if he doesn't like his monkey biscuits, you can soak them in orange juice and he'll eat them right up. He also really likes mealworms—but not too many at once."

Next, I go through how to clean Frank's crate and to make sure it double-locks. "Frank is VERY curious," I tell the camera. "If the crate isn't secure, he'll definitely be able to get out."

secure

Dad comes inside from getting the mail and nearly drops it when he sees me filming. "Please tell me you are NOT posting videos of Frank again."

I shake my head and tell him what I'm doing.

His face relaxes. "That's a great idea."

assistant

With Dad as my assistant, the rest of the video goes much faster—except the part about Frank's favorite movies and TV shows. I want to make sure wherever he is, Frank still gets to enjoy the Westerns he loves, so I really take my time.

In between shots, Dad and I talk about who Frank might end up living with next. A kid in a wheelchair like Umberto? An elderly woman who needs help getting things down from shelves? Someone with a spinal injury like our friend Michael? Whoever it is, Dad and I agree he or she will be lucky to have Frank.

After I edit the footage, Dad and

I watch the rough cut. I decide to go the extra mile and add some music, fun sound effects, and graphics. The video might only be for an audience of one, but that person will be a part of Frank's extended family, so I want to do my best.

An hour and a half later, we're laughing at the finished piece as Mom comes in, wearing her scrubs. At first she's surprised to see new footage of Frank, but as she watches, she breaks into a huge smile. When it ends, I'm shocked to see her eyes are misty.

misty

"I'm going to miss him too," she says. "Very much."

We spend our last weekend with Frank taking turns holding him, watching TV, and giving him his favorite snacks. Bodi continues to sense something's going on because he follows Frank from room to room like a shadow.

Matt and Carly stop over to say goodbye. Carly tells us all about the taping and that the show will air on Monday. None of us can believe she and Umberto got to meet Hugh Jackman in the green room!

Because the show is on at three—the same time as Mr. Ennis's class—he said our last class can be a viewing party. My mom's so happy for Carly that she reschedules a meeting so she can watch the show when it airs.

reschedules

With multiple visits from Carly, Matt, and Umberto, it's a busy weekend. When I put Frank in his crate Sunday night, he heads straight for his blanket to fall asleep.

From his first day with us, I knew Frank would have to leave someday. We were a foster family, a place to live with people before beginning his real work to help someone with disabilities. This day was always coming—I just hoped to put it off as long as possible.

"Good night, buddy," I tell him. "The pleasure's been all mine."

FAREWELL

Mary shows up like clockwork first thing Monday morning. Mom said I could go to school late so I can say goodbye to Frank, but I think it's because she wants me to apologize to the director in person.

clockwork

I hear them talking about Mary's flight as I walk toward the kitchen with Frank to hand him over—the same kitchen where I first met Frank two years ago.

The woman who brought Frank here then was an older woman who seemed like a grandmother. The next person from the foundation who came was named Wendie. She visited us after Frank had an "incident" with swallowing one of my action figures and getting semi-kidnapped by Swifty who used to go to my school.

This new director looks different than I expected. Her hair is short, shaved on one side with bangs falling across her face. Frank must remember her, though, because he leaps out of my arms and into hers.

nuzzles

"Why, hello there, Frank." She holds back, waiting to see if he's comfortable with her, but he nuzzles her face like he just saw her yesterday.

She takes a step toward me and

holds out her hand. "You must be Derek. I'm Mary."

Her hand barely has time to touch mine before I blurt out another apology.

She listens to everything I have to say before she answers.

"You know what we call that at monkey college?" she asks. "A teachable moment."

"That's what we call them here too," Mom says.

Mary looks me straight in the eye. "The point wasn't that you were pretending to feed Frank hot sauce, the point is that you had him on a treadmill, loose in the yard, and you were using him for your own gain. You know posting videos of your friends without their permission isn't cool, right, Derek?"

I now feel even worse than I did

when my parents first caught me. Whether it's because Mary runs the foundation, or that her voice is so calm, I really take in everything she has to say.

"It's not like Frank could sign a release form," I offer. "And he DID have fun."

greyhound

"Like a greyhound has fun at the dog track?" Mary asks. "Or elephants at the zoo—THAT kind of fun?"

Her eye contact is so intense, I want to turn away but can't.

intense

"We humans are privileged to share the planet with these special creatures," Mary adds. "First and foremost, our job is to protect them."

I feel Mom gently come up behind me and put her hands on my shoulders. "Derek's done a good job doing that for two years," she says. "I don't want the YouTube incident to take away from the fact that he helped us make a safe and happy home for Frank."

From his seat at the table, Dad gives me a slight nod to let me know he agrees. Knowing my parents are on my side—even through all my stupid mistakes—feels like the most important thing in the world right now. Bigger than my birthday and Christmas combined.

"Our capuchins make a lot of mistakes also," Mary continues. "We expect them to. The question is, do they LEARN from their mistakes? I've seen capuchins try to take the top off a water bottle hundreds of times," she says. "But if they really care about improving, they'll keep trying."

digital

paperwork

enormity

I could make a crack about how she's comparing me to a monkey, but even I know that would take the conversation down the wrong road.

"I made this video for whoever ends up with Frank." I hand her the DVD that Dad had to show me how to burn since I mostly use digital files. "It's full of instructions so Frank is properly taken care of wherever he goes next."

Mary smiles. "I'm sure this will be very helpful. Thanks, Derek."

She spends the next few minutes signing paperwork with Mom.

As Mary heads to the door, I ask if I can hold Frank once more before they go.

I press my forehead against Frank's and smell his monkey smell for the last time. The enormity of my loss suddenly bowls me over with sadness.

Mary must notice that I'm about to fall apart because she gently takes Frank and says a quick good-bye. As soon as she's out the door, I do something I haven't done in years. I'd call it crying, but the sounds coming out of me now are more like a wounded animal wailing than a kid sniffling through tears.

wailing

"It's okay, buddy," Dad says. "Sometimes a good cry is the best thing."

sniffling

I've got Mom hugging me on one side, Dad on the other, and Bodi on his hind legs, trying to reach me from the floor. Everybody's being kind. Everybody's being supportive.

It's just that everybody no longer includes Frank.

YOU WANT ME
TO WHAT?

After washing my face and spending some time with Bodi, Dad drives
me to school. It turns out I only
missed my first two classes. All that
emotion this morning wore me out
and I keep to myself for the rest of
the day.

All everyone else can talk about
is Carly and Umberto's appearance
on *Ellen*. Half the people jammed

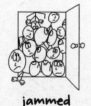

jammed

into Mr. Ennis's classroom at three o'clock aren't even in our class; they just want to see the show. Ms. McCoddle bought giant bags of candy from Costco, which she passes around in large bowls. I try to rally with my classmates but two things haunt me. First, losing Frank. And second, the conversation I need to have with Mr. Ennis after class. He's not going to be happy with how I sidestepped his rules and regulations in my YouTube channel. Not. Looking. Forward.

haunt

sidestepped

Mr. Ennis's hair is almost crew cut length as he films the proceedings with his GoPro. "This is really something," he tells Carly and Umberto. "Those of us who vlog for a living would KILL for an opportunity like this."

crew cut

Matt is throwing M&M's into the air and catching them in his mouth. Umberto's popping wheelies until he runs over Natalie's foot. Carly looks almost embarrassed by all the attention.

It's been a fun class—I learned a lot—but there's no shaking that feeling of loss too. If fighting with Carly made me feel like wearing a shirt that didn't fit, betraying my parents and Mr. Ennis and then losing Frank feels like a hole in the bottom of my gut. People say time makes everything better; I don't know if that applies to monkeys but I hope it does because this feeling of sadness and guilt really hurts.

"IT'S ON! IT'S ON!" Ms. McCoddle takes a seat next to Carly and squeezes her arm.

When Ellen dances, most of us jump up and down. The first guest is Hugh Jackman, who talks about his new blockbuster. During the commercial, everyone yells over each other, full of excitement.

The segment on YouTube kid stars is next and we all scream when Carly and Umberto come onstage.

bow tie

"You're wearing a bow tie!" Matt yells to Umberto.

"I went old-school," Umberto replies.

Ellen asks Carly what it's like to have such rabid fans. Carly answers confidently; she doesn't seem nervous at all. I'm guessing the girl jumping up and down in the first row is Power73, and sure enough, Carly tells us it is.

The audience loves Umberto's

clips too, as well as JR's, a kid from San Francisco who plays with his toys on-screen. He's been doing this for years and has three hundred million views.

Three hundred million!

When the segment is over, we all go nuts. Mr. Ennis holds up his phone. "Both Carly's and Umberto's channels are racking up colossal numbers," he says. "This week is going to be huge for you guys—NOT that that's the most important thing!"

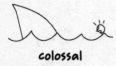
colossal

After Ms. McCoddle and the kids who aren't in our class finally leave, Mr. Ennis does a wrap-up of our work. Unfortunately, because my channel is no longer up, I come in pretty much last in every category. Luckily this elective isn't being graded.

"You guys have been great," Mr. Ennis says. "See you in the cybersphere."

cybersphere

I hang back while everyone else leaves, then approach Mr. Ennis.

"What happened to your YouTube channel?" he asks. "I didn't see it when I did a final pass of everyone's work this morning."

I begin to tell him the whole story of Monkey Love Hot Sauce.

He reaches up to shut off his GoPro. "But your parents signed the release forms giving you permission to upload that channel."

KYLE
KYLE
forged

"I forged their name on the permission slip," I confess. "I did a fake show for them—they just found out about Monkey Love Hot Sauce last week."

Mr. Ennis lets out a low whistle.

harsh

"So you lied to me AND your parents? That is harsh."

"I knew it was wrong but I did it anyway," I admit. "Like those people you warned us about, doing anything for more views."

"One of my friends has a competitive-eating channel," Mr. Ennis says. "You don't want to know how many times he's gotten his stomach pumped chasing after views. Finding that fine line of connecting with people without chasing your own tail is what this is all about."

prickly

He pulls the GoPro off his head and rubs his prickly scalp. "I have to say, Derek, I'm really disappointed."

"Join the club—it's growing faster by the day."

Mr. Ennis smiles. "When I was your age, there was no mistake I

DIDN'T make. If there were a hundred things to choose from and ninety-nine of them were good, I'd make that one wrong decision every time."

"That's pretty much how I am," I say.

"That's why I'm a big believer in second chances."

He shows me the latest video on his phone. "I was approached by a major sports drink company to make a series of YouTube videos. They want me to do my illusions but to bring in someone younger to appeal to their preteen market."

approached

preteen

Go on....

"I'm headed to Dodger Stadium this Saturday. I need a kid to toss fruits to me so I can swing at them with a bat and make it look like I'm

pitching

smithereens

turning them into the different flavors of the sports drink. I was going to ask one of my friends' kids, but how's YOUR pitching arm?"

My mind flashes forward to me on the pitcher's mound with a GoPro on my head, winding up a kiwi for Mr. Ennis to blast to smithereens. This could be gigantic! A national commercial! I take a breath and try—for once—not to get carried away. If Mr. Ennis is generous enough to give me a second chance, priority number one is to do a good job.

I tell Mr. Ennis I'd love to meet him at Dodger Stadium. "If my parents will let me," I add. "I think I might be grounded for a while."

"I just want to help you get back on the horse," Mr. Ennis says. "It would be a shame to give up on being creative just because you messed up. You did some good work in this class."

The tension in my chest releases a tiny bit. Maybe I can resurrect my YouTube channel into something good that I DON'T have to lie about this time.

After all, when it comes to You-Tube, the possibilities are endless.

releases

resurrect

THE COMFORT
OF FRIENDS

collapses

Matt must be worried that I'll be lonely without Frank because he insists on coming over even though it's a school night. First we do our homework together, which we haven't done in years. Then we take Bodi to the park and throw him his chewed-up, soggy tennis ball until he collapses on the grass exhausted.

One of the things I love about

Matt is that he never worries about looking stupid or immature; he just wants to have fun. So when the toddlers at the playground get off the slide, Matt and I take turns sliding until a mom we don't know finally tells us to move on and give the little kids a chance.

Back at my house, Mom asks if we want something to eat.

"This may sound crazy," Matt begins. "But I would LOVE a smoothie."

"Sure," Mom says. "Strawberry and banana? Chocolate and peanut butter?"

My mouth is watering just at the MENTION of Mom's famous chocolate-peanut-butter smoothie but before I can answer, Matt suggests something else.

grimaces

"I was thinking more along the lines of an apple-juice-maple-syrup-clam-chowder-bagel-lettuce-and-blue-cheese smoothie," Matt says.

Mom grimaces and throws up her hands. "You two are on your own."

I realize Matt's staying at my house to make up for Frank not being here. I also realize Matt is one of the best friends on the planet. And as much as I'd TOTALLY prefer a chocolate-peanut-butter smoothie, I pretend that our gut-busting, disgusting concoction is exactly what I want too.

We take over the kitchen and start tossing things into the blender like two mad scientists. We have to press pulse instead of on because the container is so full.

pulse

My dad sees us and looks around the room for a camera. "Is this some kind of dare? Are you guys filming this?"

I shake my head and tell him that believe it or not, we're doing this just for us.

Matt pours the brown goop into two glasses. He holds out his glass to mine. "To Frank," Matt says.

We clink our glasses.

"To friends," I say.

"To best friends," he answers.

"I'll drink to that." My dad grabs the blender from the counter, holds the container to his lips, and takes a giant swig.

swig

He immediately spits it into the kitchen sink. "That's DISGUSTING!"

"I know," I answer. "It's the blue cheese."

"Or the clam chowder," Matt adds.

yakking

Whatever it is, Matt and I spend the rest of the night yakking at the kitchen table and finishing our horrible smoothie till it's gone.

Not a bad way to spend a Monday night. Not bad at all.

JANET TASHJIAN

If you created a YouTube channel, what would be its theme? Would it be a vlog or something more experimental?

Jake and I have made lots of YouTube videos—some to promote our books, others just to goof around. No one makes sillier videos than my son, Jake. I'm not much of a vlog person; I spend so much of my time working on books that the last thing I want to do is pontificate online. But I am a firm believer that you can't just be a spectator on the internet; if you're going to consume content, you should also create it. Jake does a weekly comic strip on Instagram, and posts short videos all the time (Happy Leave a Zucchini on Your Neighbor's Porch Day!). He has much more energy than I do.

What extracurricular class (or classes) would you have loved to take in school?

As a kid, I loved making anything with my hands; I still do. I loved to sew. I made clothes for all my dolls, as well as most of my outfits in middle and high school. I am still always cutting, gluing, collaging, even writing my books in longhand. (Yes, that means using a pen in a blank notebook.) Jake's pretty much the same way—when he was in elementary school, he took a board game–making class, improv, and he did lots of stop-motion animation. He loves to take old cartoon reels, remove the sound effects, and add new ones. When we're not making our books, we're still spending most of our time creating.

What is your favorite viral YouTube video?
It's hard to pick just one viral video out of the millions on You-Tube, but "David After Dentist" still holds up. I showed it to a friend's daughter, who wasn't even born when it first came out, and she loved it so much, she shared it with all her friends.

Derek and Matt do an intense Smoothie Challenge. What is the worst smoothie combination you can think of? How about the best?
For me, the worst combination for a refreshing smoothie would be slices of bologna with marshmallows. Or maybe olive loaf and peanut butter. Anything with meat products would make a terrible shake. As far as the *best* smoothie goes, there's a place here in Los Angeles that makes french toast smoothies with almond milk, maple syrup, cinnamon, nutmeg, bananas, walnuts, and vanilla. Fantastic!

How would you finish the line "My life as _____"?
A rewriter. Like most writers, I spend more time rewriting than writing!

Are you more of a reluctant reader like Derek, or are you a big reader?
I'm a massive reader. I've been reading at least three books a week for most of my life. I can't imagine a life without books.

If you could be any living person, who would you be and why?
I'd love to be my son, Jake, for a day to see the world through his eyes. He's got such a great, original view of the world— I'm sure it would be fascinating.

You've traveled around the world. Where would you say your favorite place is?
Where I live. I love Los Angeles. I love the comedy, the music, the restaurants, the beaches, the museums, the mountains, the people. And the weather. I REALLY love the weather.

How did you come up with the My Life series?
Jake used to love books when he was young, but as books became more challenging, reading became difficult. Because he is a visual leaner, he started drawing his vocabulary words on index cards with markers to help in his learning process. When friends would see them, they'd always laugh at how funny and creative the drawings were. At the same time, I was doing school visits all around the country, listening to teachers, students, and librarians talk about reaching reluctant readers. I wrote *My Life as a Book* for Jake and other kids like him.

If you could be any cartoon character, which one would you be and why?
I mean, who DOESN'T want to be Bugs Bunny? He's unflappable, sarcastic, and has the best comebacks. Bugs totally holds up, even eighty years after he was created.

What's your favorite word Jake has ever illustrated?
It would have to be the word "colleague" from the first book in the series. He drew two guys in prison uniforms on a chain

gang, shackled to each other. Brilliant. It still makes me laugh.

Who is your favorite book character and why?
That's an almost impossible question to answer! I love Joey Pigza, I love Arnie the Doughnut, and I love Einstein the Class Hamster. Yes, the last one is one of mine, but he does have a special place in my heart. I'm a sucker for wisecracking characters.

What kind of books do you like to read?
I spend so much time in the fictional world when I'm writing that I end up reading a lot of nonfiction to balance it out. But I also keep up on what my friends are writing, as well as the latest adult fiction. I have a huge collection of vintage children's books, too.

Do you base your characters on people you know?
Sometimes I'll steal a habit or quirk from one of my friends, but never a whole character. It's much more fun to make up characters from scratch.

What is your favorite thing about writing the My Life series?
There are so many things I love about the My Life series, but first and foremost, the greatest part is getting to work with my son. When students ask about our process, I tell them I write the book first, then go through it to highlight age-appropriate vocabulary words, as well as words that would be funny for Jake to illustrate. Then he takes over, drawing more than 220 illustrations for each book in the series. His illustrations literally make me laugh out loud. I love watching him work; he's such a perfectionist and so professional. He's done more than a thousand drawings for this series!

I also like the fact that the books are read by kids all around the world in so many different languages. It's exciting that "reluctant" readers have embraced Derek, his friends, and their crazy adventures. Getting to tell Derek's story is an absolute joy. I find it funny when people talk about what a "bad" kid he is and how he always misbehaves—I know so many kids just like him, and they aren't bad at all!

Are you a fan of cartoons? Do you have a favorite cartoonist? Who and why?

I am a GIANT cartoon nerd. I'm a big fan of watching Saturday morning cartoons—even if it isn't Saturday. We have a cartoon collection that goes all the way back to the 1930s. I love print cartoons, too. Jake and I read *Calvin and Hobbes* in chronological order; it's my favorite comic strip of all time and the reason I dedicated *My Life as a Book* to Bill Watterson. I read every cartoon in *The New Yorker*; Jake reads every *Garfield.* He has a daily cartoon app on his phone so he can keep up with his favorites. I can't imagine a world without cartoons, so it's great to have a cartoonist in the family.

What did you want to be when you grew up?

Students ask me this all the time, and I wish I had a better answer. When I was young, I was too busy playing, reading, and studying to think about career goals. I envy people who knew what they wanted to be by age ten. I was not one of them.

When did you realize you wanted to be a writer?

Before Jake was born I traveled around the world, and when I got back to the States, I had to fill in some forms. One asked for my occupation and I put down "writer," even though I'd never done anything more than dabble. But deep down, I always felt being a writer would be the greatest job in the world. It took me several years after that to make that dream a reality.

What's your first childhood memory?
I remember cooking candies in a little pan on a toy stove that I got for Christmas. I was maybe three. I'm not sure if I remember it or if I just saw the photograph so often that I think I do.

What's your most embarrassing childhood memory?
I was singing and dancing in a school assembly with my first grade class when my shoe fell off. I kept going without the shoe, hopping around the stage—the show must go on.

What was your worst subject in school?
I always did well in school, but for some reason I forgot all my math skills and now can barely multiply. I'd love to know where all my math skills went.

What was your first job?
I've had dozens of jobs since I was sixteen—working on assembly lines, babysitting, washing dishes, waiting tables, delivering dental molds and telephone books, selling copy machines, working in a fabric store, painting houses. . . . I could fill a whole page with how many jobs I've had.

How did you celebrate publishing your first book?
By inviting my tenth-grade English teacher to my first book signing. The photo of the two of us from that day sits on my writing desk.

Where do you write your books?
Usually in my office on my treadmill desk. But because I often write in longhand, I end up writing everywhere—on the beach, in a coffee shop, wherever I am.

When you finish a book, who reads it first?
Always my editor, Christy Ottaviano. We've been doing books together for almost two decades; I consider her one of my closest friends.

How do you usually feel once you've completed a manuscript? Are you ever sad when a book you are writing is over?
Relieved! I don't really miss my characters; they're always with me.

Are you a morning person or a night owl?
I like waking up early and getting right to work. I'm too fried by the end of the day to get anything substantial done.

What's your idea of the best meal ever?
Something healthy and fresh, with lots of friends sitting around and talking. Definitely a chocolate dessert.

Which do you like better, cats or dogs?
I love dogs and have always had one. I'm allergic to cats, so I stay away from them. They don't seem as fun as dogs, anyway.

What do you value most in your friends?
Dependability and a sense of humor. All my friends are pretty funny.

What makes you laugh out loud?
My son. He's by far the funniest person I know.

What are you most afraid of?
I worry about all the normal mom things, like war, drunk drivers, and strange illnesses with no cures. I'm also afraid our culture is so invested in technology that we're veering away from basic things like nature. I worry about the implications down the road.

What time of the year do you like the best?
The summer, absolutely. I hate the cold.

If you were stranded on a desert island, who would you want for company?
My family.

If you could travel in time, where would you go?
To the future, to see how badly we've messed things up.

What's the best advice you have ever received about writing?
To do it as a daily practice, like running or meditation.

How do you react when you receive criticism?
My sales background and MFA workshops have left me with a very tough skin. If the feedback makes the book better, bring it on.

What do you want readers to remember about your books?
I want them to remember the characters as if they were old friends.

What would you do if you ever stopped writing?
Try to live my life without finding stories everywhere. For a job,
I'd do some kind of design—anything from renovating houses
to creating fabric.

What do you like best about yourself?
I'm not afraid to work.

What is your worst habit?
I hate to exercise.

**What do you consider to be your greatest
accomplishment?**
How great my son is.

What is your idea of fun?
Seeing comedy or music in a tiny club.

**What would your friends say if we asked them about
you?**
She acts like a fifteen-year-old boy.

What's on your list of things to do right now?
EXERCISE!

Can you share a little-known fact about yourself?
I love to make collages.

Derek Fallon has become a viral meme, but it's not long before his Internet fame spins out of control!

Keep reading for an excerpt.

MALIBU!

MATT AND I ARE SKATEBOARDING home from school, when I hit a rock and go flying onto the sidewalk. My knee gets scraped but something more valuable than a body part ends up shattered—the screen on my phone.

scraped

shattered

"My mom's going to kill me," I tell Matt. "She just had this fixed from when I broke it last time."

salvageable

It's only been a couple months since I dropped my phone out the car window trying to snap a photo of a dog in a taco costume. Thankfully, I captured one salvageable picture and was able to turn it into a LOL-worthy meme with a little help from a cool sunglasses filter.

"We need to get helmets for our phones," Matt suggests. "They take more abuse on these boards than our heads do."

I run my finger across the screen. "It looks like it's trapped in a giant spiderweb."

"It's not like you can erase the crack with your finger," Matt says. "I think you're going to have to come clean to your mom."

I tuck the phone back into the pocket of my shorts. I might have to encase my phone in something more protective—maybe bubble wrap or foam. For a minute, I think I've come up with a great invention until I realize my phone would be safe but I'd never be able to actually USE it.

encase

Even with insurance on all the family phones, Mom complains about how much money it costs to maintain them. She doesn't need to say that it's mostly me—and sometimes Dad—because she's still using the same phone she got years ago. My favorite phone accident was when we were at the Thompsons' house and Dad took my phone away because I was running around their pool. But then he didn't look where he was going and fell into the water with BOTH our phones. Dad tried to mitigate the tension in the car

protective

maintain

mitigate

by joking that our smartphones were smarter than we are, but Mom was still furious the whole way home.

After I leave Matt at the top of his street, I try to come up with a good story for yet another broken phone. Maybe some guy knocked me over and tried to steal it? Or it fell out of my pocket while I was rescuing a kid from getting hit by a car? Whatever I end up saying, Mom will probably realize I'm making it up and I'll have to tell the truth anyway. Knowing when I'm being less than honest—in other words, lying—has always been one of Mom's superpowers.

rescuing

When I get home, both my parents are cooking in the kitchen. Mom's wearing scrubs from her veterinary practice next door and Dad's in his workout clothes, which means he just got back from the gym. Mom's latest culinary obsession is using her new pasta machine and she's got Dad halfway across the kitchen holding a long string of dough that she'll cut into noodles on the wooden cutting board. Mom's had a lot of cooking fads over the years but her handmade pasta is one of the better ones. If she grounds me for breaking my phone again, at least an awesome dinner can be my consolation prize.

dough

consolation

The pasta machine is in the same place on the counter where Frank's crate used to be and every time I see it, I think about him. Frank is the capuchin monkey we used to be a foster family for until he had to go

roommate

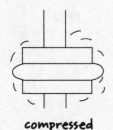

compressed

fettuccini

back to the foundation that trained him. Having a monkey as a roommate was one of the best things ever but we all knew sooner or later he'd have to go back. (Thanks to me and my dreams of YouTube stardom, it was sooner rather than later.)

Don't get me wrong—I love the pasta machine—but it's no monkey.

"Guess what?" Dad folds the compressed pasta carefully onto the counter. "Your mom made an awesome score today."

"I wouldn't necessarily call it a 'score,'" Mom says, slicing the dough into fettuccini. "It's more like I agreed to help someone out and the job comes with some nice perks."

I can see why they call them perks because that's exactly what my ears do as soon as the word leaves her mouth.

"One of my patients has a beautiful home in Malibu," she continues. "Darcy is a tech mogul, on a photo safari at a wildlife reserve in Kenya. She asked if we could dogsit at her place for the long weekend."

"She needs a veterinarian to dogsit?" I ask. "Seems a little extreme."

dogsit

Mom explains that Darcy has several go-to dogsitters, but all of them are taking advantage of the long weekend and going out of town.

"With her favorite vet in charge," Dad continues, "she won't have to worry about a thing. Malibu, here we come!"

My mind ricochets from surfing to hiking to eating clams to swimming. I've never had a bad time when we've gone to Malibu, and this time it'll include a second dog to keep Bodi company. I don't want my broken phone to change that, so I decide to put off telling my parents for a while.

"It's not going to be all fun and games," Mom says. "Poufy isn't like other dogs."

I ask Mom to explain.

"She's the only dog I know with her own Instagram account," Mom answers.

"No way!" I reach into my pocket for my phone but stop as soon as I feel the broken screen. "Wait, this isn't the person who invented that unicorn game app who comes to your office in a limo, is it?"

Mom nods and drops the fresh noodles into the pot of boiling water. "Darcy definitely spoils Poufy, but she's a longtime patient. In exchange for a free vacation in their giant house, we'll be in charge of Poufy."

"How GIANT are we talking?"
I ask.

Mom wipes the flour off her hands and scrolls through photos on her phone. "Is this big enough?"

The house in the picture is modern, constructed of floor-to-ceiling

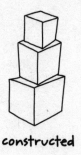

constructed

glass, surrounded by trees and mountains and with an ocean view. It's five times the size of our house. So what if I have to help take care of a spoiled dog? It'll definitely be worth it to show off pictures of me living it up in paradise.

"We'll each have our own floor!" I say.

Dad smiles. "We were thinking you might want to invite a few friends— there's plenty of room."

I know my parents want me to bring friends so they can spend time alone without worrying that I'll be bored, but I'm still excited by the offer. I immediately text Matt, Carly, and Umberto to see if they're free next weekend.

We're heading to the beach!

Now all I have to do is figure out how I'm going to fix my phone.

WHAT TO BRING

IT TURNS OUT THAT THE BEACH house in Malibu is handicap-accessible, so Umberto will be able to come after he reschedules his Saturday computer class. Carly and Matt also have to shuffle around their schedules, but by the next day at school, they're all locked in.

shuffle

"We should see if Heinz can give us surf lessons again," Carly suggests. Heinz is a surf instructor who

rugged

basically lives in the water giving lessons. His skin is so rugged from spending all his time outdoors, he looks much older than he is.

"You have to find out if the house has any gaming systems," Matt says. "Or if we should bring one of ours."

"It's MALIBU—you're crazy if you don't want to be outside," Carly says. "I think you can go three days without video games."

Umberto, Matt, and I stare Carly down over her turkey sandwich. "I think not," I finally answer.

When Mrs. Cannelini—one of the lunch crew—walks by, Umberto calls her over. "Is it my imagination or did you change the recipe for the mac and cheese?" he asks.

perceptive

Mrs. Cannelini looks at him with pride. "How perceptive! We DID—do you like it?"

While Umberto compliments her on the meal, Matt and I just shake our heads. No one has more pleasurable conversations with grown-ups than Umberto. It's actually a great quality—trying to give people a little boost to their day. Not to mention that Umberto usually gets much bigger portions at lunch than the rest of us.

pleasurable

boost

Carly, of course, has ten different apps on her phone for keeping organized, so she helps us remember some of the things we'll need for our Malibu adventure.

"Not just regular stuff like toothbrushes," she begins.

"Toothbrushes are completely optional," Matt interjects. "People got along fine for thousands of years before they were invented."

interjects

"Yeah—and they needed dentures before they were twenty."

repellent

moisturizing

getaway

Carly gives him a sarcastic smile that flashes her braces. "We'll need sunscreen, insect repellent, bathing suits, moisturizing lotion—"

"WE DO NOT NEED MOISTURIZING LOTION!" I try to grab Carly's phone but she's too fast and shoves it into her bag.

"It's better to be safe than sorry," Carly says.

"No one's going to be sorry spending three days at the beach," Matt says. "Give it a rest with the planning, okay?"

A Malibu getaway should be ONE thing my friends and I can agree on, right?

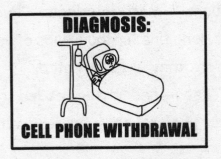
DIAGNOSIS:
CELL PHONE WITHDRAWAL

Don't miss any of the fun!

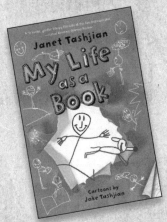

★ "A kinder, gentler Wimpy Kid with all the fun and more plot."
—*KIRKUS REVIEWS*, STARRED REVIEW

★ "Give this to kids who think they don't like reading. It might change their minds."
—*BOOKLIST*, STARRED REVIEW

The Messianic Mo

D0052879

A Field Gui
Evangelical Christians

from Jews f☆r Jesus

The Messianic Movement:
A Field Guide for Evangelical Christians
from Jews f★r Jesus

Rich Robinson, General Editor

Naomi Rose Rothstein, Contributing Editor

Purple Pomegranate Productions
A division of Jews f★r Jesus

The Messianic Movement: A Field Guide for Evangelical Christians
from Jews for Jesus
Rich Robinson, General Editor
Naomi Rose Rothstein, Contributing Editor
© Copyright 2005 by Purple Pomegranate Productions
(a division of Jews for Jesus®)
Cover design and layout by David Yapp

For more information, including reprint permission, write to:
Jews for Jesus®
60 Haight Street
San Francisco, CA 94102
USA
www.jewsforjesus.org

ISBN 10: 1-881022-62-5
ISBN 13: 978-1-881022-62-6

Introduction

What is the "Messianic movement" and what's the point of a "field guide" to it?

Hardly a day goes by that the Jews for Jesus office doesn't get calls from people asking questions pertaining to the Messianic movement. We thought that it would be helpful to put together some material that would answer many of those questions.

Though the existence of Messianic Jews dates back to the early Church—when Jewish believers in Jesus retained their distinctive Jewish lifestyle for several centuries—the specific term "Messianic" experienced a surge in popularity in the 1970s when it was used to describe a moving of Jewish people to faith in Y'shua (Jesus) in the context of Jewish culture. While the term "Messianic" was never formally defined, it was broadly used to describe someone who was both Jewish and a believer in Jesus.

Today the term "Messianic" has been adopted—and sometimes co-opted—by numerous groups and theologies. And so we constantly receive inquiries from Christians, both Jewish and Gentile, who want to know about a particular Messianic congregation, or a certain "Hebrew roots of the Christian faith" teacher, or a person who says the Church is the lost tribe of Ephraim, or someone who advocates for something called "Nazarene Judaism." It seems that when a group or congregation or teaching institution puts "Jesus" and "Jewish" together in its name or philosophy, it is seen as part of the Messianic movement.

It is because of this ambiguity that we wrote this book, which we hope will serve as a "field guide" to the Messianic Jewish movement. Given today's diverse usage of the term "Messianic," it should be clear that there is no founder or single spokesperson for the terms "Messianic," "Messianic movement," "Messianic Jew" or "Messianic Judaism." While we might prefer to restrict the term "Messianic movement" to simply mean Jews who follow Jesus, this is not possible. We will take an inclusive look at various trends and organizations that some might call "Messianic"—from the healthy to the unhealthy, from the kosher and to the not-so-kosher. Our aim is to cover not only Jews who believe in Jesus and keep Jewish customs and practices, but also any Christian group who claims to be exploring the Jewishness of the Christian faith. We also wanted to include anyone else who purports to live according to the teachings and practices of the first followers of Jesus—whether or not they accept His deity.

"Part One: The Movement" surveys the various organizations under the "Messianic" umbrella: (1) Jewish missions; (2) Messianic congregations; (3) voluntary associations; (4) umbrella organizations; (5) educational institutions; (6) philo-Semitic or "love Israel" organizations. Each chapter includes an introduction, background and analysis of the current scene. These are also followed by suggestions for further reading. Please note that all web URLs were last accessed on July 1, 2005, and some may no longer be active. For your convenience, we have listed all the URLs cited in one place at: http://www.jewsforjesus.org/publications/fieldguide

"Part Two: Movements Within the Movement" surveys some general trends that cut across many Messianic organizations. First, we look at the essential Jewishness of Christianity, especially as regards the main doctrines of the faith. Then there is a brief overview of the place of the Law in the life of

Jewish believers and, thirdly, a look at the "Torah-observant" aspects of the Messianic movement. Finally, we include an essay on the continued need for direct Jewish evangelism. And we've included some (what we hope are) helpful appendices.

This book seeks to help people think discerningly about those things that have to do with Jesus and Jews. While lines are drawn around aspects of the movement that are sub-biblical or run contrary to accepted Christian teaching, at the same time we wish to affirm the healthy diversity that comprises the movement of Jewish believers in Jesus. Any survey of this kind will end up naming particular organizations and individuals, for the various groups mentioned have for the most part promulgated their ideas publicly, thereby inviting public response. Yet, we want to emphasize that we uphold or take issue with perspectives, not people. At the time this guide was compiled, the statements herein adequately reflected the positions of the people and organizations they are attributed to. Yet we'd like to point out that we realize that people's opinions and positions are subject to change. Should a statement or position we've published no longer be the view of a group or individual cited, we would welcome hearing about it for future editions of the *Field Guide*. We also recognize that we have not included every possible group. Should you have questions not covered in this field guide, we will do our best to suggest where you might look for answers.

Our hope is to challenge followers of Jesus, whether Jewish or Gentile, to follow Paul's exhortation: "...whatever things are true, whatever things are noble, whatever things are just, whatever things are pure, whatever things are lovely, whatever things are of good report, if there is any virtue and if there is anything praiseworthy—meditate on these things" (Philippians 4:8).

—Rich Robinson

Contents

Part One

The Movement

Chapter One
Jewish Missions

INTRODUCTION

Mission agencies frequently focus on reaching specific people groups, whether geographic (missions to one region), ethnic (missions to particular tribal peoples) or socio-economic (missions to students or professionals of some kind). Likewise, there are missions particularly directed to proclaiming the gospel to the Jewish people; their missionaries are sent by and work alongside local church congregations to that purpose. Jewish missions have been affiliated with various evangelical denominations and doctrinal positions. By undertaking financial and prayer support, churches and individual Christians act as senders of the missionaries. In this, Jewish missions follow the *modus operandi* of Protestant mission agencies everywhere.

If you see someone distributing Jewish-oriented tracts in public places, or view an ad in a newspaper or magazine proclaiming that Jesus is the Jewish Messiah, or hear someone preaching a gospel sermon at a venue that Jewish people attend, or know of a Bible study group for Jewish seekers, then you have seen a Jewish mission in action. The primary tasks of Jewish mission agencies are gospel proclamation, follow-up and discipleship.

There are some aspects of Jewish missions that make the work uniquely challenging. The first challenge is geographical: Jewish people are scattered throughout the globe. The second challenge is sociological: Jewish people come from a vast array of backgrounds and belief systems, ranging from atheists to ultra-Orthodox, and everything in between. In fact, there is such a variety of worldviews represented among this one people group that there is a saying that goes, "If you ask two Jews a question, you'll get three opinions." These challenges have been present since the beginning of Jewish missions and explain in part why there have never been massive numbers of Jewish people coming to faith in Christ at one time.

JEWISH MISSIONS: A HISTORIC OVERVIEW

We know from the Book of Acts that the early Jewish believers in Jesus were missionaries—first to the lost sheep of the house of Israel, and later to the other nations, or Gentiles. In those days the question was not, "How can someone be a Jew for Jesus?" but rather, "How can a Gentile be for Jesus without first becoming a Jew?"

Before too long the Church became predominantly Gentile. While a remnant of Jewish believers remained, by and large the Jewish people were badly in need of others to extend the love of Christ to them, as the early Jewish believers did for Gentiles. Yet the concept of Jewish evangelism and Jewish missions is relatively new and is still considered somewhat controversial.

It wasn't until the 1800s that we saw the formal institution of Jewish missions. Previously, there were groups like the Moravians who felt that they should be telling Jews about Jesus. But outside of the endeavors of a few individuals, there was little organized effort to bring the message of the Messiah to the Jewish people.

Perhaps the issue was avoided for so many centuries because of the patristic antipathy toward the Jews. When we read the tirades of some of the early church fathers against the Jewish people, we should not wonder that the Church adopted a prejudiced viewpoint and viewed Jewish culture and religion negatively.[1]

There was an increase in Jewish missions activity from about 1880, at a time when anti-Semitic persecution was rising in the Russian Empire, and when Jewish immigration, especially to the United States, was reaching unprecedented levels. In order to encourage compassion for Jewish people, mission publications appealed to Christian contributors by depicting the pitiable poverty in which many Jewish people in Eastern Europe found themselves.

In Europe, missions to the Jews were founded in several countries, particularly Great Britain, Norway and Finland. The British missions sent out workers throughout Europe and overseas. The Norwegian and Finnish missions gave particular attention to the increasing number of Jews who were returning to the land of Israel. As their work in Israel developed, there was a growing desire to form indigenous Hebrew-speaking congregations in the Land.

By the early decades of the 20th century, a number of well-organized missionary societies had arisen in the USA as well: the American Board of Missions to the Jews (ABMJ, earlier known as the Williamsburg Mission to the Jews); the Presbyterian Mission to the Jews; the Chicago Hebrew Mission; the American Association for Jewish Evangelism (a 1940s breakaway from the ABMJ).

The difficulty in integrating new Jewish believers in Jesus from Eastern European cultures into largely Anglo-Saxon Christian congregations led some to favor the establishment of Hebrew Christian congregations. The Presbyterian Mission to the Jews led the way, establishing Jewish congregations in several U.S. cities: Chicago; New York; Los Angeles; Philadelphia; Baltimore.

Jewish missions have reflected a variety of Christian traditions. There have been Lutheran Jewish missions, Presbyterian Jewish missions, Christian Reformed Jewish missions, Baptist Jewish missions, Assembly of God Jewish missions and Anglican/Episcopal efforts, as well as independent missions. Among denominationally based Jewish missions, some were particularly active prior to the Second World War.

With the rise of Nazism, certain missionaries to European Jews moved to Great Britain and the United States. Some of these missionaries were apologists whose work still influences Jewish missions today.[2]

Hundreds of thousands of Jews came out of the Holocaust and arrived in the United Kingdom, America and Israel with absolutely nothing. Medical clinics were opened to care for the Jewish poor. Eventually, the governments in these countries began to assist in such relief efforts and by the middle of the century there was no longer a real need for the clinics.

Following the Holocaust, various denominations largely curtailed or ended their Jewish missions programs. Some adopted a "two-covenant" theology, which says that Jewish people have no need of the gospel, since God already made a covenant with them through Abraham (see "Further Reading" below). Even evangelicals increasingly came under the sway of this sort of thinking and embraced dialogue or friendship with the Jewish community as a substitute for proclamation. In the past few decades, however, the Lutheran Church-Missouri Synod has strongly reaffirmed the need for Jewish evangelism and has established a growing Jewish mission work, and the Southern Baptists, amidst much media coverage, have publicly endorsed Jewish evangelism. Some work also is carried on by the Christian & Missionary Alliance (C&MA), the Presbyterian Church in America (PCA) and the Assemblies of God (AOG). Alongside denominational efforts, independent Jewish missions continue, though consolidated to a handful of international

missions, such as Jews for Jesus, founded in 1973, Chosen People
Ministries, Christian Jew Foundation Ministries, Ariel Ministries,
AMF International, Friends of Israel, Christian Witness to Israel
(CWI) and The Church's Ministry Among Jewish People (CMJ).
Several local missions are currently active, including Light of
Messiah Ministries in Atlanta, Georgia; Christians Announcing
Israel's Messiah in Philadelphia, Pennsylvania; and Messianic
Good News in Wading River, New York.

JEWISH MISSIONS METHODS

Jewish mission agencies encompass a wide variety of
approaches. Few Jewish people will seek out information
about Jesus on their own, so a certain amount of creativity
and persistence is necessary. Most mission organizations
have employed one or more of the following methods.

Literature and Media Development and Distribution

Evangelistic literature development and distribution have long
played a vital role in Jewish missions. Because Jewish people
are located throughout the world, it's important to have Bibles
and other literature, including articles, pamphlets and tracts,
available in several languages. It's also crucial that these
materials be carefully constructed with Jewish sensitivities in
mind. Over the years, tracts (sometimes called "broadsides")
have become shorter and more humorous to accommodate a
more "fast food, fast everything" generation. Tracts often
contain testimonies of Jewish believers and Scripture verses.

Multimedia efforts such as videos, DVDs and CD-ROMs are
being used more effectively. Often such programs feature
moving testimonies, apologetics information, answers to
frequently asked questions or even interactive games.

As for the challenge of getting these resources into the hands
of Jewish seekers, tracts are often distributed in mass numbers

in public places where Jewish people live and work. Jewish-seeker-friendly publications (or evangelistic book or media offers) are also directly mailed to Jewish homes. Sometimes mission groups set up resource tables at events such as fairs or festivals or on college campuses, or a mission might conduct public screenings of multimedia presentations.

Messianic Music

Messianic music, in addition to its value as a valid expression of worship, has proved to be a good evangelistic tool. Jewish seekers are invited to evangelistic music concerts in secular halls, on college campuses and in churches. Sometimes Messianic music groups obtain a permit to perform in a public square or park, which almost always gathers a crowd of people and provides an opportunity to share the gospel in a creative way.

Radio and Television Ministries

Radio and television outreach continues to grow. Some of the more widely known television programs are "Zola Levitt Presents," "Jewish Voice Today" with Jonathan Bernis, "Sid Roth's Messianic Vision," and "Jewish Jewels" with Neil and Jamie Lash. These shows, which focus on educating Christians about Jews and Jewish evangelism, often reach interested Jewish people who happen to listen in. The increasing popularity of radio via the Internet has enabled radio efforts such as Messianic Bureau International's "Messianic Jewish Radio" and "Messianic Minutes." Programs typically feature testimonies of Jewish believers in Jesus, Messianic music and Bible teaching.

Cyber-evangelism

Perhaps the newest method of all is electronic evangelism. Just about every middle-class and upwardly mobile home in the western world owns or has access to a computer. Several ministries have developed and are effectively using websites and chat rooms to proclaim Y'shua.

Secular Media Campaigns

Another newer method of evangelism that has been significantly employed since the early 1980s is the publication of gospel statements in secular media, including newspapers and magazines with a large Jewish readership. Gospel statements directed to Jewish people are also found on billboards, as well as on secular radio and TV. At the beginning of this new generation of missionaries, most of the protest against the gospel stemmed from one statement: "Jews don't believe in Jesus." Now the fact that Jews do believe in Jesus is out in the open, thanks in large part to use of the secular media.

Children's Work

Evangelism to Jewish children often occurs in the context of ministry to Jewish believing children at summer camps, retreats and Bible clubs. Parents must, of course, give permission for their children to participate in these activities.

Holiday Outreaches

Jewish mission agencies and Messianic congregations conduct outreaches during the Jewish High Holy days. Constituents and congregational members are encouraged to bring Jewish friends and family to Rosh Hashanah (New Year) and Yom Kippur (Day of Atonement) services, in addition to public Passover seders. These are often worship services with evangelistic emphases. Some local ministries have developed creative initiatives for Jewish community outreach, such as hand delivering holiday gift baskets to Jewish friends.

Personal Visits

The heart of missions work is sitting down one-on-one with Jewish people who have been contacted through one of the

above methods and studying Jesus' claims with them.
Sometimes these connections are initially made on the street,
from calling Jewish people from a prepared phone list or from
making a door-to-door inquiry. Sometimes Jewish people
respond to an ad or program they saw or heard. Whatever the
case, it is this personal connection that remains the primary
goal of Jewish missions.

To read more specific information about current initiatives in
Jewish missions, we refer you to "Jewish Evangelism: A Call to
the Church" (see "Further Reading" below).

PHILOSOPHICAL ISSUES

Like all missionary enterprises, Jewish missions have had to
wrestle with issues of indigenous culture and contextualization of
the gospel. Nineteenth-century missionaries often superimposed
the culture of the sponsoring country onto the gospel message.
In the second half of the twentieth century, recognition of the
interplay between gospel and culture has allowed for indigenous
gospel proclamation and expression. This recognition has
become an integral part of the way most Jewish missions work.

There has always been a tension in Jewish missions: How
could a Jewish believer in Jesus be an integral part of the
entire Body of Christ and yet still express his or her faith in an
"indigenous" way? Typical solutions were for missions to
encourage fellowships of Jewish believers in Jesus in addition
to attendance at churches, or to sponsor Jewish holiday
events. In effect, the missions acted as a special-interest group
to Jewish believers in the same way that a campus Christian
ministry acts as a special-interest group to students, who
attend its functions as well as their own churches.

Another solution was the creation of "Hebrew-Christian
churches," the forerunners of modern Messianic

congregations. The "Hebrew-Christian churches" were sometimes independent affairs or were sometimes sponsored under the auspices of a church denomination. But the Hebrew-Christian churches sparked a lively debate of their own over whether Jewish believers should have their own separate congregations (see chapter 1.2).

Certain Jewish missions continue to plant Messianic congregations as a method for evangelism today. Some in the Messianic movement have further suggested that evangelism best takes place through Messianic congregations and have come to question the necessity for other traditional methods of proclamation.

While evangelism certainly occurs through congregations, it cannot be said that the Messianic congregational movement has seen more fruitfulness than missions. One writer states that 98% of the Jewish members of Messianic congregations came to faith in Jesus through the witness of a Gentile Christian.[3] Additionally, a significant number of Messianic congregational leaders came to faith through Jewish mission agencies.

Missions and congregations do not need to be mutually exclusive approaches; they have worked in tandem in the past and continue to do so today.

CONCLUSION

The major Jewish missions dedicated to proclamation evangelism retain close connections with the Church and remain firmly evangelical in theology. The materials, methodology and models for Jewish missions adapt according to the times, but overall, the mindset of the Jewish community has not changed, nor has our message of salvation. The mentality of those who would evangelize the Jewish people continues to be based on the mind of Christ.

The motivation to present the gospel to the Jewish people comes from faith-filled people who are propelled by the Holy Spirit and the Word of God. Moreover, Christ Jesus, whether we call Him Y'shua HaMashiach or any other of His legitimate names, will never change. He is our mandate, our motivator and our model from whom we draw our inspiration and support.

FURTHER READING

For your convenience, we have listed all the URLs in this book in one place at: http://www.jewsforjesus.org/publications/fieldguide

Rosen, Moishe. "Jewish Evangelism, Then and Now," *Jews for Jesus Newsletter*, July 1998. Available online at: http://www.jewsforjesus.org/publications/newsletter/1998_07/thenandnow_pt1

Mishkan: A Theological Forum on Jewish Evangelism 11 (1989), available at online at http://www.caspari.com/mishkan. Issue 11 is given over entirely to a discussion of "two-covenant" theology.

Mishkan 37 (2002), devoted to "19th & 20th Century Contributors to the Messianic Movement" available as a PDF at: http://www.caspari.com/mishkan/zips/mishkan37.pdf

The Digital Jewish Missions History Project, available at: www.lcje.net/history

Tucker, Ruth. *Not Ashamed: The Story of Jews for Jesus*, Multnomah Publishers, 1999.

"A Brief List of Famous Messianic Jews" at: http://www.israelinprophecy.org/live_site/english/brief_list-most_famous_messianic_jews.html

Zaretsky, Tuvya, ed. "Jewish Evangelism: A Call to the Church." Occasional Paper No. 60, Lausanne Committee for World Evangelization, 2005. Available at: http://community.gospelcom.net/lcwe/assets/LOP60_IG31.pdf

Taber, Wes. "Current Trends in Cross-Cultural Contextualization," paper presented at Lausanne Consultation on Jewish Evangelism CEO Conference, Dijon, France, May 2005, available at: http://files.jewsforjesus.org/pdf/other/taber.pdf

See Appendix E for "A Rationale for Jewish Evangelism."

See Appendix F for "The Willowbank Declaration on the Christian Gospel and the Jewish People."

Notes

1. John Chrysostom, Origen of Alexandria and Martin Luther are examples of church leaders who made statements about the Jewish culture and religion that could easily be read as anti-Semitic. See Hay, Malcolm. "Roots of Christian anti-Semitism," Anti-Defamation League of B'nai B'rith, 1984.

2. The missionary ranks of the previous generations included scholars of Hebrew and Scripture. Two of the many who deserve mention are A.J. Kligerman and his son-in-law, Arthur Kac. They contributed numerous scholarly articles and books. Many Christians know the name Jacob Jocz, but comparatively few know of his brother, Paul Yates. Paul Yates was a student of rabbinics and Scripture, but most of all he was a superb general missionary in the San Francisco Bay Area for some 40 years. Then there were Morris Zutrau, Moses Gitlin and dozens, if not hundreds, of others who could be mentioned. The last in that line of rabbinical scholars who were effective for the gospel was Rachmiel Frydland. He was a brilliant *yeshiva* (school of Jewish

education) student who came to faith just before the Germans marched into Poland. These European-born Jewish apologists argued effectively from Scripture, as well as from Jewish sources such as the Talmud and Responsa (the body of written decisions and rulings given to questions addressed) to make the case for Jesus. Others were not *yeshiva*-trained but still embodied Jewish spirit, such as Fred Kendal and Immanuel Gittell. The archetype of the scholar/missionary would be David Bronstein, Sr., of Chicago. He conducted two divergent missions and pastored what would today be seen as a Messianic congregation.

3. Wasserman, Jeffrey S., *Messianic Jewish Congregations: Who Sold This Business to the Gentiles?* Lanham, MD: University Press of America, 2000, p. 106.

Chapter Two
Messianic Congregations

INTRODUCTION

Messianic congregations are local expressions of the Body of Christ that seek to structure their service and worship along traditional Jewish lines while maintaining that Jesus is the promised Messiah. They are a large, visible part of the modern Messianic movement.

Messianic congregations can be found all around the world both in large cities and small towns, and attract Jewish and non-Jewish believers. The worship structure can vary considerably; many meet on the Jewish sabbath (Friday night or Saturday morning) while some conduct Sunday worship. Most observe the Jewish holidays, looking to Jesus as the fulfillment. In some, worshippers wear *kippot* (skullcaps) or *tallesim* (prayer shawls). In some, the music style is noticeably Jewish with a contemporary flavor; in others traditional Jewish liturgical elements are interwoven. Some congregations have auxiliary organizations such as a sisterhood, a day school or *yeshiva* (Jewish school of learning) modeled on structures similar to those in the mainstream Jewish community.

A BRIEF HISTORY OF MESSIANIC CONGREGATIONS

In the 1880s Joseph Rabinowitz formed a group in Kishinev, Moldavia, called the "Israelites of the New Covenant," which may well be the first modern "Messianic congregation."[1] Prior to the late 19th century, Jewish followers of Jesus worshiped almost exclusively in the local Lutheran or Presbyterian or Anglican churches, as in many cases it was these denominations that sponsored Jewish missions. But the late 19th century brought the rise of Zionism and the awakening of Jewish national consciousness, and it was in that context that Rabinowitz said that Jewish believers could (in fact, should) worship in a way that reflected and affirmed their Jewishness, to show the world that Jews do not cease being Jewish because they believe in Jesus, and in fact, that Jesus was one of "us."

At the same time in North America, the advent of modern Jewish missions prompted some to wonder if it would be helpful to the cause of Jewish evangelism for Jewish believers to form their own congregations that would utilize traditional Jewish forms of worship. Also, Jewish believers faced two problems: (1) they were often not welcome within the church (a situation many Christians today might have trouble picturing), and (2) they were unwelcome in the synagogue.[2]

Still, not everyone was in favor of "Hebrew-Christian churches." In 1915 the newly formed Hebrew-Christian Alliance of America (see chapter 1.3) had a lively debate over the advisability of Jewish believers forming separate congregations—or for that matter, observing any traditional Jewish practices.

However, the ideological/theological questions seemed to take a back seat to pragmatism. So Jewish missions and independent missionaries to the Jewish people in North America sometimes established "Hebrew-Christian churches," such as Jacob Freshman's Hebrew-Christian Church in New York City in the 1880s. In later years there were, among others, The Congregations of the Messiah Within Israel of Los Angeles (formed in 1955); as well as the First Hebrew Christian Church of Chicago (1934); the First Hebrew Christian Church of Philadelphia (1954); and Emmanuel Presbyterian Hebrew Christian Congregation in Baltimore (1963)—all three begun by the Presbyterian church.[3] The fact that a mainline Christian denomination began these congregations tells us that this was not a splinter move made in opposition to the Church, but done out of positive motives—to see Jews remain as Jews within the Body of Christ.[4]

In the 1970s, congregations began to prefer the term "Messianic congregation" to "Hebrew-Christian church," just as many Jewish believers in Jesus gradually began to prefer the term "Messianic Jew" to "Hebrew-Christian."[5] This change was mostly a reflection of trends in the larger Jewish community. In the late 19th and early 20th centuries there arose a sense of "national" Jewish consciousness, and the Jewish community adopted the designation "Hebrew" to express this nationality.[6] Then the rise of the State of Israel and its near-legendary victory in the 1967 war fostered a renewed sense of collective Jewish pride among many American Jews, including Jewish believers.[7] Calling oneself a "Messianic Jew" rather than a "Hebrew-Christian" was a more deliberate way of affirming one's Jewish identity.

At the same time, more Christians began to affirm Jewish believers' choice to retain their identity as Jews. After all, modern missions looked favorably on ethnic churches; there were Korean churches, Chinese churches—why not Jewish ones as well?[8]

However, not all Jewish believers flocked to Messianic congregations. In fact, most continued to attend mainstream churches, but expressed their Jewishness by joining other Jewish believers in fellowship groups that were often sponsored by local Jewish missions. Since many of those Jewish people who came to faith in the early 70s were young and had experienced tensions at home because of their faith, most looked to meet other Jews who believed, whether in Messianic congregations or fellowship groups.

MESSIANIC CONGREGATIONS TODAY

Though there are umbrella organizations for Messianic congregations, not all congregations belong to them; some are independent. Because there is no central organization or registry for all Messianic congregations, it's hard to state exactly how many there are. Jeffrey Wasserman, publishing in the year 2000, suggested that there were 200-250 congregations in North America. Some have been planted by Jewish missions or by Christian denominations. They vary widely in numbers, worship styles, training of leadership and ethnic make-up.

Some Messianic congregations in cities with larger Jewish populations have a solid, traceable history that goes back decades. Beth Yeshua in Philadelphia, Aron Kodesh in Fort Lauderdale, and Beth Israel Worship Center in New Jersey are three of the largest. Some of the other large congregations that reflect the migration of the Jewish population in the U.S. are Baruch Hashem in Dallas, Beth Hallel in Atlanta, Kehilat Ariel in San Diego, and Roeh Israel in Denver. When we say "large" keep in mind that attendance in Messianic congregations can usually be measured at most in the hundreds. On the flipside, most Messianic congregations are much smaller, with an average attendance of 100 or fewer. Some messianic congregations have only a handful of attendees.

It must be noted that most Jewish believers still attend churches, rather than Messianic congregations. Estimates as to the number of Jewish believers in Jesus in the U.S. have varied from a low of 30,000[9] to a high of 600,000 (for all of North America).[10] If one allows for 300[11] Messianic congregations in the U.S. of 60 people each, half of whom are Jewish,[12] then there would be 9,000 Jewish believers in Messianic congregations. Even with the lowest estimate, this

leaves the majority in some other context than that of
Messianic congregations.

What then is happening in the Messianic congregations? Some
missiologists have rejoiced over the Messianic congregational
movement, viewing it as evidence of growth in the number of
Jewish followers of Jesus. But a closer look reveals that few if
any Messianic congregations outside Israel are made up
exclusively of Jews. Most congregations that call themselves
"Messianic" are a mix of Jews and Gentiles, usually
predominantly and sometimes exclusively non-Jewish in
makeup. Many have non-Jewish leadership.[13]

What, then, is the difference between a Messianic
congregation and a church? Some key elements of the
Messianic congregational service might include Hebrew
liturgy, such as reading/chanting from the Torah. Like a
regular synagogue, Messianic congregations often have a
"Torah service" wherein specific portions of the Torah (the
Pentateuch) and Haftorah (the Prophetic Writings) are read in
Hebrew. Sometimes there is a Torah "processional," wherein
the Torah scroll is paraded around the congregation so people
can touch it themselves.

Other Hebrew liturgical aspects of a Messianic congregation
service may include the recitation of the Amidah (the Standing
Prayer) which is comprised of 19 benedictions and is central
to all synagogue services, the Sh'ma in Hebrew and English
("Hear O Israel, the Lord Your God is One God"); this is taken
from Deuteronomy 6:4. Also, at the end of the service, the
Aaronic Benediction may be chanted; this is taken from
Numbers 6:24-26.

The worship at a Messianic congregation will most likely
incorporate Messianic or Jewish gospel praise songs, with

Hebrew and English lyrics interwoven with Israeli folk beats, minor chords and traditional Jewish instruments, such as the dunbek, a middle eastern drum. Some Messianic congregations incorporate what is known as Messianic or "Davidic" worship dance in their services, either performed at the platform or with congregational participation.

Just as there are differences among synagogues in the mainstream Jewish community, so Messianic congregations differ in terms of how much liturgy is used, how much Hebrew is recited and how long the worship and message times are. Some reflect more structured Orthodox Jewish forms and some are more contemporary and free form, like in the Reform Jewish tradition (for more about the different streams of Judaism, please see appendix D). Often the leader of a Messianic congregation will refer to himself or herself as "rabbi"; sometimes not.

The terminology used at Messianic congregations also varies from congregation to congregation, but by and large, a visitor to a Messianic congregation will note that the pulpit is referred to as the *bima*, congregants may use some sort of *siddur*, or liturgy guide to the service, and Jesus is most often referred to as *Y'shua Hamashiach* (Jesus the Messiah) rather than as Jesus. There is usually a lack of overtly Christian symbols, such as crosses, as most congregations want to be sensitive to Jewish people who might be uncomfortable with such symbols. This is easier for some groups than others, since very few Messianic congregations own their own buildings and many share facilities with a local church. Often, the Messianic congregants cover over some of the more overt Christian accoutrements. Instead they might display a Star of David or other Jewish motifs, such as a menorah.

Whether mainstream Jews or new Jewish believers find Messianic congregations to be more comfortable than churches is really a subjective matter. There are Jewish people who have come to faith in Jesus who either weren't raised with much Jewish tradition or were "turned off" to synagogue-style services before they believed in Jesus, and so they often feel less comfortable with all the Jewish elements than one might expect. The same goes for Jewish visitors who don't believe in Jesus. In the U.S., the Jewish parts of the Messianic congregation service might put off secular Jews, and those from more religious backgrounds might feel that the Jewish aspects of the Messianic congregations aren't very authentic. When Lauren Winner, who came to Christianity from more Orthodox surroundings, first visited a Messianic congregation, she expressed her thoughts this way:

> This is how I feel all morning: that Brit Hadashah's Judaism is just raisins added to cake—you notice them, but they don't really change the cake. The structure of the service bears no relation to the Jewish liturgy, and I can't tell if my fellow worshippers think that being Jewish leads them to understand Jesus any differently from Presbyterians down the street. Add Hebrew and Stir.[14]

However, some Jews are drawn to Messianic congregations. Jews for Jesus missionary Chad Elliott claims he "found Jesus in the yellow pages"; while looking for a traditional synagogue to attend, he found one in the phone book that turned out to be a Messianic congregation! Chad kept attending and eventually came to faith in Jesus.

Messianic congregations aren't just a North American phenomenon. They exist in Europe, Russia, even in Africa. And of course, there are several Messianic congregations in Israel. The congregational movement is far from a passing trend. Though some may be fledgling and many contain more Gentiles than Jews, Messianic congregations are likely to continue for some time.

PHILOSOPHICAL ISSUES

In the early days of debating whether there should be "Hebrew-Christian churches," some feared that Jewish believers would isolate themselves from the rest of the Body and raise the "wall of partition" by emphasizing their Jewish distinctiveness. This ongoing debate centers around two questions: (1) Is it right for Jewish believers to separate themselves from the rest of the Body of Christ in this way?; and (2) Is it right for followers of Jesus to observe Old Testament or rabbinic customs and ceremonies?

The question of distinctive ethnic congregations is relevant not only to Jewish believers in Jesus; it has been an ongoing missiological question. Missiologists and church planters speak of the "homogeneous unit principle," whereby separate ethnic congregations are planted—Korean, Chinese, Native American, etc. One reason that is advanced for the validity of this approach is the claim that it leads to an increase in church growth. Others, however, think it is more biblical to form multi-ethnic congregations where the diversity in the Body of Christ is represented—since Christ has broken down the dividing wall between Jews and Gentiles and by implication, all ethnic groups.[15]

In Jewish ministry, the question also raises direct theological concerns, because unlike other ethnic groups, the Scriptures specifically say that the wall of partition *between Jews and Gentiles* was broken down in Jesus. We could say that *religiously*, there is no longer a distinction in Christ, whereas *culturally* every ethnic group is free to express its own culture as long as Scripture is not contradicted. But it is not always easy to separate the cultural from the religious elements of Jewishness, because rabbinic and Old Testament ceremonies and worship forms are utilized both religiously by Orthodox Jews and culturally by secular Jews. For example, an Orthodox Jew may observe Passover as a way to remember what God did in bringing us out of Egypt; for secular Jews, Passover becomes a cultural holiday (like the American holiday of Thanksgiving) to remember some Jewish history, visit with the family and eat.

Further, while the separateness of Israel and the Gentiles has been radically abolished in Christ, many Christians have historically believed the Scripture still teaches an ongoing uniqueness to the Jewish people. How are both facets to be resolved in terms of the congregational issue?[16]

Though these questions continue to be debated, the fact is that today the debate is largely theoretical. The whole question of whether there should be separate congregations for Jewish believers has, particularly in North America, become a non-issue, due to the fact that most Messianic congregations are comprised of Jews and Gentiles. In other words, these congregations are far from exclusive in their composition.

Instead we find ourselves with another question: Why do so many Gentiles want to worship in what they perceive is a Jewish way? We don't find a similar phenomenon with other ethnic groups. One doesn't find groups of Anglos who want to worship Korean style proclaiming that they are a "Korean church" nor groups of Caucasians attempting to worship like African-Americans. It is one thing for non-Jewish Christians to join a congregation led by Jewish believers with a substantial Jewish membership, just as one might find a few Anglos who for one reason or another attend a Chinese church. But what are we to make of non-Jews calling themselves "Messianic rabbis," heading congregations of mostly (or only) non-Jews, in areas of the country where few Jews live, who are attempting to worship in a Jewish mode?[17]

One can discern various motivations as to why some non-Jews seek to adopt Jewish practices:

• Some non-Jews have a romantic view of the Jewish people and assume that rabbis are the custodians of ancient wisdom that the Church has lost. While rabbinic Judaism can provide insights in the areas of ethics and biblical understanding, the fact is that rabbinic Judaism is the creation of the rabbis following the events of A.D.70. It is a post-biblical religion whose theology diverges in crucial ways from biblical theology. Its authority structure relies on the decisions of rabbis and it is a faith that denies the Messiahship of Jesus, the Incarnation and the possibility that God is a Trinity. The rabbis of today are not custodians of ancient wisdom that dates to the foundation of the world; what they are custodians of is the past two thousand years of Jewish legal and community decision-making. Incidentally, this kind of romanticized idea about Jewish people comes close to home. Often, Jews for Jesus receives phone calls or letters from people with a Bible question, convinced that we must have special expertise simply because we are Jewish. It may surprise them when we respond that they would do well to check a good Bible commentary; Jewishness is no guarantee that someone can explain a verse in the Bible, but good scholarship is!

• There are those who believe that by worshiping in Jewish style, they are returning to the worship of the "original Church," which is thought to be purer and unadulterated by so-called "pagan" additions. For example, there are those non-Jews who look at the cultural traditions of Christmas and Easter celebrations and expect that those traditions will be excised in the Messianic congregation model. However, it is never the case that by worshiping in a Messianic congregation, one can worship in a first-century manner, since the early Christians worshiped at the Temple in the context of priesthood and sacrifices.

• Some people have a personal need for structure and liturgy that Jewish tradition seems to provide, not just in a worship service but in daily life. While some segments of the Church could learn much from Jewish practice in areas such as ethics, family life and celebration, the use of art and ritual in reinforcing biblical truths, etc.,[18] there are certainly models within the traditional church that offer liturgy and structure.

A Messianic congregation comprised largely or entirely of Gentiles might be sincere in its appreciation for the Jewishness of the gospel, but it is misguided for them to attempt to worship like Jews and to adopt Jewish practices as their way of life. This is not to say that churches or individual Christians who appreciate the Jewish roots of their faith in Christ shouldn't, for example, celebrate Passover and incorporate the New Testament teaching from the Last Supper story. At Jews for Jesus, we actually encourage that kind of supportive involvement.

CONCLUSION

Messianic congregations vary as widely as do churches. Before attending or endorsing a particular Messianic congregation, it would be helpful to ask the following questions:

1. Does it have a statement of faith that is recognizably evangelical, especially regarding the deity of Jesus, the Trinity and the authority of the whole of Scripture?
2. Does it advocate mandatory keeping of the Law of Moses as a means of salvation or as a path to greater spirituality?
3. Is the leadership trained at a recognized institution or through a reputable course of study? Is the teaching sound and the Body life healthy?
4. Does the congregation seek to maintain ties to the rest of the Body of Christ?
5. Does it have a valid reason for existing (providing a context for Jewish believers and interested non-Jews to worship) or does it seem to be comprised largely of non-Jews who are acting Jewish?

6. Does it maintain that all Jewish believers should be worshiping in Messianic congregations and therefore that Jewish believers need to "come out of the church?"
7. Does it believe in evangelism and have an effective outreach program?

Jews for Jesus has good relationships with many Messianic congregations around the U.S. and internationally. In fact, many of our own staff attend Messianic congregations. We would be happy to recommend a congregation if you contact our Ministry-at-Large office at 415.864.2600 ext. 125 or mal60@aol.com.

As for recommending a Messianic congregation to a Jewish believer, there are many Jewish believers who would certainly benefit from attending a Messianic congregation; some very much enjoy the familiarity of such a service and would like their children to have the experience of a service that emphasizes their Jewish identity as well as faith in Christ.

For others, a Bible-believing church would be more suitable. Some Jewish believers would be more comfortable attending the church of whoever led them to the Lord. Or, they might have a non-Jewish spouse who comes from a particular Christian tradition that they'd like to further explore.

Don't assume that being Jewish automatically means that a Jewish believer in Jesus wants to attend a Messianic congregation. However, if a Jewish believer you know expresses the desire to attend a local Messianic congregation and you know one you can recommend, do so. If the only one you know of is unbiblical in doctrine or seriously deficient in some other way, affirm to your friend his or her Jewishness, but point out where the congregation falls short of a biblical standard and help them find another congregation if possible.

If you are not Jewish and are thinking of attending a Messianic congregation, ask yourself why. Your reasons may be good ones: for instance, you appreciate the Jewishness of the gospel and want to affirm Jewish believers in their faith or you are just curious to see what Jewish style worship and teaching are like. But if it's because you wish that you were Jewish or you think there is something inherently more spiritual about Jewish forms of worship, then those are not good motivations. In general, the principle "bloom where you are planted" is a good one. If your present congregation is fine, then stay there. Perhaps you can help them learn to appreciate the Jewishness of Jesus more!

FURTHER READING

Rosen, Ruth. *Following Y'shua.* San Francisco: Purple Pomegranate Productions, 2001.

Wasserman, Jeffrey S., *Messianic Jewish Congregations: Who Sold This Business to the Gentiles?* Lanham, MD: University Press of America, 2000.

Kjær-Hansen, Kai. *Joseph Rabinowitz and the Messianic Movement: The Herzl of Jewish Christianity.* Edinburgh: The Handsel Press; and Grand Rapids, MI: Eerdmans, 1995. A detailed and fascinating look at Rabinowitz and his "Israelites of the New Covenant," a precursor to today's Messianic congregations.

Zimmerman, Martha. *Celebrating Biblical Feasts: In Your Home or Church.* Grand Rapids: Bethany House, 2004.

Schiffman, Michael. *Return from Exile: The Re-Emergence of the Messianic Congregational Movement.* Columbus, OH: Teshuvah Publishing Co., 1990. Valuable for survey information on some 30 Messianic congregations, but now dated as the survey was conducted in the 1980s.

Baron, David. *Messianic Judaism; or Judaising Christianity*.
London: Morgan & Scott; Hebrew Christian Testimony to Israel,
1911. Shows there is nothing new under the sun. The same pros
and cons of Messianic congregations are debated today, but there
is far more sympathy now than Baron expresses to the idea of a
congregation worshiping in a culturally Jewish manner. But, like
Baron, most would still consider it unbiblical for a congregation
to be composed exclusively of Jews. Accessible at:
www.lcje.net/history

*Facts & Myths About the Messianic Congregations in Israel: A
Survey Conducted by Kai Kjær-Hansen and Bodil F. Skjøtt*.
Jerusalem: Published by the United Christian Council in Israel in
cooperation with the Caspari Center for Biblical and Jewish
Studies, 1999. Appeared as *Mishkan* 30-31, 1999.

Jews for Jesus takes a stand in favor of both Messianic
congregations and evangelical churches. See the following
articles:

Brickner, David. "Why I Support Messianic Congregations."
Jews for Jesus Newsletter, September 2004.
http://www.jewsforjesus.org/publications/newsletter/2004_0
9/whyisupport

Brickner, David. "Jews for Jesus and the Church." *Jews for
Jesus Newsletter*, February 2000. http://www.jewsforjesus.org/
publications/newsletter/2000_02/jewsforjesusandthechurch

Brickner, David. "What About Jews for Jesus and Messianic
Congregations?" *Mishpochah Message*, Fall 1993.
http://www.jewsforjesus.org/publications/havurah/mm93
_10/congregations

Rosen, Moishe. "Choosing Between a Local Church and a
Messianic Congregation." *Mishpochah Message*, Spring 1989.

http://www.jewsforjesus.org/publications/havurah/mm89_0
4/churchcong

For an article on Messianic Jews attending and pastoring
Christian churches, see "To the Jew First and Also to the Gentile,"
Havurah 8:2:
http://www.jewsforjesus.org/publications/havurah/8_2/jewfirst

For a directory of Messianic congregations, see
www.messianictimes.com or www.yashanet.com

Notes
1. For the history of this movement, see Kai Kjær-Hansen, *Joseph
Rabinowitz and the Messianic Movement: The Herzl of Jewish
Christianity.* Edinburgh: The Handsel Press; and Grand Rapids, MI:
Eerdmans, 1995.
2. Zeidman, Morris, "Relationship of the Jewish Convert to the
Christian Church," pp. 87-92 in *Christians and Jews: A Report of the
Conference on the Christian Approach to the Jews, Atlantic City,
New Jersey, May 12-15, 1931* (New York; London: International
Committee on the Christian Approach to the Jews; International
Missionary Council, 1931).
3. Kaplan, Jonathan. "A Brief History of Presbyterian Ministry
Among Jewish People: 1820-2001." Available at:
www.theologymatters.com/TMIssues/Kaplan01.PDF. Emmanuel
began in 1915 as an interdenominational Jewish mission, though
Jewish Presbyterians were associated with it from the beginning.
4. On the other hand, a Hebrew Christian congregation was formed
in Kishinev in 1928, after Rabinowitz was gone from the scene, and
in this case it arose from an exodus of Jewish believers from the
local Baptist church.
5. It was not a new term. "Messianic Judaism" had been a phrase
used and argued over for decades, usually referring to an expression
of Christian faith that involved keeping the Law, albeit voluntarily,
and retaining many traditional Jewish forms of life and worship.
6. Hence, dating from those years, we have the Hebrew Union

College in Cincinnati, Hebrew National hot dogs, and innumerable Hebrew Homes for the Aged and similar social service agencies.

7. For an interesting take on this, see "Tough Jews: A Dissent" by Andrew Furman at www.tikkun.org

8. This point was argued against in 1911 by David Baron, who said that Jews were unlike any other nation, and thus one could not extend the validity of an ethnic church to Jews as one could to other ethnic groups. (See Further Reading).

9. Perlman, Susan. "Statistically Speaking: What's New in Jewish Community Demographics," *Havurab* 6:1, 2003. (http://www.jewsforjesus.org/publications/havurah/6_1/statistics), where the estimate of 30,000-75,000 Jewish believers in the United States is given.

10. Kravitz, Bentzion, *The Jewish Response to Missionaries Counter-Missionary Handbook* (Los Angeles: Jews for Judaism, 2001), p. 9. "According to a 1990 Council of Jewish Federations population study, over 600,000 Jews in North America alone identify with some type of Christianity." A mediating figure of 100,000 is given by the Jewish Community Relations Council Task Force on Missionaries and Cults (http://www.tfmc.us): "More than 100,000 American Jews have been converted by missionary groups in the past 20 years, and a disproportionate number of Jews have joined cults."

11. "More than three hundred" in the U.S. is a figure given by Louis Goldberg, "Introduction: The Rise, Disappearance, and Resurgence of Messianic Congregations," p. 25 in *How Jewish is Christianity? Two Views on the Messianic Movement*, ed. Louis Goldberg (Grand Rapids: Zondervan, 2003). In 1996 Jeffrey S. Wasserman surveyed 200 messianic congregations in the U.S. and Canada for his thesis, now the book *Messianic Jewish Congregations: Who Sold This Business to the Gentiles?* (Lanham, MD: University Press of America, 2000), p. 74.

12. Wasserman writes: "My survey showed 60% Gentile membership [in the messianic congregations surveyed]. Schiffman's 1987 survey revealed Gentile membership between 75% and 50%." Wasserman, *Messianic Jewish Congregations*, p. 100, note 25.

13. In Michael Schiffman's 1980s survey of 30 Messianic congregations (see Further Reading), "most . . . have percentages of Jewish membership between twenty-five to fifty percent" (Schiffman, p. 119), which means 50-75% Gentile membership. Wasserman came up with 60% Gentile membership (Wasserman, p. 110, n. 25).

14. Winner, Lauren F., *Girl Meets God: A Memoir*, Random House, 2003.

15. See Ortiz, Manuel, *One New People: Models for Developing a Multiethnic Church* (Downers Grove: InterVarsity Press, 1996), p. 147-48.

16. These are not always easy questions to resolve. We would affirm the propriety (and often, the wisdom) of Jewish believers being free to worship in a Jewish way, a different question from whether "separate" congregations should be formed. And regarding the idea of multi-ethnic congregations, one could after all argue that even a congregation made up of Jewish people could be multi-ethnic, if it were a matter of bringing together Russian Jews, Ethiopian Jews, Sephardic Jews, and European Jews each with their own kind of worship and their own mutual mistrusts to overcome.

17. See "The Phenomenon: Gentiles in Synagogues," chapter 6 in Stan Telchin, *Messianic Judaism is Not Christianity: A Loving Call to Unity* (Grand Rapids: Chosen Books, 2004) and also Karabelnik, Chapter Four, "Dealing with the Foreigner in our Midst: Reactions to Gentiles." (See chapter 1.3, Further Reading).

18. In *Mudhouse Sabbath* (Paraclete Press, 2003), a recent book by Lauren Winner, she explores just these kinds of learning areas—but the rationale for the author living "Jewishly" while maintaining Christian faith is that she was raised as an Orthodox Jew.

Chapter Three
Voluntary Associations

INTRODUCTION

Voluntary associations, comprised of like-minded individuals meeting for a common purpose, have always played a prominent role in American life, and this includes the life of both the American church and the Jewish community. From the YMCA to InterVarsity Christian Fellowship, Christian voluntary associations—what some might call fellowship organizations, but which have larger goals than simply fellowship—have been formed to meet the special needs of specific groups. The concerns of various ethnic groups within the Church have also been addressed by voluntary associations such as Chinese or Korean Christian fellowships for college students.

The Jewish community has a rich history of voluntary associations, such as the *landsmanshaftn*, the immigrant associations which were once active on the Lower East Side of New York City, and which functioned as would modern support and relief groups or networks.[1]   Hillel, the campus group for Jewish students, is another example of a voluntary association.

Jewish believers in Jesus likewise have developed voluntary organizations to address common concerns, share common interests and provide mutual support.

A HISTORY OF MESSIANIC VOLUNTARY ORGANIZATIONS

The early history of voluntary organizations among Jewish believers is sketchy. In 1903, German Jewish Christian pastor Louis Meyer wrote a one-paragraph summary of the nineteenth century attempts to form such "brotherhoods," as he called them. Meyer mentioned ten such groups that existed between 1823 and 1887, each of which "were failures, and none existed more than two years."[2] He also noted that some of them consisted of non-Jews, perhaps foreshadowing a similar situation in the modern Messianic congregations.[3] But he really gives nothing but a few names and dates. Jewish believer Harcourt Samuel, who was a pastor and General Secretary of the International Hebrew Christian Alliance, goes back to 1813 in his very brief recap of such organizations.[4]

The main catalysts that led to the formation of Jewish Christian voluntary associations seem to have come towards the end of the 19th century, when the rise of Jewish national consciousness intersected with the experiences of Jewish believers within the Church to produce a new dynamic, particularly in Britain and America. On the one hand, the rise of Zionism and the influx of Jewish immigrants to America created a milieu in which Jewish Christians asserted their Jewish identity while affirming their faith as Christians. On the other hand, and perhaps due to this very assertion, Jews who believed in Jesus were not always comfortable or accepted within the church.

The first voluntary organization that lasted any length of time was the Hebrew Christian Alliance of Great Britain, founded by Dr. Carl Schwartz in 1866. It met every two weeks, produced two publications, *The Scattered Nation* and *Jewish Christian Magazine* and grew steadily until the death of Dr. Schwartz four years later. It wasn't until 1882 that the Hebrew Christian Prayer Union was formed, which dwindled down in numbers after 14 years and in 1901 was amalgamated with the Hebrew Christian Alliance.

Some Jewish believers were looking to do more than assert their ethnic identity; they advocated for voluntarily continuing some of the religious observances of traditional rabbinic Judaism. In 1901, a certain Dr. E. S. Niles of New England convened the "Hebrew Messianic Conference," which had an attendance of 25 and advocated keeping the Law of Moses as a means of evangelism to Orthodox Jews. Others had substantial disagreements with this approach and undertook to form their own committee, which Louis Meyer was appointed to head.

Meyer's committee convened in 1903 in Maryland with a variety of viewpoints represented, especially over the matter of keeping the Law (following the commandments found in the first five books of the Old Testament, traditionally enumerated as 613), advocated in particular by John Mark Levy of London.[5] Yet there was also an underlying call for unity among the participants and a delineation of the benefits to be derived from an alliance of Jewish Christians: a witness to the uniqueness of Israel in God's plan; an influence in reaching other Jews with the gospel; and a positive influence upon the Church.

It took another 12 years, but in 1915 the Hebrew Christian Alliance of America (HCAA) was founded, followed by the establishment of the International Hebrew Christian Alliance (IHCA) in London in 1925.[6] Under their auspices, various other national Hebrew Christian alliances came into being.

In the 1970s, the self-perception of many Jewish believers, especially of the younger generation, changed to reflect the attitude of many other Jewish youth; there were more overt expressions of Jewishness, and people expressed more pride in being Jewish—much of this stemming from the rise of the State of Israel and especially Israel's stunning victory in the 1967 Six-Day War. With this change in self-perception came a change in self-designation—"Messianic Jew" became the description of choice, replacing the earlier "Hebrew-Christian"—and a change in the name of the HCAA. In 1975, by popular vote, the name

became the Messianic Jewish Alliance of America (MJAA).
Similarly, the International Hebrew Christian Alliance is today
the International Messianic Jewish Alliance.

VOLUNTARY ASSOCIATIONS TODAY

The purposes of the Messianic Jewish Alliance of America
(MJAA) are currently stated as the following:

> 1. To testify to the large and growing number of Jewish
> people who believe that Yeshua (Jesus) is the promised
> Jewish Messiah and Savior of the world.
> 2. To bring together Jews and non-Jews who have a shared
> vision for Jewish revival.
> 3. Most importantly, to introduce our Jewish brothers and
> sisters to the Jewish Messiah Yeshua.[7]

The trademark of the MJAA is the annual summer "Messiah
Conference," held on the campus of Messiah College in
Grantham, Pennsylvania. These vibrant affairs host a variety
of speakers, bring in Israeli or other Jewish-style music
groups, and include animated discussions and workshops, not
to mention jam-packed plenary sessions. For many Jewish
believers, a Messiah Conference was the first time they met
large numbers of other Jews from around the world who also
believe in Jesus. Throughout the year there are also regional
MJAA conferences taking place, which are more intimate.

One does not need to be Jewish to join the MJAA or attend the
Messiah Conference. Non-Jews can join as "honored associates."
The MJAA website encourages non-Jewish people to join: "Both
Jewish and non-Jewish believers in Yeshua are welcome to join
the MJAA, from churches as well as Messianic congregations
and synagogues. Each person plays a specific role in this
prophetic ministry." All members pay yearly dues and in return
get discounts on admission to the Messiah Conference.

The MJAA is governed by an executive committee that oversees the various ministries of the MJAA, which include relief efforts for Russian and Ethiopian Jews as well as the poor in Israel, and a Young Messianic Jewish Alliance (YMJA), which "seeks to establish and develop ministry to Messianic Single Adults, college and career groups, young married couples, and teen groups."

As for the IMJA, there are today some 14 countries comprised within the membership.[8] Joel Chernoff is the President, Paul Liberman the Executive Secretary and John Fischer and Natalio Krauthamer are Vice-Presidents.[9] The IMJA gives this description of itself:

> Membership in the IMJA is open to all Jewish believers in Yeshua who accept the Word of God as contained in the Old and New Covenants, and fellowship with other believers in a community of faith. Non Jewish believers who identify with the ministry of the IMJA are associate members and play an important and vital role in God's work through this ministry.[10]

Furthermore,

> Some of the world-wide ministries of the International Messianic Jewish Alliance include . . .
> • Bringing relief to any Jewish believer or group who has been ostracized because of his or her faith in Yeshua
> • Establishing alliances in every region of the world where there is a community of Jewish believers
> • Fostering the spiritual growth of every Jewish believer in such a way that they will live a life for the Glory of God.
> • Providing assistance to churches in restoring Jewishness of their faith and an understanding of the Jewish people.[11]

Over the years, the Alliances have attempted to meet the needs of Jewish believers around the world. Of particular note is the help the International Alliance extended to Jewish believers fleeing Hitler's Germany and to those seeking to make *aliyah* (immigrate to Israel) after the Second World War. The current direction of the MJAA appears to focus on humanitarian projects (e.g., The Joseph Project) as their primary way to "introduce our Jewish brothers and sisters" to Jesus.

In its modern history, the MJAA has become closely identified with Beth Yeshua, a vigorous Messianic congregation in the Philadelphia area. The vision and steering leadership for the MJAA for over three decades has been actively led by the leaders of that congregation, first Martin Chernoff and today his son, David. Joel Chernoff, David's brother, is the current General Secretary of the MJAA.

Curiously, while essential elements of theology are becoming a major issue among some Messianic congregational umbrella groups (see chapter 2.5), not so in the MJAA (nor the IMJA) whose theological statement of faith could be accepted by any evangelical Christian where it talks about the person of Christ and the nature of God. If there is a point of departure in which some Jewish believers feel the Alliance does not represent them, or which departs from traditional evangelical Christian understandings, it is in the area of practical theology. The Alliance, as it exists today,

- Is strongly in favor of Jewish believers attending Messianic congregations rather than mainstream churches.[12]
- Believes that it is incumbent upon Jewish believers to observe the Jewish holidays, as written in their statement of faith under the rubric of "Messianic Judaism": "We observe and celebrate the Jewish Holy Days given by God to Israel, with their fulfillment in and through the Messiah Yeshua."[13]

The organization is today strongly charismatic in its theological orientation; one of the MJAA's humanitarian programs, The Joseph Project, is said to have originated by a prophecy.[14] One writer has characterized the dual emphases of the MJAA as being "restoration" (returning to an allegedly first-century mode of faith, with later expressions being seen as impure accretions) and "revival" (in which the current move of Jews to the person of Jesus is related to prophecies of the end times and of the restoration of the nation of Israel).[15]

PHILOSOPHICAL ISSUES

In the early days of the Jewish Christian voluntary associations, the main obstacles to unity included (1) theology, particularly how appropriate it was for Jewish believers to continue observing the Law; and (2) social rivalries, especially between the wealthier, more assimilated German Jews vs. the poorer, more traditional Eastern European Jews.

The issues discussed among Jewish believers today are rather different. Most would probably be in agreement that Jewish believers can choose to keep whatever aspects of the Law and rabbinic tradition they like (as long as they don't violate biblical principles). A hundred years ago, some Jewish believers were glad to be free from what they saw as rabbinic burdens imposed by Orthodox Judaism; today, tradition and Law are often viewed within today's multi-ethnic world, not as rabbinic burdens, but as entree points into understanding one's roots and culture and as identity markers.

While the MJAA and the IMJA have been the main voluntary associations for Jewish believers for many decades, a new organization, the International Jewish Evangelical Fellowship (IJEF) was created as a conscious counterpoint to certain trends in the Messianic movement.[16] It is headed by Baruch Maoz, who is on the staff of a British-based Jewish mission,

Christian Witness to Israel, and also pastors the Grace and Truth Assembly in Israel. IJEF members particularly raise cautions with regard to incorporating rabbinic tradition, and they support the participation of Jewish believers in churches rather than Messianic congregations. The four "goals and purposes" of the IJEF as stated on their website are:

1. To promote a clear presentation of the Gospel to our people, unencumbered with rabbinic religious authority, and in terms our people can understand.
2. To call upon, encourage and assist Jewish Christians to be an active part of local Christian churches, rather than of ethnically and culturally focused congregations.
3. To create an alternative to Messianic Judaism by encouraging Jewish Christians to maintain, cultivate and express their Jewish national identity in cross-congregational contexts rather than within the context of church life and worship, and by inculcating in Jewish Christians an affection and a respect for the work of God in and through the Church throughout the ages.
4. To create a distinctly Jewish Christian voice that will address the church, the world and our people.[17]

The IJEF has sponsored annual conferences since 2003 and has produced a series of papers. It is too early to say what influence the IJEF will bring.

CONCLUSION
Much like in the Christian community, there is no voluntary organization that meets the needs and concerns of all Jewish believers in Jesus and "unites" them all. This should not be surprising; Christian unity is rarely achieved organizationally.

As part of the Messianic movement, the MJAA represents some Jewish believers, not all; in fact it would be safe to say that the majority of Jewish believers are not formal members. It calls itself "the largest association of Messianic Jewish believers in Yeshua (Jesus) in the world," but that, after all, is different than representing all Jewish believers. And in its development from the early days when it was the Hebrew Christian Alliance, it has come to represent primarily a charismatic form of expression, with an emphasis on restoration, as well as a "Messianic congregation only" position in regards to where its members should worship. Its agenda, too, is rather different than in the early days. But interestingly, a look back suggests that at no point in its history did the Alliance represent a broad base of Jewish followers of Jesus. Harcourt Samuel said of even the earlier IHCA, "Regretfully, only a small percentage of Jewish believers have become members."[18] This is very instructive, because it underscores the fact that no one can hope for one organization to be all things to all people, nor was there ever a "golden age" when Jewish Christians were all united under one banner. However, there remains a family feeling among many in the voluntary associations and the missions that is, perhaps, a more important mark of unity than organizational membership.

FURTHER READING

Karabelnik, Gabriela. "Competing Trends in Messianic Judaism: The Debate Over Evangelicalism." Unpublished senior thesis, Department of Religious Studies, Yale University, 2002. Compares and contrasts the MJAA and the UMJC (the latter discussed in Chapter 1.4).

Warnock, James. "All These Efforts were Failures: Alliances of Hebrew Christians." Paper presented at the Lausanne Consultation on Jewish Evangelism (North America), 2001. Available as a PDF download at: http://www.lcje.net/papers/2001/Warnock.pdf

Samuel, Harcourt. "The History of the International Hebrew Christian Alliance," *Mishkan: A Theological Forum on Jewish Evangelism* 14 (1991), pp. 74-79.

Winer, Robert I. *The Calling: The History of the Messianic Jewish Alliance of America 1915-1990.* Wynnewood, PA: Messianic Jewish Alliance of America, 1990. Contains much valuable historical information and primary quotes, but highly colored by the author's enthusiasm for the current MJAA: "the true calling of the Alliance [has been] unfulfilled until my generation." Unfortunately too, in the primary source material, he has chosen to replace terms used by the original authors, using "Jewish believers" instead of the original "Hebrew Christians," etc.—markedly lessening their value as historical evidence. Even so, there's a great deal of value in the sources he has brought together. But a more objective history has yet to be written.

ONLINE RESOURCES
Messianic Jewish Alliance of America: http://www.mjaa.org
International Messianic Jewish Alliance: http://www.imja.com
International Jewish Evangelical Fellowship:
http://www.ijef.org

Digital Jewish Missions History Project: http://www.lcje.net/history. Here you can find the *Minutes of the First Hebrew-Christian Conference of the United States* from 1903.

Notes
1. See Soyer, Daniel, *Jewish Immigrant Associations and American Identity in New York, 1880-1939* (Harvard University Press, 1997) and the brief review by Leonard Dinnerstein at http://www.24hourscholar.com/p/articles/mi_m2082/is_4_61/ai_56 909109
2. Meyer, Louis. "Hebrew Christian Brotherhood in America," *The Jewish Era*, April 15, 1903, p. 65.

3. See Chapter 1.2.

4. See Samuel, Harcourt. "The History of the International Hebrew Christian Alliance," *Mishkan: A Theological Forum on Jewish Evangelism* 14 (1991), p. 74. See also the survey in Warnock, James, "'All These Efforts Were Failures': Alliances of Hebrew Christians." Lausanne Consultation on Jewish Evangelism, North America, 2001. Warnock's paper is available at http://www.lcje.net/papers/2001/Warnock.pdf

5. *Minutes of the First Hebrew Christian Conference of the United States* (Mountain Lake Park, MD, 1903), pp. 40-51, section entitled, "The Scripture Method of Preaching the Gospel 'to the Jew first,'" by Mark Levy.

6. For a history of the HCAA (today the MJAA), see Winer, Robert I. *The Calling: The History of the Messianic Jewish Alliance of America 1915-1990*. Wynnewood, PA: Messianic Jewish Alliance of America, 1990. The IHCA's story is briefly recounted in Samuel, "History," cited above. Both were authored by those involved in their particular organizations. For an outsider's view of the HCAA/MJAA along with the UMJC (see chapter 1.4), see Gabriela Karabelnik, "Competing Trends in Messianic Judaism: The Debate Over Evangelicalism," unpublished senior thesis, Department of Religious Studies, Yale University, 2002.

7. http://mjaa.org/mjaa.html

8. http://www.imja.com/affiliated.html

9. http://www.imja.com/execom.html

10. http://www.imja.com/Intro2.html

11. Ibid.

12. "Should Jews really attempt to assimilate into churches and forego their Jewish identity when they choose to put their faith in the Jewish Messiah? Messianic Judaism answers, 'No!'" (http://mjaa.org/mj.html). Its statement of faith is integrated with the statement of faith of its sister organization, The International Alliance of Messianic Congregations and Synagogues (http://mjaa.org/StatementOfFaith.html).

13. Ibid.

14. "On the morning of February 13, 1996, the Lord sent a strong prophetic word to the General Secretary of the Messianic Jewish Alliance of America (MJAA). This message was written down and

according to Scriptural standards and confirmed by the leadership of the MJAA and various Christian leaders outside of the MJAA. As a result, the Joseph Project was born." See http://josephproject.org/

15. See Karabelnik, various places.
16. http://www.ijef.org
17. http://www.ijef.org/about/goals.php
18. Samuel, "History," p. 79.

Chapter Four
The Umbrella Organizations

INTRODUCTION

In the 1970s and following, as Messianic congregations proliferated amid much advocacy and encouragement in some quarters, there also emerged moves to form congregational associations for the purposes of mutual encouragement, accountability and pooling of resources.

This, of course, was nothing new in the history of congregations and synagogues. All sorts of structures, from denominations to loosely affiliated fellowships, have characterized Christian churches and the various branches of Judaism. For the most part, the Messianic congregational umbrella groups have avoided trying to become denominations, but neither have they been completely unstructured.

It should be noted that some Messianic congregations have been planted by existing church denominations and look primarily to their denomination for support. Most of the congregations that are part of one of the umbrella groups mentioned in this chapter have been independently formed or planted by a Jewish mission rather than by a church denomination. Finally, it should be noted that some Messianic congregations do not belong to an umbrella group at all. So just as the MJAA (Messianic Jewish Alliance of America) cannot be said to represent all Jewish believers, neither do the congregational groups represent all the Messianic congregations. However, a majority of all Messianic congregations belong to one of these two groups.

In this chapter we will also look at an umbrella group formed for Jewish missions, the Lausanne Consultation on Jewish Evangelism.

MESSIANIC JEWISH CONGREGATIONAL UMBRELLA GROUPS

While the idea of voluntary associations for Jewish believers goes back to the early 19th century, the oldest of the congregational umbrella groups was formed in 1979. It is called the Union of Messianic Jewish Congregations (UMJC). According to one history of the UMJC/MJAA by a Messianic Jewish leader, the UMJC was created as a spin-off group by some in the MJAA who did not take under advisement the call of Martin Chernoff, then-president of the MJAA, to delay forming such an organization until more maturity and growth had been evidenced by the various congregations.[1]

It was not until 1986 that the MJAA itself officially founded another umbrella group—the International Alliance of Messianic Congregations and Synagogues (IAMCS). The IAMCS has come to function as "essentially the pastoral arm of the MJAA." [2] There was tension between the two groups for some time, until they officially reconciled in 1994, with the signing of the *UMJC/MJAA Agreement of Reconciliation and Commitment.*[3]

The two umbrella groups agree to disagree in some theological and practical areas.[4] Both groups acknowledge current and historic ties to evangelicalism, yet both seek to emphasize their Jewishness. Some have observed that the IAMCS is more willing to be openly identified with evangelicalism[5] while the UMJC is seen as more concerned with maintaining ties to the Jewish community.[6] Some would describe the UMJC as less charismatic than the IAMCS and more interested in keeping rabbinic forms and customs.

Jewish believer Gabriela Karabelnik elaborates in her thesis:

> While the UMJC acknowledges certain ties to evangelicalism historically and theologically, a

conscious and increasing disassociation from it is
taking place. Within the UMJC, restorationism[7] takes
on a different form or is minimized altogether, as is the
intense focus on the end time [both of which are
characteristic of the MJAA/IAMCS]. The Union seeks to
enter into dialogue with Jewish traditions over the
ages, valuing rabbinic contributions and often adopting
their rituals and liturgy to a greater extent and
sometimes without specific Messianic adaptation or
justification. Mosaic law and Jewish tradition are kept
not so much to point to Messianic content within it,
but because they are inherently valuable as God's law
and as tokens of Jewish heritage. Furthermore, large
parts of Mosaic Law are considered to be a continued
obligation for Messianic Jews and not merely a matter
of personal conscience. All of these distinguishing
marks of the UMJC serve the central goal of building
bridges with the Jewish community by creating a
maximally "authentic" and "credible" form of Judaism.[8]

To that end, theologically, the UMJC leadership has allowed
some questionable ideas to come under its rubric (see chapter
2.5 for more on this). This has resulted in some congregations
pulling out of the UMJC.

While the UMJC and IAMCS are the two major congregational
umbrella groups, there have been others. In 1986, there was
another group formed with a non-charismatic emphasis called
the Fellowship of Messianic Congregations (FMC), led by
Louis Lapides, pastor of Beth Ariel Fellowship in Sherman
Oaks, California. The FMC emphasized unity through doctrinal
maturity. Its four purposes were stated as:

1. To encourage and assist in the establishment and growth
   of Messianic congregations.

2. To develop cooperation among like-minded congregations through their leaders.
3. To represent a biblically and theologically sound Messianic faith to the body of the Messiah and to society at large.
4. To carry the message of redemption to the entire world by practicing and promoting the priority of the Gospel to the Jew first and also to the gentile.[9]

Due to its small size and limited membership and resources, the FMC disbanded in the late nineties.

In 2003, the Association of Messianic Congregations (AMC) was formed. Some have regarded it as the successor association to the FMC. Their purpose statement reads as follows: "The Association of Messianic Congregations exists to strengthen Messianic Congregations by providing resources, teaching and fellowship that promote Biblical values, proclaims personal faith in Yeshua as the one Atonement for all humanity, and encourages worship through the diversity of Jewish expressions of faith."[10] The AMC describes itself as "grace-embracing"; its statement of faith includes the view that the Law of Moses is no longer mandatory upon Jewish or any believers to observe.[11] In addition, this group presents itself as a non-charismatic alternative to the charismatic/Pentecostal orientation of the MJAA and IAMCS. It was spearheaded by Steve Shermett, who leads the Messianic congregation Beth Sar Shalom in Tucson, Arizona and who serves as President; Pete Koziar of Baltimore's B'nai Abraham Congregation is Vice-President; Mottel Baleston who heads Messengers Messianic Jewish Fellowship in New Jersey serves as Board Secretary.[12] Of the eleven congregations listed in their online directory,[13] one is in Israel, another in Montreal, Canada and a third is in the UK. As of the writing of this booklet, an AMC-Europe is opening up under the leadership of Dr. Alan Poyner-Levison.

THEOLOGICAL AND PHILOSOPHICAL CONCERNS

As stated above, in the past few years there have been signs of ferment within the UMJC, mainly having to do with issues of theology. This has already caused some congregations to pull out of the UMJC and has raised red flags among others. This is particularly true in the area of ecclesiology, the doctrine of the Church. For more on this development, please see Chapter 2.5.

Another umbrella group that raised concerns in the past was a Maryland-based group known as the "Association of Torah-Observant Messianics" (A.T.O.M.). Torah-observant groups—which believe that keeping the Law of Moses is mandatory or spiritually necessary—are discussed in Part Two. A.T.O.M. described itself as "an international organization of followers of Yeshua who believe that the Torah is, always has been, and always will be G-d's perfect standard for our lives."[14]

The history of A.T.O.M. is a cautionary tale. In December of 1997 their statement of faith made reference to the Father, Son and Spirit, although not in standard evangelical phraseology; affirmed the inspiration of the Old and New Testaments; spoke of Yeshua as the Messiah whose death atoned for our sins; affirmed the sin nature and the need to trust in Yeshua for forgiveness. In addition it included statements on the Torah (in terms which many evangelicals could agree with) and added a charismatic-flavored statement on spiritual gifts. By 2001 the organization was known as A.T.O.N., the Association of Torah-Observant Nazarenes under the auspices of netzarim.org, a theologically heterodox organization. By 2002 Steve Heiliczer, the founder of A.T.O.M., had renounced his faith in Jesus altogether, changed his name from Steve to Yeshayahu, and published his story online.[15] His website, teshuvah.com, is now a completely Orthodox Jewish site and links to anti-missionary organizations and mainstream Jewish sites.

JEWISH MISSIONS UMBRELLA GROUPS

The Fellowship of Christian Testimonies to the Jews (FCTJ) was formed in the early 1950s by Fred Kendal and Emil Elbe. Kendal was General Director and founder of a Jewish mission called Israel's Remnant that was based in Detroit. Elbe was Superintendent of the Midwest Messianic Center in St. Louis. Meeting every one or two years at various locations in the U.S. and Canada, the FCTJ was intended for those engaged in Jewish ministry in those countries to be of mutual encouragement to one another and to exchange ideas on methods and issues in Jewish evangelism. Of particular note was its production of *Ha'Or*, an evangelistic publication used by various mission agencies for about twenty years. Fred Kendal was the first editor, followed by his son-in-law Avi Brickner in the late sixties. Brickner (father of David Brickner of Jews for Jesus) was also elected president of the FCTJ at that time.

Perhaps the most interesting moment in the history of the FCTJ was in 1970 when Jewish rabbi Sid Lawrence was invited to speak to its annual conference. When asked what the image of missionaries to the Jews was in the Jewish community, he replied that they had no image! His words served as a challenge to the various Jewish missionaries (among them Moishe Rosen, who later founded Jews for Jesus) to be more visible and effective.

The FCTJ was originally a somewhat loose association of individuals who had the right to vote on various issues. Some of the mission boards felt they did not want to see that kind of power in the hands of individuals rather than mission boards. In the early 1970s, there was discussion of making the organization to be an association of missionary societies in order to develop the kinds of standards in ethics and operations that other mission organizations shared. The FCTJ constitution was changed so that only mission boards could be members.

Around that time the FCTJ began objecting to certain trends that it saw among some in the Messianic movement. At the annual meeting in 1975, a resolution was put forth that essentially took issue with many of these trends, such as those who would declare Messianic Judaism to be a fourth branch of Judaism. The resolution was authored by Harold Sevener, then with the American Board of Missions to the Jews; William Currie, director of the American Messianic Fellowship; and Marvin Rosenthal who headed the Friends of Israel.

The FCTJ went out of existence in the 1980s. One reason for its demise was the conservatism of the organization; some of its members became closed to new approaches. Another reason was that when it stopped being an organization of individual missionaries and changed so that only mission societies could be members and vote, the attendance at the conferences dwindled to mostly mission leaders. The new constitution also required unanimous approval for all new member organizations. None was approved after the new constitution was put in place.

In a sense, the FCTJ was the forerunner to the Lausanne Consultation on Jewish Evangelism (LCJE). The story of the LCJE begins in 1980, when the Lausanne Committee for World Evangelization (LCWE) sponsored the Consultation on World Evangelization (COWE) in Pattaya, Thailand. "Reaching Jews" was one of the 17 mini-consultation groups at that event.[16] The enthusiasm of the leaders in the field of Jewish evangelism in attendance to expand the network gave rise to the formation of a task force, which became the LCJE. The basis for cooperation through the LCJE is agreement by its members to the Lausanne Covenant. Today, the LCJE is the main umbrella group for Jewish Missions.

LCJE meets for international consultations every four years, and more often on a regional basis. There are chapters in North

America, Europe, Israel, South Africa, Australia, Japan and Latin America. A quarterly, the *LCJE Bulletin*, is published to keep its members abreast of what is happening in between consultations. Many Jewish evangelism agencies, congregations engaged in Jewish evangelism, scholars and writers in the field, individual agency workers, and congregational leaders belong to the LCJE. Some Messianic congregational leaders attend LCJE conferences, and these meetings can provide a forum for dialogue between mission leaders and academic figures. A list of LCJE member organizations appears as Appendix C.

CONCLUSION

In a later chapter, we will discuss in more depth the quandaries facing congregational umbrella organizations. For now, it is important to note that the Messianic movement is still finding itself in terms of its identity, and will probably continue to struggle for some time.

FURTHER READING

Karabelnik, Gabriela, "Competing Trends in Messianic Judaism: The Debate Over Evangelicalism." Unpublished senior thesis, Department of Religious Studies, Yale University, 2002. Discusses the history of the UMJC and MJAA and highlights their distinctives.

Winer, Robert I. *The Calling: The History of the Messianic Jewish Alliance of America 1915-1990* (Wynnewood, PA: Messianic Jewish Alliance of America, 1990.) This book also has some helpful information on the formation of the IAMCS.

Lapides, Louis S. "Do We Need the Fellowship of Messianic Congregations?" *Mishkan* 6/7 (1987), pp. 121-134.

Juster, Daniel C. "The History of the Union of Messianic Jewish Congregations." *Mishkan* 2 (1985), pp. 63, 68.

ONLINE RESOURCES

Union of Messianic Jewish Congregations:
http://www.umjc.org

International Alliance of Messianic Congregations and
Synagogues: http://www.iamcs.org

The Association of Messianic Congregations:
http://www.messianicassociation.org

Lausanne Consultation on Jewish Evangelism:
http://www.lcje.net
Here you will find many of the LCJE conference papers and
the *LCJE Bulletin*.

The Lausanne Covenant:
http://www.lausanne.org/Brix?pageID=12891

Notes

1. Winer, Robert I. *The Calling: The History of the Messianic Jewish Alliance of America 1915-1990* (Wynnewood, PA: Messianic Jewish Alliance of America, 1990), p. 64.
2. Ibid. p. 65.
3. Hocken, Peter. "The Rise of Messianic Judaism," online at http://www.BaruchHaShemSynagogue.org/resources/riseofmj.html
4. One Jewish believer, writer Gabriela Karabelnik, has helpfully detailed the history and distinctives of the UMJC and the IAMCS in her thesis (see Further Reading).
5. Karabelnik observes that the MJAA/IAMCS shows "greater willingness to identify officially with evangelical movements," being "more typically evangelical/charismatic than the Union in its attitude towards theology, [and] also in its self-presentation." In contrast, "the Union is more reluctant to link itself with evangelicalism." See "Competing Trends," Part One, section "The MJAA versus the UMJC."

6. Ibid. "one of the clear goals of [the UMJC] is to identify more fully with the Jewish community, both historically and in the present."

7. At several points in her thesis, Karabelnik describes rather than defines "restorationism," e.g., "the claim that everything after Jesus was corrupt and that Messianic Jews are repristinating the biblical faith that other groups have lost." She nuances this by also describing "full" vs. "modified" restorationism.

8. Karabelnik, Chapter 5, "Facing our Brethren: Reactions to Non-Messianic Jews," section "The UMJC Challenging the 'Saved' versus 'Unsaved' Dichotomy."

9. For details on the FMC including the full text of its constitution, see Lapides, Louis S. "Do We Need the Fellowship of Messianic Congregations?" *Mishkan* 6/7 (1987), pp. 121-134.

10. http://www.messianicassociation.org/about.htm

11. http://www.messianicassociation.org/believe.htm

12. http://www.messianicassociation.org/board.htm

13. http://www.messianicassociation.org/directory.htm

14. This sounds like something that many Christians would agree with—surely everything in the Bible reflects "God's perfect standard"—but the practical outworking was something far different than what evangelical Christians would have in mind. http://web.archive.org/web/19980504010126/teshuvah.com/organizations/atom/membership.html

15. http://web.archive.org/web/20030810051135/www.teshuvah.com/articles/journey.htm

16. The document is available at: http://www.lausanne.org/Brix?pageID=14607. Jewish missions continue on the radar of the LCWE. In 2004, again meeting in Pattaya, the forum on Jewish evangelism produced "Jewish Evangelism: A Call to the Church," downloadable at: http://community.gospelcom.net/lcwe/assets/LOP60_IG31.pdf

Chapter Five
Educational Institutions

INTRODUCTION

It naturally follows from a discussion of congregations and congregational institutions, that there must exist programs to train congregational leaders as well as those in Jewish mission work. This section highlights these institutions, beginning with the Jewish mission training institutes that were birthed as early as the 18th century.

In a later chapter we will address another aspect of Messianic education: the "Hebrew Roots" teaching movement, which functions more as a vehicle for the layperson than as a means of training leaders.

EARLY EDUCATIONAL INSTITUTIONS

The first modern institution for training missionaries to the Jews is generally agreed to be the Institutum Judaicum, founded in 1728 by Professor Johann Heinrich Callenberg in the University of Halle, Germany. Callenberg was part of the German Pietist movement of the 18th century, and the Institutum was established even before the rise of modern missions. It began on quite a small scale, as an attempt to publish a Yiddish-language missionary tract. It would seem that rather than offering a formal program of studies with a set curriculum and so many years of classwork, Callenberg's Institutum fielded some 20 missionaries, provided Christian literature in several languages, and offered instruction to new Jewish believers in Jesus. But because it was connected with the University of Halle, the academic setting was serious and rigorous and "set high standards for informed and qualified missionary work."[1] The areas of study included languages (Hebrew, Yiddish) and rabbinics. The Institute lasted until 1792.

Yet even before Callenberg, suggestions were made for schools in which Jewish Studies would be taught as an adjunct to the work of convincing Jewish people that Jesus was the Messiah (the term "Jewish missions" had not yet entered the vocabulary). In the 17th century, Johann Christof Wagenseil, Professor of History at Altdorf University, detailed his plans for a Christian institute of Jewish studies, training students in the languages, in rabbinics, and in what today would be called apologetics.[2] It was partly as a result of momentum developing from Wagenseil and others that Callenberg began the Institutum Judaicum.

Around 1880, the scholar Franz Delitzsch began another Institutum Judaicum in Leipzig, Germany. Just a few short years afterwards, in 1886, a similar institute was started in Berlin by Professor H. L. Strack. By the time of the publication of the *Jewish Encyclopedia* in 1906, these institutes were still in existence as Jewish missionary training centers. In that encyclopedia, we read that:

> The institutes of Leipsic and Berlin have courses in New Testament theology with reference to the Messianic passages in the Old Testament, and they also give instruction in rabbinic literature; they further publish works helpful to their cause, as biographies of famous converts, controversial pamphlets, autobiographies of converted Jews, and occasionally scientific tracts. The Berlin institute has published Strack's "Introduction to the Talmud," his editions of some tractates of the Mishnah, and a monograph on the blood accusation. A special feature of its publications is the New Testament in Hebrew and Yiddish translations.[3]

It is apparent from this description that the curriculum was wide-ranging and that the institutes relied on recognized scholars: Strack's *Introduction to the Talmud* remains a standard work to this day, while Franz Delitzsch's writings, and especially his Hebrew translation of the New Testament, are of enduring value. Both institutes also produced periodicals.

Much of the resources of these institutes were destroyed during the Second World War. Today, the Leipzig organization has been reborn, not as a missionary training center, but as a school for the study of Judaism, and is called the Institutum Judaicum Delitzschianum, now located in Münster.

CURRENT TRENDS IN MESSIANIC EDUCATION

In the 20th and 21st centuries, the locus of Messianic Jewish or Jewish missions education has largely moved from Europe to the United States, with Israel as a secondary center. In America as well as elsewhere, modern missionaries to the Jewish people usually receive their theological education at evangelical Bible schools or seminaries, in addition to which a mission agency might have its own internal training course.

There are some Bible schools that offer Jewish studies degrees or emphases within their curricula. On the undergraduate level, Moody Bible Institute's Jewish studies program in Chicago has long been a vehicle for training missionaries to the Jewish people (though one doesn't have to be a missionary in training to enroll). The program began in 1923 as the Jewish Missions Course, which was a three-year program under the auspices of the Hebrew Christian Alliance of America before becoming part of Moody. Subjects included Hebrew and Yiddish, rabbinics, Jewish history, and Messianic prophecy, as well as Jewish holidays and customs. Solomon Birnbaum, a Jewish believer in Jesus, was the first director. In 1940, Max I. Reich took over leadership of the program, and he was succeeded in turn by Nathan J. Stone in 1946, Louis Goldberg in 1966, and Michael Rydelnik in 2001.[4] Moody's program remains the most extensive of its kind, at least in the United States. Today, in keeping with changed times, course requirements no longer include Yiddish, but have added Contemporary Jewish Literature, the Holocaust, and the History and Thought of Modern Israel, along with continuing requirements of Hebrew, Jewish history and Messianic prophecy.[5]

Shorter programs include Philadelphia Biblical University's "Friends of Israel Institute of Jewish Studies," which has been in place in Langhorne, Pennsylvania since 1996, in association with The Friends of Israel, a Jewish mission agency that originally ran the program under their own auspices from 1987-96.[6] This program is one year in duration, taught in modules and includes a study trip to Israel. Youth With a Mission (YWAM) conducts an in-depth, 12-week School of Jewish Studies and brings in respected faculty to teach its intensive courses. Also available is an additional internship in mercy ministries, intercession, education in the USA and abroad.

On the graduate level, a masters program in Jewish missions was taught at Fuller Theological Seminary's School of World Mission in the 1990s in partnership with Jews for Jesus, through which dozens of Jews for Jesus missionaries and others interested received degrees. It is no longer offered; however, Jews for Jesus has now partnered with Western Seminary in offering a Master of Arts in Specialized Ministry in Jewish Evangelism degree at their San Jose campus. The Specialized Ministry programs are intended for students seeking specialized, graduate, theological education. The program is slated to begin in the Fall of 2005. Faculty will include Tuvya Zaretsky of Jews for Jesus and Galen Peterson, who is an adjunct instructor in Intercultural Studies at Western and heads the American Remnant Mission, a Jewish outreach in the San Francisco area.

Then there is the Pasche Institute of Jewish Studies at Criswell College in Dallas, Texas, formed in 2004. It offers an M.A. in Jewish Studies as well. Named after members of First Baptist Church in Dallas, the institute's vision is "to multiply and strengthen Kingdom leaders for ministry to the Jewish people and to significantly contribute to the scholarship of Jewish studies." As of this writing, faculty include one full-time (Todd Bradley) and five adjunct (Arnold Fruchtenbaum, J. Randall Price, Michael Rydelnik, Jim Sibley and Tuvya Zaretsky).

Israel has also become a place for similar studies. In a formal, degree-granting setting, Israel College of the Bible (formerly King of Kings College) also includes Jewish studies within its bachelors and certificate programs. It offers courses in Hebrew, Russian, Amharic and English. Based in Jerusalem since 1990, this interdenominational school is accredited through the Asian Theological Association and the European Evangelical Accrediting Association. It has a student body of indigenous Israelis, as well as short-term course offerings for non-Israeli residents. Its stated purpose is "to equip and to develop leaders for serving the Lord and to provide a unique understanding of the Jewish roots of the Faith in Yeshua (Jesus)." [7]

Also in Israel, the Caspari Center is "an educational institute for academic study and training where Messianic Jews and Gentile Christians work in cooperation. The staff consists of local Israelis working together with Christians from the nations . . . The Israeli focus is in providing local believers with serious theological education and training. . . ." [8] The Caspari Center was founded in 1982 by the Norwegian Church Ministry to Israel to fill a need for Hebrew-language training.

It was named after Carl Paul Caspari (1814-1892), a Jewish believer who was professor of Old Testament at the University of Oslo and first chairman of the Committee for the Mission among the Jews in that city.

The Caspari Center functions today as a study center and think tank, offering lectures and seminars "with the possibility of academic credit," publishing the journal *Mishkan: A Forum on the Gospel and the Jewish People*, and currently sponsoring a multi-volume scholarly project, "History of the Jewish Believers in Jesus from Antiquity to the Present" under the editorship of Oskar Skarsaune, professor of church history at the Norwegian Lutheran School of Theology in Oslo. Though not a formal degree-granting institution, the Caspari Center maintains a high academic caliber in its offerings and projects.

In addition to the above institutions, various other vehicles have been created to train aspiring leaders in the Messianic movement, particularly leaders of Messianic congregations, and others who might be interested. The newest undergraduate program is the Messianic Jewish concentration offered at Nyack College in New York, as a track within the Pastoral Ministry program. Nyack's program, spearheaded by Messianic Rabbi David Rosenberg, is "designed for students who are desiring to be Rabbis of Messianic Jewish congregations. All streams of the Messianic movement will be welcomed and represented in the courses of this concentration."[9]

The Messianic Jewish Training Institute (MJTI) was established in 2002 as the training arm of the UMJC congregational leaders (see chapter 1.4 on the UMJC). MJTI has a faculty of seven, five of whom have earned doctorates. MJTI consists of two schools: The School of Jewish Studies (SJS) and the Rabbinical Ordination Institute (ROI). The School of Jewish Studies offers academic courses and concentrations in Scripture, rabbinics, theology, history, and spiritual life, all taught from a Messianic Jewish perspective. The Rabbinical Ordination Institute supplements the SJS curriculum by offering practical courses in rabbinical leadership. ROI also provides spiritual and vocational direction for rabbinical candidates. MJTI is based in Ann Arbor, Michigan. Week-long intensive courses are taught in Michigan and at regional campuses in Virginia, Connecticut and Pasadena. In addition, MJTI is linked to the Netzer David International Yeshiva in Clearwater, Florida, which is headed by Dr. John Fischer and attached to the recently accredited St. Petersburg Theological Seminary.

MJTI's stated purpose is to "serve the Messianic Jewish movement by providing advanced education and training for those seeking ordination within the UMJC." So, for instance, applicants to the rabbinical ordination program must submit "reflections on the official UMJC statement, 'Defining Messianic Judaism.'" [10]

The congregational wing of the Messianic Jewish Alliance of America, the International Alliance of Messianic Congregations and Synagogues (IAMCS), does not have a formal educational institution, but provides courses at its conferences and on tape for its members. [11] There doesn't seem to be a formal educational track for the leaders of MJAA to receive their ordination and rabbinic titles as there is for the UMJC leaders. Another institution is the Messianic Bible Institute-Yeshiva [12] in Newport News, Virginia, which is run by David Hargis, which is further discussed in the next section.

EVALUATING THE STATE OF MESSIANIC JEWISH EDUCATION

When it comes to evaluating Messianic Jewish education, it's important to keep in mind that while the programs offered are small, this does not mean they aren't quality. The question is not the size of the institution, but the value of faculty and education offered.

Missionaries to the Jewish people have typically been trained in evangelical schools and seminaries that are well established and are known for offering a high quality education. More recently, many Messianic congregational leaders have been trained through their own institutions, such as the Messianic Bible Institute-Yeshiva and MJTI, or through specialized but non-accredited courses. As these newer institutions purport to be training present and future leadership of the Messianic movement, they deserve close scrutiny.

In the case of the Messianic Bible Institute-Yeshiva, their accreditation is through the Transworld Accrediting Commission, an agency, which has been described by one writer as an "accrediting mill."[13] Yet the Institute offers degrees through correspondence courses that one would normally require accreditation for: Bachelor of Bible, Master of Divinity, Master of Theology in Messianic Studies, and Master of Theology degrees in Rabbinic Studies. Under Virginia law, they are allowed to offer such degrees. Thus the question is not one of legality, but of the value of the degrees granted. The Institute also offers ordination as a Messianic rabbi, even though, unlike the UMJC, they are not a congregational organization. Their credentials come with a peculiar disclaimer that "MBI does not make any claim that the qualifications are infallible, nor that their credentials necessarily proves the qualifications and ability of anyone to do the work of ministry."[14]

The catalog from MJTI describes an impressive array of courses whose descriptions reflect a high caliber of thought. The faculty are known to many within the Messianic movement. Some hold masters degrees and doctorates from recognized institutions. Mark Kinzer, who heads up the MJTI, holds a Ph.D. from the University of Michigan. The MJTI offers perspectives on the Jewishness of the Bible and theology that may not be found in most mainstream Christian seminaries, and also highlights particular issues (alleged anti-Semitism in the New Testament, for instance) that those ministering among Jewish people need to understand.

However, many evangelicals would describe Mark Kinzer as theologically liberal in some of his views, and indeed he espouses some very non-traditional positions, most notably on matters of ecclesiology (see chapter 2.5). The program of MJTI is stronger on Bible courses and courses on rabbinic writings than on theology. The theological categories are placed in terms that Jewish thinkers have chosen to interact on, rather than on traditional categories as taught in evangelical seminaries. That is not wrong in itself, as we should always be looking for contextual ways to present abiding truth.

However, if one is looking to find new ways of doing theology and Bible study, the least one should do is expose students to the traditional ways of thinking that they are attempting to change. It is noteworthy that while theology courses are in the MJTI catalog, the only history taught is Jewish history; the history of the Church, Christian theology and reflection are not explicitly addressed. One wonders if traditional Christian viewpoints are adequately represented.

CONCLUSION

For those interested in attending a school (or classes) to learn more about Jesus and the New Testament from a Messianic Jewish perspective, or about the Jewish backgrounds to Christianity, see if there is a local evangelical seminary or Bible college offering such a course. If you are considering attending a local Messianic "yeshiva" or an institute such as the MJTI, recognize that unless a school is properly accredited, you cannot count on earning a degree that will be generally recognized, if that is what you are after.

Whether it is a local Messianic institute or a course offered through an evangelical seminary or Bible college, learn something about the school and the faculty. Some salient questions to ask are: What is the institute's statement of faith? Do faculty members have degrees and from which institutions? What is their theological perspective? For example, are they part of the current theological ferment in the Messianic movement? Are they presenting "new" and untested approaches to Bible and theology that do not also present the traditional approaches? Would their views be considered idiosyncratic or non-evangelical were they to be subjected to scrutiny by evangelical scholars? What affiliations do they have? That is, are they members of recognized evangelical associations and agencies? Affiliations are one of the most helpful tests for an institution's general theological outlook.

Do not assume that because the instructor is Jewish or affiliated with a Messianic organization, or because they are presenting a "Jewish perspective," that they therefore have the best "take" on things. Some non-Jewish scholars have done some of the best and most enduring research on the Jewishness of the gospel. Lastly, do not assume that because a Jewish perspective is being taught, that therefore the instructor is unlocking "secrets" never before revealed. Most serious Bible scholarship is well aware of, and interacts with, the Jewish backgrounds to the New Testament.

FURTHER READING

Rosen, Moishe. "Reflections on Missionary Training." Paper delivered at the Lausanne Consultation on Jewish Evangelism of North America, 2004. Available at: http://www.lcje.net/papers/2004/rosen.doc

Dillan, Vicky. "The MBI Yeshiva and the Hargis Clan" on the Seek God website: http://www.seekgod.ca/mbiyeshiva.htm. In the genre of investigative reporting and overall a good site, but not all will agree with the theological conservatism of the author—she is opposed to "ecumenism" as well as various trends in modern evangelicalism and hence also calls Jews for Jesus, the Lausanne Consultation on Jewish Evangelism and others into question.

ONLINE RESOURCES
Educational institutions discussed above (listed alphabetically):

Caspari Center: http://www.caspari.com
Friends of Israel Institute of Jewish Studies at Philadelphia Biblical University: http://www.pbu.edu/programs/ijs/
IAMCS Yeshiva: http://www.iamcs.org/Yeshiva.php
Israel College of the Bible: http://www.israelcollege.com
Messianic Bible Institute-Yeshiva:
http://www.Messianicbureau.org/mbima/
Messianic Jewish Theological Institute (training arm for the UMJC): http://www.mjti.org/
Moody Bible Institute: http://www.moody.edu
Nyack College's Jewish Studies Concentration:
http://www.nyack.edu/2005.php?page=PMNConcentrations
The Pasche Institute: http://pascheinstitute.org/about.html
Western Seminary's program:
http://www.westernseminary.edu/AcademicPrograms/SJ/MASM.htm

Notes
1. Clark, Christopher M., *The Politics of Conversion: Missionary Protestantism and the Jews in Prussia 1728-1941*. Oxford: Clarendon Press, 1995, p. 51; and see pp. 47-57, section "The Institutum Judaicum in Halle."
2. For this and further details, see Mevorah, Barouh, "Precursors of the Pietist "Institutum Judaicum," *Immanuel* 21 (Summer 1987), pp. 99-105.

3. Deutsch, Gotthard, "Institutum Judaicum," *Jewish Encyclopedia*, 1906. Online at: http://www.jewishencyclopedia.com/view.jsp?artid=156&letter=I

4. See Getz, Gene A., *MBI: The Story of Moody Bible Institute* (Chicago: Moody Press, 1969), pp. 101, 162.

5. http://mmm.moody.edu/GenMoody/Media/MediaLibrary/UGCatalog0406rev_3.pdf, p. 170

6. http://www.pbu.edu/programs/ijs/, with further information in the "IJS Links" section.

7. http://www.israelcollege.com/showpage.php?cat=1

8. http://www.caspari.com/about.html

9. http://www.nyack.edu/2005.php?page=PMNConcentrations

10. Catalog, p. 4, available as PDF download at http://www.mjti.org/mjti/catalog.pdf

11. http://www.iamcs.org/Yeshiva.php

12. A "yeshiva" is a traditional Jewish school of learning.

13. See discussion at http://www.seekgod.ca/mbiyeshiva.htm.

14. http://www.messianicbureau.org/mbima/

Chapter Six

Philo-Semitic Organizations*

INTRODUCTION

Christian anti-Semitism has been one of the greatest obstacles to effective Jewish evangelism over the centuries—not to mention simply being a moral evil. Though anti-Semitism existed long before there were Christians (e.g., Pharaoh and Haman), to many Jewish people, Christianity as an institution has become synonymous with the Crusades, the Inquisition, Martin Luther's anti-Jewish polemics and even Adolf Hitler. Although the Nazi regime was no friend of Christianity either, many German churches were nevertheless complicit in the events surrounding the Holocaust. On a more personal level, many older Jewish people have childhood memories of being called "Christ-killers" by people they knew who claimed to be Christians.

It is in the context of the history of anti-Semitism that a number of philo-Semitic, or for want of a better term, "Love Israel" organizations have arisen. Their goal is to show the Jewish world that true Christians who embody the spirit of Christ love the Jewish people, and to persuade Christians to support Israel. Such organizations are often perceived to be part of the Messianic Movement.

A BIT OF BACKGROUND

Demonstrations of love for Israel and the Jewish people are not new. Even in the early church, much anti-Jewish writing was directed not against Jews, but against "philo-Semitic" Christians. These Christians came from the ranks of the "God-fearers," that

(*organizations that promote a love for Israel)

is, those who already had an attraction to Judaism and the Jewish people. It is the anti-Jewish writing that has survived, but its very existence underscores the early existence of what one scholar calls a "grass-roots" philo-Semitic movement.[1]

In more recent times, modern Jewish missions arose out of a concern for the Jewish people that embraced the desire to see them come to know Christ and attempted to meet their physical needs. The Jewish perspective was, unsurprisingly, rather different. Attempts to share Christ with Jewish people were viewed as anything but acts of love. Material help, especially of a medical nature, was more welcome. However, today, at least in the West, Jewish people are well provided for, and in fact have produced a large number of physicians.

In the late 19th century, the rise of Zionism found many advocates among Christians who believed that a Jewish homeland would be a fulfillment of prophecy. Humanitarian motives played a part as well. To this day the Jewish community usually welcomes Christians who support Israel, though some question the motivations of evangelical Christians who also believe that Jewish people need to hear the gospel.

In entering a discussion of philo-Semitism, it must also be noted that during the Holocaust individual Christians often reached out to Jews, hiding them or facilitating their escape. They number among the "righteous Gentiles" that Jewish tradition honors.

Over the years, the vision and position of some philo-Semitic organizations and people have modified. When Jewish evangelism was still strongly on the agenda of Christian churches, evangelistic efforts were united with social programs to share God's love in Christ. In contrast, the newer philo-Semitic organizations have arisen at a time when many Christian denominations have openly repudiated the need for the proclamation of the gospel to Jewish people.

Even among evangelical Christians, pressure to refrain from Jewish evangelism has come from several fronts—not just the Jewish community. First, the past several decades have seen an emphasis on dialogue over what is pejoratively called "proselytism," that is, evangelism. Second, postmodernism and pluralism have influenced a softening of theological positions regarding the necessity of faith in Christ for salvation for anyone, not just for Jewish people. Third, there has been an increasingly widespread promulgation of "Two-Covenant" or "Dual-Covenant" theology— the idea that Jews already have a relationship with God through the covenant with Abraham and therefore have no need for Jesus. These forces have all combined to erode evangelical support for Jewish evangelism.[2] Consequently, the most recent expressions of love for the Jewish people tend to downplay or disavow evangelism altogether.

CURRENT PHILO-SEMITIC EFFORTS

It is with this background in mind that we look at some of the better-known philo-Semitic organizations.

The International Fellowship of Christians and Jews (IFCJ)

IFCJ has perhaps the highest profile of any of the modern philo-Semitic organizations. Unlike some of the others described below, IFCJ is headed not by Christians, but by Yechiel Eckstein, a mainstream Jewish rabbi who is not a believer in Jesus. Among the programs of the IFCJ is "Stand for Israel," which promotes prayer for Israel and Christian advocacy for the State of Israel. On an FAQ page of IFCJ's website,[3] the question is asked, "Does the Fellowship evangelize or share the gospel with those they help through their programs?" The answer: "While we affirm the right and duty of evangelical Christians to share the gospel, we are not an organization that seeks to convert people to either Christianity or Judaism. Our mission of building bridges between Christians and Jews would be compromised if we endorsed any conversion efforts."

While Rabbi Eckstein perhaps affirms the "right and duty" of sharing the gospel on his website, elsewhere he speaks of Jewish evangelism in the harshest terms: "When directed at Jews, however, Christian missions conflict with and even jeopardize the central ethic guiding Jewish life today—Jewish survival. While Christians have sought to convert Jews to Christianity for almost two millennia, after the holocaust those attempts are regarded as especially pernicious threats to Jewish survival—indeed, a form of spiritual genocide."[4]

Rabbi Eckstein is simultaneously soliciting support from evangelical Christians and isolating Jewish believers in Jesus from the support of the Church at large. Not only has he gone on record as opposed to Jewish evangelism, but he also has harsh words for Jews who follow Jesus. One writer who has studied some aspects of the Messianic movement wrote in the *Journal of Ecumenical Studies*:

> Orthodox Rabbi Yechiel Eckstein, another national participant in interfaith dialogue, believes that Messianic Jews engage in deceptive proselytizing . . . Eckstein asked, 'Is it any wonder that Jews are so deeply offended by such groups and tend to regard them as essentially no different from cults?' This author spoke with a representative of Eckstein's organization, the International Fellowship of Christians and Jews, in September, 1998, who indicated that Eckstein's position on Messianic Jews had not changed.[5]

Despite his characterization of evangelism of the Jewish people as "spiritual genocide," and his disdain for Jews who believe in Jesus,

Rabbi Eckstein is endorsed by some leading evangelical Christians. In 2003, Jews for Jesus issued a statement authored by Executive Director David Brickner, which read in part:

> Some well-known pastors and Christian leaders have either endorsed those who oppose Jewish evangelism or have carefully avoided endorsing anyone who does engage in effective gospel outreach to Jewish people. Some are flattered by the affirmation rabbis bestow on them. Others fear that standing with those who believe in Jewish evangelism might jeopardize their friendship with these rabbis. Many simply don't think through the implications or realize that those they are endorsing oppose Jewish evangelism. In any case, the cause of Christ among the Jewish people is hurt.
>
> You can find examples of good Christians endorsing people who oppose our efforts on the web site of Rabbi Yechiel Eckstein. As director of the International Fellowship of Christians and Jews, Eckstein has diverted tens of millions of dollars in mission giving to his non-missionary efforts. Yet Lloyd Ogilvie, . . . Jerry Falwell, Pat Robertson and Pat Boone as well as the late Bill Bright are all listed on his site with quotes that sing the rabbi's praises. The quotes may not reflect their knowledge of Eckstein's anti-evangelism stance, or even portray their sentiments today, but they are there just the same. Many lay Christians depend on such leaders to help determine if a cause is "kosher." No wonder evangelicals are duped into supporting Rabbi Eckstein.[6]

Unknown to the many evangelical Christians who support Eckstein, his organization does not directly disburse funds to indigent Jews or to Jews wishing to immigrate to Israel. Instead he gives funds raised to other Jewish organizations who then do the acts of charity in their own name. Among the organizations that are recipients of funds are Colel

Chabad, a humanitarian organization related to the Lubavitcher Hasidim, an ultra-Orthodox group that is active not only in humanitarian projects, but in anti-missionary work as well. One can be sure that any Jewish recipient of aid from such an organization who speaks favorably about Jesus or relates an encounter with a Christian missionary will be quickly talked out of considering Jesus.[7] It is significant that Christians sometimes mistake Rabbi Eckstein's organization for a Christian one. At Jews for Jesus, many of us have met at least one person who thought they were supporting a work like Jews for Jesus because they were already supporting the IFCJ. Furthermore, they were unaware that Eckstein was a rabbi and not a Christian evangelist! Some of the endorsements by Christian leaders have contributed to this confusion, as they refer to Eckstein as "brother" or "man of God" or proudly announce that he has spoken in their pulpit.[8]

We commend Christians who want to join in supporting the Jewish people, and we don't intend to tell Christians which causes they should and should not support. Nevertheless, it seems to us that Rabbi Eckstein is deliberately seeking to blur lines, with the effect that many evangelical Christians are persuaded that he is one of them.

Bridges for Peace

Headed by Clarence H. Wagner, this organization seeks to encourage among Christians a love for Israel and a concern for the Jewish people. Their publications include material on the Jewish background of the gospel and have also included strong statements in support of Israel and against replacement theology (the doctrine that the Church has replaced Israel in God's plan).

Bridges for Peace is evangelical in its leadership. Its goals are listed on its web site:

We are committed to the following goals:
- To encourage meaningful and supportive relationships between Christians and Jews in Israel and around the world.
- To educate and equip Christians to identify with Israel, the Jewish people, and the biblical/Hebraic foundations of our Christian faith.
- To bless Israel and the Jewish people in Israel and worldwide, through practical assistance, volunteer service, and prayer.
- To communicate Christian perspectives to the attention of Israeli leaders and the Jewish community-at-large.
- To counter Anti-Semitism worldwide and support Israel's divine God-given right to exist in her God-given land.[9]

All this is commendable, yet it should be pointed out that Bridges for Peace does not include sharing the gospel among the ways one should show love to Jewish people. A perusal of some of their printed materials suggests that they do believe that Jesus is the way of salvation and hints at the fact that some day "all Israel will be saved" (Romans 11:26), yet for now the calling of the Church is only to "bless" and "love" Israel. Anecdotal accounts suggest that Christians visiting Israel under the auspices of Bridges for Peace are encouraged *not* to share their faith.[10] It is noteworthy that Rabbi Eckstein's book mentioned above is listed on the Bridges for Peace recommended reading list.[11]

The International Christian Embassy Jerusalem

Formed in 1980, the ICEJ originated as a counterpoint to a widespread lack of support for Israel as evidenced by the refusal of a number of countries to have their embassies in Jerusalem. The ICEJ attempted to express Christian support and love for the state of Israel "as an evangelical Christian response to the need to comfort Zion according to the command of Scripture found in Isaiah 40:1-2."[12]

However, the organization does not embrace evangelism.[13]
Their website explains their goals in these terms:

> The International Christian Embassy Jerusalem is a
> worldwide, non-profit ministry with a prophetic calling to
> be a source of comfort to Israel and the Jewish people. The
> Bible is clear about the attitude Christians should have
> towards the Jews. Genesis 12:3 says we should "bless
> them." Isaiah 40:1 commands us to "comfort them." Psalm
> 122:6 says we should "pray for the peace of Jerusalem."
> Romans 11:31 tells us to "show them mercy."[14]

In 1990, the Israel branch of the Lausanne Consultation on
Jewish Evangelism issued a statement that included this remark:

> We commend those Christians who are reaching out to
> Israel by humanitarian labors of love and concern.
> However, history cannot excuse the church from its duty to
> preach the Gospel to Israel, nor can Israel be comforted
> truly apart from her Messiah. No good deeds can atone for
> the past, nor may we replace the finished atoning work of
> Messiah with expressions of our love.[15]

Acts of social and personal care are to be welcomed. As
Baruch Maoz, an Israeli Jewish-Christian pastor who authored
the above statement, said elsewhere in the same journal, "Jews
have never suffered from an overdose of Christian affection."
At the same time, the retreat of gospel proclamation to a back
issue or side issue is cause for concern in organizations that
claim to represent the love of Christians for Jews.

Exobus

Founded in 1991, Exobus describes itself as "an international,
prophetic and practical ministry."[16] Headed up by Phil Hunter,

who is the managing director of Good News Travels, a Christian coach company based in England, Exobus raises funds to bring Jewish people to Israel from Russia and Ukraine. They see this as their way to fulfill "the call of God on Jews to return home [meaning the land of Israel]." The coaches (buses) transport Jews from Russia to Poland and then they are carried by other transport to Israel. Like the above groups, Exobus doesn't engage in or specifically encourage Jewish evangelism. While clearly expressing faith in Jesus and the need for worldwide spiritual revival, Exobus seems to believe that the Jewish people need first to return to the Land of Israel in unbelief, after which God will spiritually revive the nation. No mention is made of a present need for Jewish people to hear about Jesus.[17]

CONCLUSION

We live in a time when anti-Semitism seems to be on the rise, particularly in Europe and in many Islamic lands. The current generation has no firsthand recollection of the Holocaust or the rise of the State of Israel. The voices of those who can speak of personal experiences in the Holocaust are becoming fewer and fewer, and propaganda often preempts rational discussion of Israel's right to exist.

In this climate any expression of love, care and concern for the Jewish people is to be encouraged. That is why the modern philo-Semitic agencies pose a dilemma. On one hand, they undoubtedly help Jewish people. Who can argue with praying for Israel, providing material support for immigrants to Israel or encouraging understanding of the State of Israel?

Yet if the gospel is never spoken of by organizations operating under the banner of evangelicalism, misimpression is inevitable— among both Jewish people and evangelical Christians. One might think that as far as Jewish people are concerned, Christianity requires no more than mutual understanding and social concern.

It is difficult to pin down the reasons for this neglect of evangelism. Do these agencies consider evangelism to be necessary, but best done by others? Do they hold to something akin to a two-covenant theology? Do they believe that it is, so to speak, God's job to bring Israel to faith in Jesus while it is the Church's job to only "bless" Israel? Baruch Maoz's comment concerning the International Christian Embassy is apropos:

> It is readily acknowledged that not all evangelical bodies must be involved in evangelism. Indeed, some such bodies definitely should not. Their callings are different, and should be conducted accordingly. There would be no difficulty if the Embassy issued a statement to the effect that, while it believed in the necessity of evangelism *per se*, it did not itself engage in such activity. But the Embassy's repeated hedging on this issue gives credence to the growing conviction of some that the Embassy believes political and economic support in the name of Christ are all that is needed, and that evangelism is, at best, peripheral.[18]

Previous generations embraced liberalism to the extent that the basics of the gospel were replaced with the "social gospel." Will this generation purposely embrace a political and social love for Jewish people without proclaiming Him who is our only political, social and spiritual hope? One is reminded of Jesus' saying that certain things should be done without neglecting the others (Matthew 23:23).

Jews for Jesus encourages people to consider practical ways of expressing love to Jewish people they know. But we also consider sharing the gospel with a Jewish person the ultimate reflection of care and concern, even though it often involves risking relationships.

We would never want to dictate to anyone where their support should go. But at least let those who support the philo-Semitic organizations understand who and what they are supporting, especially when it comes to the question of the most loving thing you can do for a Jewish person—that is, proclaiming the gospel. Jews for Jesus is in touch with forthright Christian relief efforts to the Jewish poor in Israel and elsewhere, and will supply such information upon request.

FURTHER READING

On Rabbi Yechiel Eckstein:
> The War on Jewish Evangelism
> http://files.jewsforjesus.org/pdf/other/war_on_je.pdf

> Moishe Rosen concerning "On Wings of Eagles"
> http://www.jewsforjesus.org/publications/newsletter/1997
> _03/sayings

> Moishe's Musings on Lifestyle Evangelism
> http://www.jewsforjesus.org/publications/newsletter/2000
> _11/moishesmusings

On Philo-Semitic Organizations:
> Goldberg, Louis, "Historical and Political Factors in the Twentieth Century Affecting the Identity of Israel." In *Israel: The Land and the People: An Evangelical Affirmation of God's Promises*, edited by H. Wayne House. Grand Rapids, MI: Kregel Publications, 1998.

> Skarsaune, Oskar, "The Neglected Story of Christian Philo-Semitism in Antiquity and the Early Middle Ages," *Mishkan: A Theological Forum on the Gospel and the Jewish People*, vol. 21, 1994, 40-51.

> *Mishkan: A Theological Forum on Jewish Evangelism* 12, 1990, issue including material on the Christian Embassy. http://www.caspari.com/mishkan/contents/contents11.html#12

On loving the Jewish people:
  Bärend, Irmhild, "Why I, a German, Love the Jewish
  People." *ISSUES* 13:7.
  http://www.jewsforjesus.org/publications/issues/13_7/whyi
  lovethejews
  Damato, Catherine, "Why I, a Gentile, Love the Jewish
  People." *ISSUES* 11:1.
  http://www.jewsforjesus.org/publications/issues/11_1/whyi
  lovethejews

Notes

1. See Oskar Skarsaune, "The Neglected Story of Christian Philo-
Semitism in Antiquity and the Early Middle Ages," *Mishkan: A
Theological Forum on the Gospel and the Jewish People* 21
(1994): 40-51. Skarsaune also references scholars John Gager and
Stephen Wilson in support.

2. On Two-Covenant theology see *Mishkan:* 11 (1989). The entire
issue was given over to this subject.

3. http://www.ifcj.org/site/PageServer?pagename=programs_faq

4. Eckstein, Yechiel. *What Christians Should Know About Jews
and Judaism* (Waco: Word, 1984), p. 287.

5. Samuelson, Francine K. "Messianic Judaism: Church,
Denomination, Sect, or Cult?," *Journal of Ecumenical Studies* 37:2
(Spring 2000), p. 174, citing *What Christians Should Know*, pp. 297-
298; and "Joan Watson, telephone conversation with author,
September 15, 1998."

6. Brickner, David, "The War on Jewish Evangelism," 2003, online as a
PDF at: http://files.jewsforjesus.org/pdf/other/war_on_je.pdf.
A website that brings together many relevant quotes by Eckstein
and his supporters can be found at:
http://www.myfortress.org/RabbiYechielEckstein.html

7. For a complete list of 2003 recipients of IFJC's aid, see their
annual report available at:
http://www.ifcj.org/site/PageServer?pagename=whoweare_annualreport

8. http://www.ifcj.org/site/PageServer?pagename=endorsements
and http://www.myfortress.org/RabbiYechielEckstein.html

9. http://www.bridgesforpeace.com/h2n.php?fn=whoarewe.html

10. Goldberg, Louis. "Historical and Political Factors in the Twentieth Century Affecting the Identity of Israel," pp. 113-141 in *Israel, the Land and the People: An Evangelical Affirmation of God's Promises*, ed. H. Wayne House (Grand Rapids: Kregel, 1998), p. 131.

11. http://www.bridgesforpeace.com/h2n.php?fn=research.html# JEWISH-CHRISTIAN%20UNDERSTANDING

12. http://www.icej.org/

13. Goldberg, "Historical Factors," pp. 131-32.

14. http://www.icej.org/comfort/index.html

15. "A Statement on Christian Zionism," *Mishkan* 12 (1990), p. 6.

16. http://www.exobus.org

17. http://www.exobus.org/featuresstory.asp?id=286&section=reg3

18. Maoz, Baruch. "The Christian Embassy in Jerusalem," *Mishkan* 12 (1990), pp. 2-3.

Part Two

Movements Within the Movement

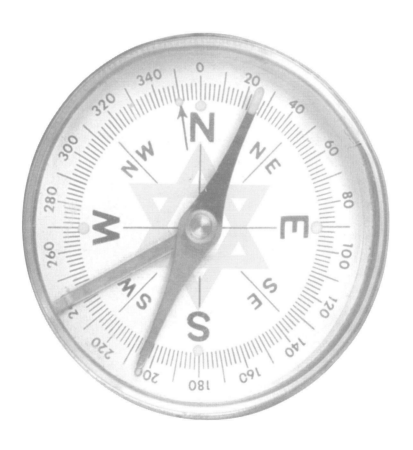

Chapter One
Questioning the Jewishness
of Christian Theology

INTRODUCTION

In an effort to "restore" or emphasize the Jewishness of the gospel, a teaching has surfaced among some in the Messianic movement who maintain that the cardinal doctrines of Christianity such as the Incarnation and the Trinity are pagan in origin, and that observances such as Christmas and Easter are based in paganism and are to be rejected as unbiblical or "unJewish."

The first thing to keep in mind is that the gospel is cross-cultural, and this means that Jewish forms of worship and lifestyle are not mandatory for the Church at large. Jewish believers may enjoy expressing their faith in Jewish terms by, for instance, celebrating the Passover and holding a seder in their home or displaying Jewish art. Such practices should be encouraged. But these activities are not incumbent on Korean, Malaysian or Nigerian Christians.

The charge of paganism, though, pertains less to what Christians should do or believe; rather, it seeks to tell Christians what they should *not* do or believe. And charges of paganism might not be thorough-going; some who question the appropriateness of celebrating Christmas might not challenge the doctrines of the Incarnation or the Trinity; they may be quite orthodox in that regard. This chapter looks at the various allegations of paganism in Christian thought and practice.

RESPONDING TO THE CHARGES OF
PAGANISM OF CHRISTIAN PRACTICES

First, let's consider the charge that believers shouldn't observe

Christmas and Easter because they were pagan in origin.
There are several problems with this approach.

One problem has to do with the use of symbols. Symbols
are a language and, as with any language, their meaning
depends on usage, not origins. God's people have long used
pagan or secular symbols and institutions with new,
sanctified meanings. For example, in the Old Testament,
sanctuaries, temples, priests and sacrifices existed among the
pagan nations long before Israel was formed. God, however,
took those institutions and turned them into sanctified
symbols that reflected who He was and how He wanted His
people to live.

In the New Testament, Jesus took post-biblical customs such as the
four cups of wine at Passover and the water-drawing ceremonies
of Sukkot and invested them with new meaning concerning
Himself (or, as some might phrase it, He explained their old
meaning with application to Himself). In more recent history,
Johann Sebastian Bach was known to take secular drinking songs
and convert them into church hymns to the glory of God.

The date on which Christmas is now celebrated, December
25, did indeed coincide with a pagan holiday. It is quite
possible, however, that the date was deliberately adopted by
the Church in order to sanctify the day, invest it with new
meaning and perhaps even reach out evangelistically. The
same holds true for Easter, whose name derives from the
Saxon goddess Eostre, but which may have been intended to
be a Christian replacement for a pagan celebration rather than
an accommodation to one. But again, the origins are not as
important as the present meaning associated with the holiday.

Further, once you say that you can't celebrate Christmas or
Easter because of their pagan origins, where do you stop? The

seven days of the week are, in the English language, named for pagan Norse gods. To be consistent, those who advocate abandoning Christmas or Easter on the grounds of pagan origins should stop calling the days of the week by their common names. The planets are likewise named after Roman gods and common words like "odyssey" have their origins in non-Christian, pagan literature. But of course none of these things pays homage to Greek or Norse gods in daily usage. Origins do not determine meaning.

One pastor and historian sums it up this way:

> The regular worship of the church in the early centuries has been closely studied by scholars. Its changing forms have been carefully documented. Such changes are no cause for alarm, in themselves. The Passover celebrated by Jesus embraced a traditional course of four wine cups which was not specified in the Law. Furthermore, Jesus appears to have taken part in the Feast of Dedication (Hannukah), referred to in John 10:22f, which was an inter-testamental celebration recalling the days of the Maccabees. These traditions were acceptable because [they were] not alien to what the Law *did* require. This fact is helpful when considering customs in worship and Christian observance (such as Christmas), which are not commanded in Scripture.[1] [emphasis in the original]

Saying a particular worship form or holiday isn't culturally Jewish is one thing, though one can argue that celebrating the Messiah's birth or resurrection is in fact Jewish. But to go further and call them unbiblical is quite another.

RESPONDING TO THE CHARGES OF PAGANISM OF CHRISTIAN DOCTRINES

Claims that Christian concepts such as the Incarnation and the Trinity are of pagan origin are not new, nor are they specifically

Jewish assertions. In the context of this book, it should be noted that some who make these claims are at times identified as being part of the Messianic movement—but their theology, insofar as they reject the Incarnation and the Trinity, is not evangelical. In fact, in that regard their thinking is quite similar to that of anti-missionaries and many secular scholars.

There are resources available that explain how these doctrines did not originate in paganism; some of them are listed at the end of this chapter. But few accounts go further and demonstrate that these doctrines are *distinctly Jewish*.

The Doctrine of the Incarnation

One scholar who has done much work in this area is Oskar Skarsaune, professor of church history at the Norwegian Lutheran School of Theology in Oslo, Norway.

In his book, *In the Shadow of the Temple*,[2] Skarsaune observes, "Jewish scholars in antiquity, the Middle Ages and modern times have almost unanimously claimed that the idea that Jesus is the incarnate Word of God is un-Jewish, a product of Christianity's transplantation from a Jewish milieu to a Gentile-Hellenistic milieu." (And, we add, not just mainstream Jewish scholars, but as indicated above, some who might be considered part of the Messianic movement also hold this view.) However, the evidence substantiates the opposite conclusion, as Skarsaune goes on to show:

> Let us begin with an observation on the typical Hellenistic reaction to the dogma of the incarnate Son of God. [Orthodox Jewish scholar Pinchas] Lapide would have us believe that this was something Gentile Hellenists would really appreciate, something they craved for, something

they would embrace enthusiastically. But we have several authentic reports on the Gentile Hellenistic reaction, and it does not correspond to this picture at all. The available evidence shows, on the contrary, that most Hellenists reacted with disgust and contempt at the very idea of a divine incarnation, and with charges of blasphemy when they heard that the incarnate Son of God had suffered the uttermost shame of crucifixion.[3]

Skarsaune traces the roots of the doctrine of the Incarnation to the Jewish concept of the Wisdom of God in the Old Testament and inter-testamental periods.[4] And he gives us a rather startling quote from Pinchas Lapide:

> I used to think that becoming incarnate was impossible to God. But recently I have come to the conclusion that it is un-Jewish to say that this is something the God of the Bible cannot do, that he cannot come that close. I have had second thoughts about the incarnation.[5]

The Doctrine of the Trinity

Similarly, research on the doctrine of the Trinity shows its essentially Jewish character. A case in point is the work of Larry W. Hurtado. Hurtado is professor of New Testament Language, Literature and Theology at the University of Edinburgh's School of Divinity and director of the Centre for the Study of Christian Origins. Hurtado has written extensively on the early Christian understanding that Jesus was divine. For the full argument, interested readers can refer to his books in the section on further reading. The following, however, summarizes his conclusions:

> Devotion to Jesus as divine erupted suddenly and quickly, not gradually and late, among first-century circles of followers. More specifically, the origins lie in Jewish

Christian circles of the earliest years. Only a certain wishful thinking continues to attribute the reverence of Jesus as divine decisively to the influence of pagan religion and the influx of Gentile converts, characterizing it as developing late and incrementally.[6]

In other words, the doctrine of the deity of Jesus is not some fourth century development foisted on the Church by Gentile believers. There is no "non-divine Jesus" in first-century Christianity that needs to be "restored" in the name of Jewishness. It is true that the doctrine did not take the form in which we know it for a few centuries after Jesus' ministry.

But the doctrinal problem they [church councils] worked on was not of their making. It was forced upon them by the earnest convictions and devotional practices of believers from the earliest observable years of the Christian movement.[7]

Hurtado, in his wide-ranging study, traces the early devotion to Jesus as a "variant" of exclusive Jewish monotheism, in sharp contrast to typical pagan ideas of "apotheosis" (the transformation of a human being into a god). In other words, we are dealing with a case where God becomes man, not where man becomes divine. Interestingly, he quotes first-century Jewish writer Philo, responding to the emperor Gaius Caligula's claim to be divine: "Sooner could God change into a man than a man into God." Hurtado remarks that this quotation is illustrative of the Jewish attitudes of the time.[8]

CONCLUSION
In the end, study of Scripture and the history of theological ideas shows the Jewishness of Christian doctrine, as well as the propriety of sanctifying non-Christian practices to the service of God.

Some in the Messianic movement use the history of anti-Semitism within the Church as a justification for avoiding the contributions made by the largely non-Jewish Church in the centuries after Christ. But those who wish to bypass, neglect, or replace the fruit of 2,000 years of theology fail to appreciate that God has worked within the Church in spite of its failings. Furthermore, the inclusion of Gentiles within the people of God was part of God's purposes since He proclaimed in Genesis 12:1-3 that through Abraham, the entire world would be blessed. If God intended Gentiles to become part of God's people, how then can we neglect their contributions or stereotype them as pagan? Those who neglect the fruit of Gentile theologians are guilty of the very same thing as those they accuse of neglecting Jewish thought.

FURTHER READING

Hurtado, Larry W., *Lord Jesus Christ: Devotion to Jesus in Earliest Christianity.* Grand Rapids and Cambridge: Eerdmans, 2003.

Nash, Ronald H., *The Gospel and the Greeks: Did the New Testament Borrow from Pagan Thought?* P & R Publishing; 2nd ed., 2003.

Skarsaune, Oskar, *In the Shadow of the Temple: Jewish Influences on Early Christianity.* Downers Grove: InterVarsity Press, 2002.

Skarsaune, Oskar, *Incarnation: Myth or Fact.* Concordia Publishing House, 1991.

Davies, W. D., *Paul and Rabbinic Judaism: Some Rabbinic Elements in Pauline Theology.* Fortress Press, 4th edition, 1980. Originally published 1948.

Nash, Ronald, "Was the New Testament Influenced by Pagan Religions?"

http://www.iclnet.org/pub/resources/text/cri/
cri-jrnl/web/crj0169a.txt

Nash, Ronald. "Was the New Testament Influenced by Pagan Philosophy?"
http://www.iclnet.org/pub/resources/text/cri/cri-jrnl/web/crj0163a.html

Miller, Glenn. "Was Jesus Christ just a CopyCat Savior Myth?"
http://www.christian-thinktank.com/copycat.html

Miller, Glenn. "Were the New Testament authors influenced by pagan legends?"
http://www.christian-thinktank.com/copycat2.html

Notes

1. Jackson, Jeremy C., *No Other Foundation: The Church Through Twenty Centuries* (Westchester, IL: Cornerstone Books, 1980), p. 53.
2. Skarsaune, Oskar. *In the Shadow of the Temple: Jewish Influences on Early Christianity*. Downers Grove: InterVarsity Press, 2002.
3. Ibid., p. 323.
4. See also his earlier book, *Incarnation: Myth or Fact* (Concordia Publishing House, 1991).
5. Skarsaune, *In the Shadow*, pp. 335-36, citing "Norwegian television, April 1978. There seems to be no taped copy of this interview preserved by Norwegian Broadcasting, but Lapide's words made such an impression upon me that they stuck in my mind."
6. Hurtado, Larry W., *Lord Jesus Christ: Devotion to Jesus in Earliest Christianity*. Grand Rapids and Cambridge: Eerdmans, 2003, p. 650.
7. Ibid., p. 651.
8. Ibid., pp. 91-92, citing Philo, *Embassy to Gaius,* 118.

Chapter Two
About "Torah Observance"

INTRODUCTION

Among those groups that are sometimes considered part of the Messianic movement are those organizations and congregations that call themselves "Torah-observant" or emphasize obedience to the Law of Moses by another term. As a random sampling, such groups may include educational organizations, such as the First Fruits of Zion, individual congregations, such as Petah Tikvah in Rochester, New York or associations such as the Observant Messianic Jewish Rabbinical Association.[1] These groups can vary from the theologically orthodox regarding the person of Christ and the Trinity, to theologically aberrant. Essentially, these groups present themselves as following the Old Testament Law of Moses, thereby living a life they believe more closely resembles that of first-century followers of Jesus, or is more in keeping with God's will for today.

LOOKING AT THE LAW

Martin Luther once observed that no sooner does someone fall off a horse on the right side, than they get back on and proceed to fall off on the left side. The Torah-observant groups are in part a reaction against negative views of the Law found in some Christian circles. It is the unfortunate case that in much of evangelical Christianity the Old Testament is hardly taught, rarely preached on and little understood by the average congregant. Where the Law is mentioned, it is often portrayed as merely a burden from which Christians are now free.

The biblical picture of the Law is quite different. The Law in the Old Testament is spoken of as a gift from God, a guide to

life, something to be cherished and enjoyed, as well as
something to be obeyed under penalty of disobedience. It is
intimately bound up with the covenant wherein God
graciously reiterated His relationship with His people.

In the New Testament, the Apostle Paul reminds us that the Law
is good.[2] The idea of obedience is continually highlighted, from
the Sermon on the Mount to Jesus' words in John's Gospel[3] and
in the Epistles.[4] In fact, nine of the Ten Commandments are
explicitly reinforced in the New Testament.

The Law itself is not bad; it is sin, the misuse of the Law, and
the way that human traditions can end up supplanting the
Law, that are bad. The principles of the Law, especially the Ten
Commandments, have become the bedrock of Western
civilization and of the Church itself—even those churches that
portray the Law negatively.

Having said this, the Christian church has universally
recognized that the Law of Moses is not meant to be kept as a
body of law by Christians today.[5] The Law of Moses was part
of a covenant that God made with Israel at a particular time
and in a particular place. With the coming of Christ, the New
Covenant prophesied by Jeremiah has come into effect and we
are no longer under the Old Covenant.

The fact is that for the past two thousand years it has been
impossible to observe all the commandments of the Law of
Moses because so many of them depend on the existence of a
Temple, a priesthood, animal sacrifices and living as a
theocratic nation within the Land of Israel. Orthodox Judaism
recognizes this, and when the Temple was destroyed in A.D.
70, Judaism was reconstructed as a religion without a Temple
or a priesthood, a religion dependent on the authority and
decisions of the rabbis. Reform Judaism, a recent movement

of the past 250 years, views the Law as often antiquated and outdated, but useful as a reminder of our history, a symbol of our people and a source of ethics.

It is, however, equally important to note that the recognition that we are not intended to keep the Law of Moses today does not mean that Christians believe in lawlessness! The specific commands of the Law of Moses each reflected something of the nature of God, and behind each commandment is a principle. Those principles, reflecting God Himself, are still incumbent on all Christians today. See more on this point in the following section.

A RESPONSE TO TORAH-OBSERVANT GROUPS

In evaluating the "Torah-observant" groups within the Messianic movement, there are several things worth considering. To be sure, the exact nature and function of the Law of Moses are debated among Christians, but with an understanding that the Church, including both Jewish and Gentile members, is not mandated to keep the entire Law of Moses. The following then, is not intended as a final word by any means (as if it were possible in just a few paragraphs!), but is meant to give food for thought, and hopefully pause to those who would rush into attempting to observe the Law of Moses today.

1. It is no longer possible to keep all 613 (if we accept the traditional rabbinic enumeration) laws because we no longer have a Temple, or a priesthood, or live as a theocracy in the Land of Israel. Because of this, the Torah-observant groups end up being extremely selective in their "law-observance." For the most part, the emphasis is on holy days—Sabbaths and festivals—with perhaps some attention given to other parts of the Law. In essence, these are not so much Torah-observant as festival-observant groups. And since the Temple and

priesthood are gone and a majority of Jews live in the diaspora (outside the land of Israel), even the festivals, for instance, must be observed differently than they were in biblical times. Perhaps without their realizing it, Torah-observant groups must either depend on rabbinic tradition, which is distinctly post-biblical, or must construct their own traditions. For instance, members of such groups do not send their men to appear before the Lord in Jerusalem, as required in the Law of Moses, nor do they offer sacrifices. So there can be no question of this being an authentic, first-century way of observance.

Moreover, among the commandments of the Law are penalties for its violation, including the death penalty in many cases. Torah-observant groups do not apply the death penalty to those who are not Torah-observant. Indeed they cannot, for if they did, they would be subject in modern society to criminal charges in a court of law! We no longer live in a theocracy subject to the penalties of God's Law.

2. One gets the impression that far more than they emphasize faithfulness to Christ, the Torah-observant groups emphasize "Torah-observance" as their distinctive, and in fact imply that they are being more obedient to God, or have a deeper spirituality, than other believers in Jesus. Perhaps they would argue that their obedience to the Torah *is* faithfulness to Christ, but there is a distinct imbalance in their approach. Inadvertently, perhaps, they have created a two-tier system of believers: the more spiritual ones who observe the Law and the less spiritual ones who do not. This is not only unbiblical, but it also separates these groups from the rest of the Body of Christ in an unhealthy way.

3. Since much of the Torah-observant movement is a reaction to negative teaching about the Law, there is likewise a failure on the part of this movement to recognize that large segments of the Church take a very positive view of the Law. This is

particularly true of Reformed and Presbyterian churches, which include a positive emphasis on God's law within their confessional statements, and in their preaching and teaching. What they mean by God's law, however, is not the specific 613 commandments of the Law of Moses—which was part of the Mosaic covenant intended for that time in redemptive history—but the principles that God intends for us and commands us to live by. For many of these churches, those principles are embodied especially in the Ten Commandments, which comprise the standard for all Christian obedience.

4. Actually, the obedience required under the New Covenant is more radical than that under the Old Covenant. For instance, in Deuteronomy 22:8, it is required for one to build a parapet around the roof, a safety feature in a time when the roof functioned as both a living room for entertaining and a bedroom. I doubt that the Torah-observant groups require such parapets. But under the New Covenant, *much more* is required. That particular commandment is an example of how to follow the general rule to love our neighbor and is an outworking of the Sixth Commandment, "You shall not murder." In principle, its application today would range from preserving safety for our family and guests all the way to working for national security or in public policy. The New Covenant broadens and deepens the requirements of the Law of Moses: "For everyone to whom much is given, from him much will be required" (Luke 12:48). To stress obedience to the Law of Moses without stressing the fuller applications of the principles embodied in those laws is to miss the point (Galatians 3:24).

5. The Torah-observant groups justify their position on the basis of selected verses, while ignoring others. Much is made of the term "forever" used in regard to some Old Testament laws, while verses such as Hebrews 8:13, that speak of the first covenant as being "obsolete," are not dealt with. Further,

they ignore what theologians commonly call the "history of redemption," the progress of God's dealings with humankind throughout history. Jesus has indeed brought something new, but the Torah-observant groups minimize the newness that the coming of the Messiah has meant. In addition, they minimize the way much Old Testament Law functioned to distinguish Israel from the nations. While there is indeed distinctiveness to the Jewish people, not all the Old Testament distinctions apply. For example, one can make a good argument that the food laws were intended to symbolize the separation of Israel from the nations. Under the New Covenant, Jewish and Gentile believers in Jesus become one in the Messiah (Ephesians 2:14) in a way not realized under the Mosaic Covenant. As a result, one can build a good case that the mandatory keeping of kosher laws is no longer required for a Jewish believer in Jesus.[6]

6. Many in Torah-observant circles are not Jewish. Thought should be given as to why non-Jews are so eager to observe a law never intended for them, and to the New Testament teaching on the place of the Law of Moses in the lives of Gentile Christians.

CONCLUSION

With Jewish observances, questions arise about whether or not particular observances are proper for a follower of Jesus, and these questions have been debated among Jewish believers. One problem is that it is often hard to separate cultural from religious expressions. For an Orthodox Jew, celebrating Passover is a fulfillment of a divine command, and is done in accordance with the accretions of 2,000 years of rabbinic tradition and rabbinic law. For a Reform or secular Jew, celebrating Passover is often simply an opportunity to enjoy doing something Jewish: having a get-together with the family, going through a few traditions familiar from childhood and sharing a meal. Is Passover then a cultural expression or a religious one? Similar questions arise pertaining to other aspects of Judaism, because Judaism today is not a monolith when it comes to religious and cultural expression.

Therefore, a word needs to be said about the place of the Law of Moses in the life of a Jewish believer. Some Messianic congregations have a *Sefer Torah*, a scroll of the Law. Many, even if they do not own a *Sefer Torah*, incorporate readings from the Torah that correspond to the passage being read that week in synagogues in their services. Many Jewish believers choose to celebrate the holidays or keep kosher. Usually, though, this is something quite different from the intentions of the Torah-observant groups. For instance, all the above examples might be done to show solidarity with the rest of the Jewish community, to express worship in a Jewish manner, to be a testimony to other Jewish people, or simply as a mark of personal Jewish identity. If done voluntarily, without a belief that one accrues higher favor with God for doing so, there is freedom in Christ to do these things. However, the emphasis of Torah-observant groups is on mandatory law-keeping as an expression of greater obedience to God. So in their case we are dealing with something quite different.

A word also about churches that enjoy such celebrations as Passover: this is also something quite different from the Torah-observant groups. Churches that have an annual Passover Seder generally do so as a teaching and worship tool, with fulfillment in Christ as the focus, and an emphasis on enriching the observance of Communion. In such circumstances, it is not done as part of a mandatory requirement to observe the Law of Moses. As such, this activity should be encouraged.[7]

In summary, if you hear of a group calling themselves "Torah-observant," keep in mind the above responses and remember that it was never the Law, only its misuse, that the New Testament criticizes.

FURTHER READING

Strickland, Wayne G., ed., *Five Views on Law and Gospel.*
Zondervan, 1996. A helpful though challenging read on
different views among evangelical Christians of the place of
the Law of Moses for the Christian.

Wenham, David., "Jesus and the Law: An Exegesis on Matthew
5:17-20." *Mishkan* 8/9, 1988. Available at:
http://www.caspari.com/mishkan

Kaiser, Walter C., Jr. "James' View of the Law." *Mishkan* 8/9, 1988.

ONLINE RESOURCES

Lieske, Bruce J., "Jewish Feasts in Gentile Congregations." *Papers
for August 8-9 from the Lausanne Consultation on Jewish
Evangelism, Fourth International Conference, Zeist Holland,*
1991. 247-51. An example of an approach from a Lutheran pastor
that finds educational and worship value in the Jewish festivals
without advocating them as mandatory, necessary for obedience
to God, or indispensable to Christian growth. Available at:
http://www.jewsforjesus.org/publications/lieske

Shore, Alan M., "The Torah of God: Road Back or Road Block?
A Look at Law in Judaism and Christianity." *ISSUES* 6:2, 1988.
Includes a look at how the Law functions in rabbinic Judaism
and the relationship of Jesus to Torah.
Available at:
http://www.jewsforjesus.org/publications/issues/6_2/torahofgod

Mishkan 4, 1986. Available as a PDF download at:
http://www.caspari.com/mishkan/zips/mishkan04.pdf
Includes "Paul, the Law and the Covenant" by Ray Kearsley
(response by Stephen Notley) and "Jesus, the Kingdom and the
Torah" by Ole Chr. M. Kvarme (response by Ronald H. Lewis).

TORAH OBSERVANT GROUPS MENTIONED ABOVE
First Fruits of Zion
www.ffoz.org

Petah Tikvah
http://www.petahtikvah.com

Observant Messianic Jewish Rabbinical Association
http://www.omjra.org

Notes
1. See for instance the listing at:
http://www.omjra.org/Members.html
2. Romans 7:12, 16.
3. "If you love me, you will obey what I command" (John 14:15).
4. For instance: "But the man who looks intently into the perfect law that gives freedom, and continues to do this, not forgetting what he has heard, but doing it—he will be blessed in what he does" (James 1:25); "If you really keep the royal law found in Scripture, "Love your neighbor as yourself," you are doing right" (James 2:8); "What good is it, my brothers, if a man claims to have faith but has no deeds? Can such faith save him?" (James 2:14).
5. Many divide the Law into civil, ceremonial and moral laws. Whether those are valid distinctions is another matter, but it is instructive that no one insists that we need to keep them all. Most Christians who view the Law along those three divisions accept an ongoing validity to the moral law, particularly as embodied in the Ten Commandments. A minority view is that of Theonomists, who believe that the civil law with its penalties should continue to function in some way today.
6. For a good discussion of the laws of kosher food in Leviticus, see Wenham, Gordon J., *The Book of Leviticus* (New International Commentary on the Old Testament; Eerdmans, 1979).
7. See Lieske, Bruce J., "Jewish Feasts in Gentile Congregations," at http://www.jewsforjesus.org/publications/lieske/

Chapter Three
The Hebrew Roots Movement

INTRODUCTION

The Hebrew Roots movement, sometimes also called the Hebraic Roots or Jewish Roots movement, is one indicator of an increased interest on the part of Christians in exploring the Jewishness of their faith. One definition, from within this movement, is this:

> The Hebrew Roots movement is composed of a diverse variety of believers and ministries, united in the conviction that our understanding of the New Testament, our relationship with our Savior, and the mission of the Church can all be enhanced by a greater knowledge of the Jewish background of Christianity.[1]

So far so good. It turns out, however, that a great deal is encompassed in the word "diverse" in the above definition. A more specific description might go like this: The Hebrew Roots movement is a movement of organizations, closely networked, that hold in common an emphasis on studying, participating in, or "restoring" the Jewishness of Christianity through some or all of the following: studying the Bible in its Jewish context; observing the Torah; keeping the Sabbath and festivals;[2] avoiding the alleged "paganism" of Christianity; affirming the existence of original Hebrew language gospels and denigrating the Greek text.

Some organizations that are part of this movement emphasize *study*; some add *practice*, especially of the Old Testament festivals; others are interested in what they term *restoration*—getting the Church back to what they understand to be the "original" Jewishness of the Christian faith.

A BIT OF BACKGROUND

So what sets the Hebrew Roots movement apart? After all, most Jewish missions and Messianic congregations want to teach their constituency something about the Jewishness of the gospel (study); many hold demonstrations of the Jewish holidays, or have full celebrations of them (practice); and most would like to see the church recognize its Jewish roots. As will become apparent below, the Hebrew Roots movement often goes beyond an appreciation of Christianity's Jewishness to more controversial areas.

It is difficult to trace a history of the Hebrew Roots movement, which seems to have mushroomed since the advent of the Internet. Undoubtedly, several influences have been at work in its growth. One is the increasing appreciation for the Jewishness of Christianity, both among Jewish and Christian scholars. This interest has been a hallmark of some Jewish scholarship since the Enlightenment, but has been given added impetus by the post-Holocaust move away from evangelism toward dialogue (hence, the desire to find commonality in the Jewishness of Jesus), the rise of the State of Israel (encouraging archaeological explorations, including those related to Christianity), and the discovery of the Dead Sea Scrolls (further highlighting the Jewish background of the New Testament).

To that mix, add the increasing appreciation for Jesus' Jewishness among evangelical Christians. Some Jewish believers of past generations complained about anti-Semitism in the churches and a refusal to allow Jewish believers the freedom to express their faith in a Jewish way. In today's evangelical churches, the response to hearing about Jews who come to faith is likely to be positive, and churches often explore the Jewish background of their faith by, for instance, holding an annual Passover Seder. Many Christians, too, have become ardent supporters of the modern State of Israel. With this background, it is not hard to see how the Hebrew Roots movement has grown.[3]

Geographically, many Hebrew Roots organizations are based in the Midwest and South (Ohio, Oklahoma, Texas, Arkansas, etc.), in areas where there are relatively few Jews.

Despite the fact that one website cites interest in Jewish evangelism as a factor behind the rise of the Hebrew Roots movement, that interest is not plainly seen in most of the ministries involved. Rather, their emphasis is on learning and doing Jewish things. Some, such as John Garr's Restoration Foundation, explicitly promote Jewish-Christian dialogue, with no mention of evangelism.

RESPONDING TO HEBREW ROOTS GROUPS
Many Christians would be enriched to rediscover the Jewishness of Jesus. For this reason, it is regrettable that words of caution need to be said in regard to the Hebrew Roots movement. These warnings fit into two categories: first, regarding the indiscriminate networking and linking among the organizations; second, regarding the actual teachings of some of the organizations.

Networking and Linking
The average evangelical Christian who approaches a website such as www.hebroots.org may think that all the organizations and resources listed are evangelical in orientation, especially if his or her first contact with the movement came via an evangelical Hebrew Roots ministry. But the networking among Hebrew Roots groups is often without regard for orthodoxy. For example, the Restoration Foundation links to The Friends of Israel Gospel Ministry (an evangelical mission to Jews), Netivyah (an evangelical teaching ministry in Israel),

a host of Hebrew Roots organizations (of varying perspectives) and news reports produced by Jerusalem Bible College (an evangelical Bible college in Israel). Another listing of "Hebrew/Jewish Roots Christian Ministries" includes groups as disparate as First Fruits of Zion (a Torah-observant group), Marvin Wilson (an evangelical Christian college professor), Bridges for Peace (a non-evangelistic "love Israel" organization), a homeschooling site, and the International Fellowship of Christians and Jews and its ministry On Wings of Eagles (whose director, Rabbi Yechiel Eckstein, is an adamant opponent of Jewish evangelism and Messianic Jews). What do all these have in common? They all merely have something to do with Jews and Jesus.

It's not that Christians should only be exposed to evangelical teachings. The concern is that indiscriminate networking may give the impression that all such organizations are evangelical teaching ministries, sound in doctrine and practice—when in fact the converse is sometimes the case.

Specific Teachings and Practices

It is difficult to characterize the Hebrew Roots movement as holding to any one set of doctrines. Some organizations offer statements of faith that are evangelical concerning the doctrines of Christ and of salvation, although they add points that most Christians would consider unbiblical concerning the need to keep the Law of Moses or the Jewish festivals. Several espouse the idiosyncratic (but influential) "Two-House Theory," which asserts that the Church is the lost tribe of Ephraim, the idea being that many or all Gentile Christians are descendants of the so-called "Ten Lost Tribes" (see Chapter 2.4). In fact, there is a good amount of affiliation and overlap between many Hebrew Roots and Two-House organizations. For instance, Edward Chumney, who has written in support of the Two-

House theory, is news director for "Restore!" a magazine published by the Restoration Foundation. Similarly, the Hebrew Roots of Christianity Global Network website links to materials on the Two-House theory.

One teaching institution that is part of the Hebrew Roots movement is the American Institute of Middle Eastern Studies (formerly called the Arkansas Institute of Holy Land Studies), headed by Ron Moseley. Faculty members include Roy Blizzard, Marvin Wilson and Brad Young. Not all are evangelical. To be sure, there are many things one can learn from non-evangelicals or non-believers in an academic setting. What is disconcerting is not that the faculty come from a variety of theological viewpoints, but that in a ministry that is promulgated to evangelical Christians, and suggests that it is Christian in basis, there is no mention of its faculty's theological positions. Marvin Wilson is an evangelical scholar at Gordon College and Brad Young teaches at Oral Roberts University. On the other hand, Roy Blizzard's view of the Trinity is not evangelical: "And now we have the Father, Son, and Holy Spirit. That idea is a very late development in Christian theology. As a matter of fact, it's not developed to any degree until the fourth century. When it is put forth by the church, they argue over it for about 40 years before it is finally adopted. The man who proposed it initially was banished eight times for heresy. It's not Hebrew."[4] But who would know that from the website?

Having said this, it's time to delve further into the three areas related to the Hebrew Roots movement mentioned above: study, practice and "restoration."

Study
The study of the Jewishness of the Christian faith is to be encouraged. Unfortunately, the way in which the Jewishness of Christianity is presented in much of the Hebrew Roots

movement does not always accurately reflect what most scholars believe. For instance, one organization within this network is HaKesher, the ministry of Robert Lindsay. Lindsay is one of the scholars who helped promulgate the "original Hebrew gospels" view, which states that the gospels as we have them in Greek are only translations of documents originally written in Hebrew.

In *Mishkan* 17-18 (1992/1993), respected Jewish Christian apologist Michael L. Brown responded to this view of the New Testament with a "discommendation" of the book *Understanding the Difficult Words of Jesus* by Blizzard and Bivin, and with a stern word of warning concerning the overall approach of the Jerusalem School of Synoptic Research to biblical reliability. The "original Hebrew" view of the gospels is not accepted by most scholars, not because of anti-Jewish bias, but because in their view the evidence does not support it. Furthermore, these scholars are quick to point out that if the "original Hebrew" hypothesis is believed, then the inerrancy of Scripture must be questioned.

On the same topic of study and learning, the Hebrew Roots movement appears to be rather ingrown. While the work of those involved is given continual prominence, in some of the ministries it is rarely suggested that one can learn much about the Jewishness of Christianity from mainstream Christian sources. The fact is that any good commentary will give Jewish backgrounds and explanations; whole series of books have been written on the Jewish (and Greek/Roman) backgrounds to the New Testament. Gentile scholars such as W. D. Davies and Jewish ones such as David Daube have written extensively on the Jewishness of Jesus. Periodicals like *Mishkan: A Theological Forum on Jewish Evangelism* have been produced for some twenty years, focusing on the Jewishness of Jesus. But one hears hardly a word about any of this from many in the Hebrew Roots movement. It is almost as if they alone have rediscovered the Jewishness of the gospel. Now, some ministries within the movement do recommend a more broad-based program of study. But shouldn't a movement intending to encourage understanding of the Jewishness of the gospel, especially one this highly networked, draw on all the many resources available?

Practice

The Hebrew Roots movement presents itself partly as an educational movement. Indeed, some organizations, such as Brad Young's Gospel Research Foundation, seem to be more strictly educational in nature; it has sponsored conferences, one of which was held at Oral Roberts University, Our Lady of Sorrow Convent and Temple Israel in Tulsa, and included the participation of local rabbis and cantors.

Likewise, education is the focus of the mission statement of HaY'Did: "To train, educate and equip both the Jew and the non-Jew for study of the rich Biblical/Hebrew Heritage of our faith." But it is evident that HaY'Did is concerned with more than study. Their website continues: "HaY'Did (*The Friend* in Hebrew) is a neutral clearing house which reviews and stocks educational materials dealing in the subject matter of the Jewish roots of the Christian faith. In addition to providing our subscribers with these educational materials at the lowest possible price, HaY'Did sponsors various teaching seminars on the relationship of Biblical festivals and their relationship to Christian practice, and other teaching seminars all over the world."

Part of their educational thrust includes encouragement to certain practices. The Jewish holidays should be observed; the most "Biblically correct" period for worship is Friday night to Saturday night; Christmas, Easter and Halloween need to be "abandoned"—but HaY'Did is tolerant towards those who disagree.[5]

On the part of some Hebrew Roots organizations, there is a call to a "Torah-observant" or at least a "festival-observant" lifestyle as essential in the life of a Christian, as it brings the Christian into greater conformity with Jesus. As an example, reading the website of Awareness Ministry raises plenty of questions: "Feast day celebrations must not be limited to serving as mediums for worship and praise. We have discovered and aggressively teach that within these Biblical Memorial days such as Passover, Pentecost and Tabernacles is expressed every spiritual lesson that is needed to bring the Church to the knowledge of the full counsel of God."[6] Michael Rood of the program "A Rood Awakening" espouses a similar view. They are leaving out the fact that knowing Jesus is really the way to a relationship with God.

"Restoration"
Some in the Hebrew Roots movement encourage a "return" or a "restoration" of so-called "original" first-century Jewish practices. This necessitates a rejection of much else as non-Jewish and therefore wrong. This is wrongheaded both practically and theologically because:

• It is *not necessary* to observe Old Testament festivals as a means to a higher spirituality. The New Testament is clear that the Old Testament ceremonial laws, including the festivals, were pointers to the coming Messiah and were not intended for all time. Certainly the moral undergirdings of the Law of Moses are still in force, but the Hebrew Roots organizations seem more concerned with Sabbaths and festivals than with any other aspects of the Law.
• Neither is it *possible* in many cases to return to first-century practices. There is no longer a Temple or priesthood; the Church

is not the theocratic nation of Israel; and the culture has changed from that of a first-century agricultural world to a postmodern 21st-century world of technology and globalism.

• Nor is it *advisable* to try and observe Old Testament or first-century practices to the exclusion of other cultural forms. The Hebrew Roots movement shows little understanding that the gospel can function among various cultures. In essence, they function as a kind of Jewish variation on those Christian denominations that have sought to get back to "original New Testament Christianity." They confuse gospel content with culture. Thus, Garr's magazine says, ". . . practices which are not grounded in the Hebraic heritage of the faith of Jesus are not authentically Christian. They represent accretions which have been added from cultures which were founded on philosophies that are incompatible and inimical to the holistic worldview and mindset of the Biblical Hebrews."[7] But why can't "non-Hebraic" practices be acceptable, as long as they are not contrary to Scripture? The gospel can function across a multitude of cultures.

When it comes to excluding Christmas or Easter as pagan, we need to see that symbols can be sanctified. There were temples, priests and sacrifices before ancient Israel ever appeared on the scene, but God sanctified those pagan customs in the Old Testament. Even Christmas may have been originally instituted to *displace* the pagan holiday by offering a Christian alternative at the same time—not because Christianity became pagan.

One of the Hebrew Roots organizations, Awareness Ministry, says, "We declare the necessity of returning to the Old Testament for the purposes of establishing New Testament truth concerning moral and ethical standards as well as Biblical church orders. [We have seen] a dramatic increase of interest in such things as the use of banners in worship, dancing, the Christ centered celebration of Biblical feast days, observing the 'Hours of prayer', drawing lessons from Biblical Jewish customs and values that are impacting personal and family... many of these things are not essential to personal salvation, but they are *essential to growth* as we conform to the image of Christ, anticipating and preparing for Messiah's return [emphasis added]." [8]

Not only is Old Testament ceremonial worship not "essential to growth" under the New Covenant, but it is indeed questionable whether banners and dancing were typical of Old Testament worship. Sacrifices, priestly ministrations and singing were far more typical. The result of the above statement is that extra-biblical practices that have more in common with modern charismatic worship than Old Testament worship are called "essential to growth"—the very sort of thing the Hebrew Roots movement condemns.

In summary, while some organizations that place themselves within the Hebrew Roots movement may be sound biblically, many display some key problems. Beyond the most obvious one of advocating mandatory law-keeping (which usually seems to mean festival-keeping), there are other problems as displayed by some of the Hebrew Roots organizations:

• The movement's network includes both those who appear sound in Christology, soteriology and their view of Scripture, and those whose doctrine has been called into question in one or more of these areas, giving the impression that these are all evangelical Christian teaching ministries.
• The movement similarly shows little awareness that plenty of material has already been written on the Jewishness of the New Testament.

• Rather than being content with explicating the Jewish background as a way to understand the Biblical text, many wish to make first-century observances mandatory for the body of believers. The irony is that Christians simply cannot keep the law as it was kept in the first century, nor can they observe the festivals either as they were done in A.D. 30 or as they were done in 1000 B.C. The result is something quite removed from "original first-century" Jewish practices.

• The movement rejects anything that is allegedly "Greco-Roman," forgetting that the first-century church also grew up in such a context—with no call by the apostles for the Greco-Roman believers to "recover" their Jewish roots.

• The movement shows little understanding that the gospel can function among various cultures.

• The movement shows little interest in evangelism of Jewish people. Geographically, many of these organizations are removed from any substantial Jewish community.

Some in the Hebrew Roots movement are aware of problems with certain ministries and tendencies, and have spoken for a balanced view. Unfortunately, even among those who are not particularly engaged in controversial areas, some seem to lend tacit approval to those who are, by extensive networking via website links, conferences, and so on.

CONCLUSION

It is unwise to assume that all Hebrew Roots ministries are evangelical in doctrine. If you are interested in taking advantage of opportunities and resources to learn more about the Jewishness of the gospel from Jewish missions, Messianic congregations and good books, or from a Hebrew Roots organization, approach them with discernment. Jews for Jesus may be able to help evaluate particular resources.

Avoid any ministry where it seems that . . .
- people adulate (rather than appreciate) Jewishness or the teaching of rabbis
- people forsake Jesus for Jewishness
- Christians must observe Old Testament holidays and/or avoid celebrating Christmas and Easter, either because "God commanded it" or because it is seen as a superior path to lead one closer to God
- it is implied that by following certain worship practices one is returning to the worship of the early Church

Where many Hebrew Roots groups go astray is in their insistence that certain practices and preferences be made mandatory for all believers. As always, the Bible should be our first and foremost resource for determining which things are commanded and which are not.

FURTHER READING

Katz, Stephen., "The Jewish Roots Movement: Flowers and Thorns." *Havurah*, March/April, 2001. Published by Jews for Jesus http://www.jewsforjesus.org/publications/havurah/4_1/jewish roots

Daube, David., *The New Testament and Rabbinic Judaism*. Hendrickson, 1994. A classic by the late Jewish law professor at the University of California, Berkeley.

Mishkan: A Forum on the Gospel and the Jewish People 17-18, 1992-93. Issue devoted to "The Jerusalem School of Synoptic Studies." Articles pro and con, so you get both sides of the picture. Available by ordering online at: www.caspari.com/mishkan/contents/contents16.html#17-18.

Davies, W. D., *Paul and Rabbinic Judaism: Some Rabbinic Elements in Pauline Theology*. Philadelphia: Fortress

Press; or Sigler Press, 1980. A classic, though the average layperson will probably find it heavy reading.

ONLINE RESOURCES

http://www.isitso.org/guide/hebroot.html
A well-written response to the Hebrew Roots movement from a non-Jew and a former member of the Worldwide Church of God. It is quite extensive, and a good supplement to the material in this section. One of the most valuable sections is an exploration of the attraction that the Hebrew Roots movement holds for Christians from Sabbatarian and non-Sabbatarian backgrounds, followed by a word of personal testimony from the author, who is a Sabbatarian Christian in the Church of God.

http://www.empirenet.com/~messiah7/spl_rood.htm
A page about Michael Rood, prepared in 2003 by John Juedes, pastor of Messiah Lutheran Church of Palmdale, California.

Notes

1. http://graceandknowledge.faithweb.com/roots.html
2. The site in the previous footnote has as its banner sentence at the top of its web page, "A growing number of Christians are coming to an appreciation of the Jewish roots of Christianity and a love for the Sabbath and biblical festivals."
3. The site referred to above gives three reasons for this interest: the Holocaust, which has made Christians aware of anti-Semitism and the need to understand their Jewish neighbors; the increasing interest by Bible scholars in placing Jesus within the Jewish framework of His time; and the desire on the part of Christians to evangelize Jewish people. The Internet has helped this along, as most organizations in the movement now have a presence on the web and consequently the potential for a high profile and easy promulgation of their views.

4. Hanegraff, Hendrik H., "What's Wrong With The Faith Movement—Part One: E. W. Kenyon and the Twelve Apostles of Another Gospel." *Christian Research Journal* (Winter 1993), online at: http://www.iclnet.org/pub/resources/text/cri/cri-jrnl/web/crj0118a.html. See footnote 66.
5. See their "Statement of Tolerance," http://www.haydid.org/toleranc.htm
6. http://home.hiwaay.net/~aware/atglance.htm
7. http://www.restoremagazine.org/volume_1/122.htm
8. http://www.awarenessministry.org

Chapter Four
The "Two-House" Organizations

INTRODUCTION

One non-adherent describes the movement known as "Two-House" or "Messianic Israel," as centering on the idea that "the membership of the Church is largely made up of people who are descended physically from the lost tribes of Israel."[1] A more extended description is given by Angus and Batya Wootten, two of the more prominent proponents of the movement: "Messianic Israel deems the Jewish people to be the identifiable representatives and offspring of Judah and 'the children of Israel, his companions,' and that non-Jewish followers of the Messiah from all nations have been, up to now, the unidentifiable representatives and offspring of Ephraim and 'all the house of Israel, his companions.'"[2] In other words, non-Jewish believers are of one "house" of Israel, and Jewish believers are of the other "house"—hence, "Two-House" theology.

Put more bluntly, this movement maintains that Gentile Christians are beginning to realize their true identity as physical descendants of Israel.

The goal of the movement is stated as follows: "Messianic Israel is a people whose heart's desire is to fully reunite the olive tree of Israel—both branches— Ephraim and Judah—into one, redeemed, nation of Israel—through Messiah Yeshua. They seek to arouse Ephraim from obscurity, and by example, to awaken Judah to the Messiah—and thus to hasten both Yeshua's return to Earth and the restoration of the Kingdom to Israel."[3]

The Woottens' description indicates that "Messianic Israel" sees its role as helping to fulfill biblical prophecy of the "restoration" of the entire nation of Israel through non-Jewish believers recognizing their true descent, and thus being an example to the Jewish people.

A BIT OF BACKGROUND

Angus and Batya Wootten are generally recognized as the "founders" of "Messianic Israel."[4] Non-Jewish themselves, the Woottens became believers in Jesus in the 1970s and met up with many in the growing movement of Jews who were for Jesus. As they thought through the place of Jews and non-Jews in God's plan, they report that in their experience, Gentile Christians were treated like second-class citizens in the Messianic Jewish community. They write that Gentiles were "being rejected" by Messianic Judaism. They concluded that Scripture taught that there were two houses of Israel, Judah and Ephraim. In their books, they say that God is "restoring" the two houses, that Jewish believers are the house of Judah and non-Jewish or Gentile believers are the house of Ephraim.

Using Paul's statement in Romans 11:25, the Woottens' organization, Messianic Israel Ministries, writes that, "'blindness in part' has happened to all (both houses) of Israel, and as the blinders are lifted, non-Jewish followers in Yeshua will gain insight into their role as Ephraim, they will become defenders of Scriptural Torah and of Judah, and due to this character change, many Jewish people will accept Yeshua as Messiah. This process has already begun as indicated through the Messianic Jewish movement (Judah), the Christian Zionism movement (Ephraim), and the Messianic Israel movement (union of Judah and Ephraim)."[5] The Woottens publish a regular newsletter (*The House of David Herald*) and have authored several books vigorously advocating their viewpoint.

The 1980s saw the birth of Your Arms to Israel, headed by Moshe (or Marshall) Koniuchowsky based in Broward County, Florida. According to information at Koniuchowsky's website, his work began in New York City in 1984 as a Jewish evangelism agency called Messiah is God Ministries. An evangelism campaign was conducted in 1991 in South Florida under the name "Operation Joshua." Both he and his wife claim to be Jewish believers. Somewhere along the line they adopted the theology of "Messianic Israel," i.e., the "Two-House theory."

Koniuchowsky writes, "Messianic Nazarene Yisrael does in fact teach that Ephraim's seed has fulfilled the promise of physical multiplicity given to the patriarchs and views the re-gathering of the latter day 'gentiles,' as consisting mostly of lost Israelites."[6] And, "that Ephraim's recognition of their identity and restoration with brother Judah is the truth that will become the salvation of all Israel (Ezekial [sic] 37:16-28)."[7] It seems that this movement, which has a small but vocal following, teaches that rather than direct evangelism, the "coming out," so to speak, of Ephraim will lead to Israel's salvation.

IS IT HERESY?

Other names connected with the Two-House movement are David Hargis, Ed Chumney, and Monte Judah. One website contains a statement by Chumney and Judah regarding their theology and a response by Dan Juster, a Messianic Jewish author and pastor.[8] In their statement, Chumney and Judah speak of Two-House theology as part of the "Messianic/Hebrew roots movement." Juster disagrees with much that Chumney and Judah advocate, but concludes that, contrary to his earlier fear, they are not heretical.

Though the theological ideas expressed by the Woottens, Ed Chumney and the others may not be "heretical," they are distinctly idiosyncratic and ultimately unbiblical. Take for instance the umbrella organization, the Union of Nazarene Yisraelite Congregations. In addition to advocating Two-House theology, their website includes a statement of Torah-observance and sacred-name theology. They have this to say:

> Today hundreds of thousands of unsaved and unbelieving traditional Jews and wayward Ephraimites continue to reside in all of Miami Beach from the North Miami Beach sight [sic] of our new facility down to South Beach, unable to relocate, with little or no Gospel witness representing the Messianic Nazarene Yisraelite movement. While there are still plenty of churches ready, willing and able to convert Jews, and reinforce Ephraim in pagan error, there are no known vibrant English speaking Messianic synagogues in Miami Beach. A true Messianic synagogue ordained by Yahweh must introduce Yahshua's blood atonement as the only means of eternal life, and the Torah as the only true basis and instruction manual for holy living by the redeemed community of Yahweh. Our restoration calling is commissioned to reintroduce the Father Yahweh's true eternal Name, as well as that of the Son of Yahweh.[9]

The "Two-House" movement can be criticized on several grounds:

1. Understanding of Bible Passages and Theology

Under the auspices of the International Messianic Jewish Alliance, Kay Silberling, Daniel Juster and David Sedaca have written a concise but thorough refutation of the teaching of the Two-House movement.[10] In their paper they point out several fallacies of interpretation. The Two-House movement is wrong in asserting: (1) that the word *goy* always means Gentile and that therefore Genesis 48:19 refers to Ephraim becoming Gentiles; (2) that the number of descendants of Abraham being as "the sand of the sea" precludes its fulfillment by the Jewish people alone; (3) that the northern Israelites taken into captivity by Assyria are never called Jews.

In addition, the authors point out that the Woottens and Moshe Koniuchowsky present ambiguous evidence for all Christians in history being physical descendants of Israel. They also note that the basis for this claim is often entirely subjective on the part of the Gentile believer: Wootten says regarding how one can know if he or she is a physical descendant of Ephraim, "you knew in your 'knower.'"

Theologically, the "Two-House" proponents and organizations run the gamut from those that are theologically orthodox, except in their idiosyncratic doctrine of the Church, to those that are aberrant. Some that are evangelical regarding Christ hold to these views out of a misplaced desire to in some way have a greater connection with the Jewish people. Some have statements of faith that appear evangelical as to the person of Christ, though written in a kind of pseudo-Jewish nomenclature; other statements of faith are written in such a way that one cannot quite tell what they believe about the Trinity, the deity of Jesus and salvation.[11] At worst, some espouse non-evangelical theology and practices.

The Woottens believe in the deity of Jesus, and in salvation by faith in Him. One might almost overlook their idiosyncratic view of the relationship of Jews and non-Jews in the body of Christ, were they merely personal views. But now there is a whole "Two-House" network. Some organizations that are part of the movement promote Torah-observance or promulgate teachings on the alleged paganism of Christianity.

2. The Driving Question
The Two-House proponents are not alone in their desire to be part of the nation of Israel. Sadly, some non-Jews earnestly

wish that they were Jewish. For some of the motivations in this area, see: http://www.isitso.org/guide/hebroot.html, section "The Allure." [12]

The desire of the Woottens to see all believers in Jesus treated equally is an admirable one. But it would seem that the driving question from which the movement originated—how Gentiles can find acceptance among Jewish believers—has controlled their scriptural understanding, rather than scriptural understanding controlling their response to the perceived lack of acceptance.

3. Aberrant Ideas

The Your Arms to Israel site advertises a "Sefer Yahshar," [13] purporting to be the Book of Jasher mentioned occasionally in Scripture in such places as Joshua 10:13. Unfortunately, Koniuchowsky's claim that the book was first translated into English in 1840 is totally spurious. All existing claims to be the "Book of Jasher" are recent or spurious compositions. Yet Koniuchowsky offers this book and "is more convinced than ever, that this book or scroll in particular must and should be reinstated in the scriptures." Never mind that it never *was* in the Scriptures. He will include it in his Bible, known as the "Restoration Scriptures."

And what is the Restoration Scriptures? "We then proceeded to correct obvious anti-Yahshua redactions, shamefully tampered with by the Masoretic editors. Moreover, we reinserted the true Name back into this foundational source." [14]

Unlike many crafty translators and their translations that do not admit to an underlying agenda in their publications, *The Restoration Scriptures True Name Edition Study Bible* has an overriding and clear agenda in publishing this project. We admit that! ...We desire that *The Restoration Scriptures True Name Edition Study Bible* will lead to a repentance and return to YHWH for many, so as to experience life in His sight as a practicing Torah-keeping born-again Yisraelite.[15]

No reputable Bible scholar agrees that there is a legitimate Sefer Yahshar, nor that the biblical canon should be corrected, nor that the Masoretes were in grave error. This may not be theological heresy, but it does not speak well of the Hebrew Roots/Messianic Israel movement that it freely links to such resources as legitimate sources of knowledge and information.

4. Ingrown Nature

Just as problematic as the teaching about Ephraim and Judah is the fact that the movement has become ingrown, with its own conferences, directories,[16] music teams, speakers, etc., which mirror mainstream Messianic Jewish ministries. In essence, the movement has placed itself against, rather than alongside, other believers.

CONCLUSION

It's important to understand that the teaching that the visible Church is largely descended from the northern tribes cannot be substantiated historically or biblically. It's safe to say that Two-House movement adherents place far too much importance on trying to claim a Jewish identity. All believers in Jesus should be treated equally as full citizens within the body of Christ. Neither being Jewish nor descended from the tribes of Israel counts any more than being non-Jewish in God's sight.

FURTHER READING

Websites of Two-House Organizations:

House of David *aka* Messianic Israel Ministries (Angus and Batya Wootten)
http://www.mim.net/

Your Arms to Israel
http://yourarmstoisrael.org/

Responses:
Juster, Daniel C., "Is the Church Ephraim?" Previously available at http://www.umjc.org, but now only on the Wayback Machine:
http://web.archive.org/web/20000308231905/http://umjc.org/index.html
From there, click on "Documents" in the lower frame, then scroll for the link to the paper. *Counter-response:* We can also no longer locate online "Resolving Issues," by Angus Wootten.

"The Ephraimite Error: A Short Summary" by Kay Silberling, advised by Daniel Juster and David Sedaca. A concise and thorough refutation through an examination of the relevant biblical passages.
http://66.70.185.249/biblicaljudaism/EphraimiteErrorSummary.html

"The Ephramite Error," same authors, a longer version (PDF download)
http://66.70.185.249/biblicaljudaism/EphraimiteError.pdf
The most extensive response I have seen.

Counter-responses:
Koniuchowsky, Moshe Joseph, "The Truth About All Israel: A Refutation of the M.J.A.A. Position Paper on the Two Houses of Israel" (PDF):
http://yourarmstoisrael.org/The_Truth/THE_TRUTH_ABOUT_ALL_ISRAEL_by_Rabbi_Moshe_Koniuchowsky.pdf

The Messianic Israel Movement is mentioned with a brief critique in "Something Old, Something New: The Messianic Congregational Movement" by Bruce Lieske, Christian Research Journal 22:1 (June-August 1999). Available through the Christian Research Institute:
http://www.equip.org/free/DJ440.htm

Notes

1. Juster, Daniel C., "Is the Church Ephraim?" at:
http://web.archive.org/web/20000308231905/http://umjc.org/inde
x.html
2. http://www.mim.net/Beliefs.shtml
3. Ibid.
4. See http://www.mim.net/Who.shtml#Our%20History.
5. *We Declare These Truths to Be Self-Evident* (St. Cloud, FL:
Messianic Israel Alliance, 2002), at:
http://www.mim.net/Books/DeclaredTruths/WeDeclareScreen.pdf
6. http://yourarmstoisrael.org/Articles_new/restoration/
?page=12&type=10
7. http://yourarmstoisrael.org/misc/official_statements/
?page=doctrinal_statement&type=2
8. http://www.hebroots.org/twohousemeeting.htm
9. http://yourarmstoisrael.org/misc/?page=by/index
10. http://66.70.185.249/biblicaljudaism/EphraimiteErrorSummary.html
11. For example, see the Messianic Church of God in Royal Oak, MI, at:
http://www.messianics.us/statementoffaithMCOGfolder/StatementF
aith.htm, linked to from www.mim.net.
12. This site is compiled by someone affiliated with a Sabbatarian
Church of God denomination, but has much of value.
13. http://store.yourarmstoisrael.org/Qstore/
Qstore.cgi?CMD=011&PROD=1082997719
14. http://www.restorationscriptures.org/page.php?page=home
15. Ibid.
16. For example, http://www.mim.net/MIA/Directory/index.html

Chapter Five
The Hashivenu Group

INTRODUCTION

Within the structure of the Union of Messianic Jewish Congregations (see chapter 1.4), an organization called "Hashivenu," Hebrew for "bring us back" (to God), was formed in 1997. Its founders provide some of the theological direction for the movement. Hashivenu is a sort of think tank comprised of well-educated and theologically creative people, who have been calling for what they term a "mature Messianic Judaism." The theological and practical ideas emanating from Hashivenu have led to a good degree of ferment within the UMJC, so much so that some congregations have even pulled out.

What does Hashivenu mean by a "mature Messianic Judaism"? In their own words:

> We seek an authentic expression of Jewish life maintaining substantial continuity with Jewish tradition. However, Messianic Judaism is energized by the belief that Yeshua of Nazareth is the promised Messiah, the fullness of Torah. Mature Messianic Judaism is not simply Judaism plus Yeshua, but is instead an integrated following of Yeshua through traditional Jewish forms and the modern day practice of Judaism in and through Yeshua. Messianic Judaism will only attain maturity when it has established communal institutions which are capable of expressing its ideals and transmitting them effectively to ourselves, to our children, and to a skeptical world.[1]

In this chapter we'll unpack some of these ideas and see why Hashivenu is causing such ferment.

A BIT OF BACKGROUND

Hashivenu was formed by Stuart Dauermann, rabbi of
Messianic congregation Ahavat Zion in Beverly Hills, California.
The Hashivenu group includes Dauermann as President, G.
Robert Chenoweth, Susan C. Chenoweth, Mark S. Kinzer,
Richard C. Nichol, Ellen B. Quarry, Paul L. Saal and Michael H.
Schiffman. Kinzer heads the Messianic Jewish Theological
Institute (see Chapter 1.5 on educational institutions) and also leads
congregation Zera Avraham in Ann Arbor, Michigan. Kinzer
serves with the theology committee of the UMJC and has, for
all practical purposes, become the leading theologian within
Hashivenu. Nichol is rabbi of Congregation Ruach Israel in
Needham, Massachusetts, while Saal heads Congregation
Shuvah Yisrael in Simsbury, Connecticut. Both Nichol and Saal
are part of the New England Messianic Jewish Council, whose
address is that of Congregation Simchat Yisrael, headed by
Tony Eaton, who also serves as treasurer for the UMJC. These
congregational leaders are among the most articulate and
erudite in the Messianic movement.

There is no one explicit platform or statement of theology
that comes from Hashivenu, but there are some overarching
ideas, chief of which has to do with identification with the
Jewish community.

A QUESTION OF BELONGING

There have always been two somewhat competing positions
in the Messianic movement concerning how Jewish
believers in Jesus are to relate to the Jewish community at
large. Some have been eager for the Jewish community to
recognize the legitimacy of Jewish belief in Jesus and to
grant validity to Jewish believers in Jesus. Much of the
impetus for developing the Messianic congregational
movement has been to "show" the Jewish community that

we are "real" Jews; hence the trend to naming assemblies "synagogues," calling the leaders "rabbis," etc.

There is an important caveat here: not every expression of Jewishness on the part of Jewish believers or the Messianic community is intended to gain acceptance from the larger Jewish community. Jewish expression can be a personal statement or a matter of one's own convictions or community identification, regardless of how others respond. Some believe that maintaining a visible expression of Jewishness reflects the ongoing distinctiveness of the Jewish people in God's plan.

But when such expressions *are* intended to gain acceptance, how effective are they? At least one non-Messianic Jewish scholar, Dan Cohn-Sherbok, who has been a featured speaker at UMJC conferences, seems prepared to accept Messianic Judaism as a variety of Judaism in today's pluralistic world.[2] Yet it is unclear to what extent he would allow a theology that includes the Incarnation and the tri-unity of God to go under the rubric of Judaism. Another Jewish writer, Dennis Prager, has gone on record as affirming Messianic Jews as Jews, provided that they deny those doctrines.[3] Jewish author David Klinghoffer recently penned an article for the *Forward* reluctantly accepting the Jewishness of Jewish believers in Jesus on the grounds that it is inconsistent to accept secular Jews and not Messianic Jews.[4] Messianic Judaism is still far from being accepted in the mainstream Jewish world.

The other position taken by the Messianic movement has been described by detractors as "adversarial" and by others as being in the position of "underdog" or "outsider." These Messianic Jews do not hope for acceptance from the larger Jewish community, but in fact expect to *not* be accepted, just as Jesus and the apostles were largely rejected, and for that matter so were Moses and the prophets. In short, as Jesus was rejected (as prophesied in Isaiah 53), so His followers can expect the same. Some Jewish believers remember that when they came to faith, they attempted to continue attending their family synagogue in addition to Christian fellowships, in an attempt to maintain ties with their Jewish community. But once it was known that they were believers in Jesus, they were sometimes asked outright to leave.

These are broadly painted portraits of both views. And, as stated above, not every expression of Jewishness is a bid for acceptance. Some Jewish believers feel that they will always be a part of the Jewish community—accepted or not—and seek to live out a Jewish expression of their faith. As far as Hashivenu is concerned, they have strongly come down on the side of acceptance and seek to identify with the Jewish community in a way that goes beyond what most Jewish believers would considered necessary. For example, consider this statement on Messianic Jewish conversion by Tony Eaton, that both broaches the desire for acceptance and hints at the broader Hashivenu agenda of identifying almost entirely with the Jewish community:

> Can we ever expect acceptance from the wider Jewish community if we insist on bypassing the way that people have for centuries been received into the community? . . . The challenge for our movement as we enter the new millennium is to develop and institute a conversion process for our non-Jewish members. Without this process, we will find it difficult—perhaps impossible—to *justify ourselves* as a Judaism to the wider Jewish community, the wider world, and perhaps in time, even to ourselves.[5] [emphasis added]

IMPLICATIONS FOR THEOLOGY AND PRACTICE

Kinzer, Dauermann, and Nichol all believe that the primary community to which a Jewish believer in Jesus must be committed is the Jewish people. By this they mean being a Jewish believer in Jesus means "locating" oneself, not primarily within the Church composed of both Jews and Gentiles, but within the Jewish community—even though a Jewish believer shares faith in Jesus with non-Jewish believers. Since the Jews are a people, "to be part of a people means embracing its history and tradition as one's own." [6] In Kinzer's words, Judaism is to be seen as "genus," and Messianic as "species."

It is from this basic premise that Hashivenu's core values are derived as follows:

1. Messianic Judaism is a Judaism, and not a cosmetically altered "Jewish-style" version of what is extant in the wider Christian community.
2. God's particular relationship with Israel is expressed in the Torah, God's unique covenant with the Jewish people.
3. Yeshua is the fullness of Torah.
4. The Jewish people are "us" not "them."
5. The richness of the Rabbinic tradition is a valuable part of our heritage as Jewish people.
6. Because all people are created in the image of God, how we treat them is a reflection of our respect and love for Him; therefore, true piety cannot exist apart from human decency.
7. Maturation requires a humble openness to new ideas within the context of firmly held convictions. [7]

A fuller explanation of these values is available on the Hashivenu website. It is not so much with these values that one might be inclined to take exception. However, other writings and statements from Hashivenu leaders have created cause for concern.

Implications for Ecclesiology (the Doctrine of the Church)

Mark Kinzer has been the one to set the theological agenda for Hashivenu and for the UMJC. In the past several years, Kinzer has developed a new ecclesiology that is quite different from traditional thinking.

Kinzer maintains that God made a covenant with the Jewish people, which is ongoing and continuous. Because that covenant still exists, all of its obligations and responsibilities exist as well. Therefore, God calls Jewish believers in Jesus to make the Jewish people their main community of commitment. And He calls all Jews to the obligations of observing the 613 commandments of the Torah.

According to Kinzer, Galatians 2:7-10 indicates that there was not only a separate mission for Jews and Gentiles, but also "two distinct sets of communities resulting from those missions, and two distinct leadership structures overseeing those missions and communities."[8] Kinzer calls this a "binitarian ecclesiology."[9] He concludes that the primary locus of a Jewish believer's community commitment is to the Jewish community; and that the primary locus of a Gentile believer's community commitment is to the Church. While both Jewish and Gentile believers in Jesus form aspects of the one people of God, they each have their own spheres of existence. They may come together in cooperation and make joint efforts, but there is *not* one unified Jewish-Gentile community of all believers. As Dauermann asserts on his web log, "Togetherness does not mean sameness."[10]

Rich Nichol underscores this emphasis when he writes that, "the irreducible dyad of human existence is Israel and the nations."[11] Commenting on this point, Dauermann states:

> The irreducible dyad that Rich Nichol mentions is intensely biblical. Why else, for example, would G-d have appointed and Scripture have highlighted two apostolates—one to the circumcision and the other to the uncircumcision (Galatians 2:9)? . . . in the purposes of God, it is only these two spheres which are mentioned, and they remain distinct.[12]

However, we would counter, the irreducible dyad of Scripture ultimately, and certainly clearly set forth in the New Testament, is the redeemed and the unredeemed.[13]

At least one person has concluded that the natural outworking of the Hashivenu point of view means there should be two separate religious systems, one for Jewish believers and one for non-Jews![14] While Kinzer and others have distanced themselves from any such statement, it's little wonder that this "binitarian" ecclesiology has led some in that direction and led others to reconsider the traditional (and we would argue biblical) doctrine of salvation.

Implications for Soteriology (the Doctrine of Salvation)

There are some in the Hashivenu ranks who have been less than forthcoming about the need of Jesus for salvation. While it may not have been stated explicitly, there is a concern that some within Hashivenu are prepared to allow for a *normative* salvation apart from conscious faith in Christ. Following are some questionable statements, the first from Mark Kinzer:

> Because of the validity of the Abrahamic covenant, I believe it's still as possible for a Jew who doesn't know Yeshua to have a living relationship with God, just as a Christian. But of course

Yeshua is still the Messiah and any Jew who knows him is in a better place and has more access to God than before.[15]

Kinzer also says:

We don't come as Christians bringing good news to damned souls who need to be delivered from religious bondage.[16]

Similarly, and somewhat patronizingly, Tony Eaton says:

Modern evangelicalism fixes on one aspect of things, it says if you say these four spiritual laws—that's your get out of jail free card. It says if you accept a certain concept of truth, this makes the difference for your eternal destiny. Not that I don't believe there's a certain amount of truth to that. Let me explain it this way. Among devout Jewish people, there's a concept called devakut, God consciousness, maybe Paul would say 'walking in the Spirit.' This is the highest achievement of a devout Jew. I don't think true devakut can be achieved without Messiah Yeshua, but you can get close, I suppose. But you can't get where you could have gotten.[17]

Kinzer clarified his quote above about the Abrahamic covenant in a letter addressed to Rich Robinson and Ruth Rosen who co-wrote an article for the *Havurah* publication on trends in the Messianic movement. In this letter he wrote:

Robinson and Rosen conclude that my statement "is clearly an example of two-covenant theology, which says that Jews already have a covenant with God through Abraham and so do not need Jesus in order to find salvation." Admittedly, such a statement could be an example of dual covenant theology, but it is not "clearly so." And, in the mouth of a Messianic Jewish leader, one can safely assume that there is probably a different way of construing the remark. Dual covenant theology holds that Jews and Christians have two distinct and equally valid paths to God: Christians come to God through the covenant established by Yeshua's sacrifice, whereas the relationship of Jews to God is through God's covenant with Abraham and his descendants. I do not know of any Messianic Jews who believe in dual covenant theology, for this theological framework has no place for Messianic Judaism. Despite raising the specter of "dual covenant theology," it appears that Robinson and Rosen also recognize that I do not embrace such a position, for they proceed to summarize my view as the belief that "God has already accepted them [i.e., non-Messianic Jews] *in Y'shua*" (emphasis mine).

I do believe that the Abrahamic covenant offers Jewish people access to God in and through Yeshua. That does not mean that all Jews, by virtue of being Jews, have a right relationship with God. It does mean that God's favor still rests upon Israel, and He makes a way for humble and faithful members of His people to enter His presence *through the unrecognized mediation of Israel's Messiah* (emphasis added).[18]

The phrase "unrecognized mediation" suggests that Kinzer holds to a form of inclusivism, according to which people may be saved through the work of Christ even if they have not professed conscious faith in Him. Inclusivism exists in various shades, and is associated (in one form or another) with the names of theologians such as John Hick, Karl Rahner and John Sanders.

On the other hand, the invocation of the Abrahamic covenant does have affinities to two-covenant theology, which was developed by mainstream Jewish philosopher Franz Rosenzweig in the early 20th century and adopted by some liberal theologians and even by some evangelical theologians.

According to two-covenant theology, the covenant with Abraham is a saving covenant. Non-Jews do need Jesus; Jews do not.

Kinzer's and Eaton's statements are ambiguous. Unlike some others, they add that it's better if one does believe in Jesus. Kinzer is a creative thinker and only time will tell the particulars of his views. As of this writing, he has a book forthcoming which will hopefully clarify his thinking and that of others (*Postmissionary Messianic Judaism: Redefining Christian Engagement with the Jewish People*, Brazos Press, November 2005).

There have been many responses written to two-covenant theology as well as to forms of inclusivism. We include some of the most helpful in the "Further Reading" sections of earlier chapters.

Implications for Evangelism

Stuart Dauermann's weblog criticizes certain aspects of evangelical Christianity as well as some in the Messianic Jewish movement, especially in regard to evangelism. He says that conservative evangelicals read Scripture through preconceived theological grids;[19] that the church sees the Great Commission, rather than the final consummation, as the be-all and end-all of God's will;[20] and that the church sees outreach more in terms of salesmanship than relationship.[21] While the accuracy of Dauermann's depiction is debatable, Mark Kinzer concurs and has been quoted as stating point blank that Jewish missions are obsolete.[22]

Dauermann and Kinzer are not the first to critique the Church or traditional methods of evangelism. Many churches have engaged in serious thought on the question of how relationships and proclamation interrelate, particularly those churches reaching postmodern seekers. This question is really part of the larger question framed by Richard Niebuhr, as to how Christ relates to culture.[23] To what extent should believers be involved in the world, seeking to transform it, living in it incarnationally? And to what extent are we *not* in the world, strangers and pilgrims, striving to live godly lives in the face of a sinful culture? Many would say the answer lies in a balance of both aspects; it is not a matter of either/or, but of both/and.

In Hashivenu's hierarchy, identification with the Jewish community comes before evangelism. There are both theological and sociological reasons for this. As opposed to some Jewish believers who discount most of the past 2,000 years of Jewish thought and history as having little value, Hashivenu wants to embrace this history as much as possible.[24] It then follows that traditional missions are wrong because they (supposedly) act like "outsiders" coming to proclaim a message. Kinzer and Dauermann would have Jewish believers in Jesus be such an integral part of the Jewish community that the message comes from "within." Whether such a proposal is realistic remains to be seen. After all, Jewish believers in Jesus were "insiders" in the first century, until the Jewish community effectively isolated them.[25] No Jewish believer in Jesus was seeking to be an "outsider," but we were labeled as such by the rest of the Jewish community.

Then there is a sociological reason for downplaying evangelism. Those who look for the Jewish community's acceptance sometimes eschew the more public forms of gospel proclamation and the discomfort they can bring, in favor of developing relationships with the Jewish community. Whether these relationships lead to proclamation is up for debate. However, for the Jewish believer who is not seeking inclusion in the Jewish community, forthright evangelism—public, one-on-one, as well as long-term relational interactions—is seen as an essential part of one's calling as a believer in Jesus.

Implications for Lifestyle and Relating to Jewish Tradition

According to Hashivenu's website:

> It is our conviction that HaShem brings Messianic Jews to a richer knowledge of himself through a modern day rediscovery of the paths of our ancestors—Avodah (liturgical worship), Torah (study of sacred texts), and Gemilut Chasadim (deeds of lovingkindness).[26]

Similarly, the fifth core value of Hashivenu is, "The richness of the rabbinic tradition is a valuable part of our heritage as Jewish people." In an elaboration on this statement, the writer states:

> Although weaned and wooed to believe that our New Covenant faith was based on the Bible and nothing but the Bible, "the only rule of faith and practice," we gradually discovered that living out our faith inevitably had a cultural component. The Bible cannot be understood apart from a community context, which helps one understand its deepest meanings. In this way, obedience might become incarnate in daily life. We realized that having our views shaped entirely by a non-Jewish context was leaving a foreign imprint on our hearts, minds and lives.... We also began to appreciate how our own spiritual lives stood to benefit from the fruit of thousands of years of Jewish struggle for understanding.

Those committed to the Hashivenu vision place high importance on rabbinic thought. The problem, though, is that rabbinic thought and writing are double-edged. Much rings right and true, especially in the areas of ethics, liturgy and some biblical commentary. However, much is also a departure from biblical teaching. Rabbinic Judaism came into being after A.D. 70 as a top-to-bottom reworking   of Judaism without a Temple and a priesthood. As rabbinic

Judaism continued to develop, it was influenced by factors such as its need to stand in opposition to Jewish believers in Jesus and to the gospel message. It was further influenced by Greek philosophy in medieval times, and whole areas of modern Judaism, such as the Kabbalah, are closer to Gnosticism than to biblical faith. (Kabbalah is the system of Jewish mysticism.)

It is a matter of practical theology how a Jewish believer in Jesus should relate to this accumulation of traditions, commentaries, liturgies, ways of thinking and cultural forms in Judaism. (Note here that we are not talking about relating to biblical material, such as the Law of Moses, but to the traditions of the past 2,000 years.) The fact is that many Jewish believers in Jesus find much of value in Jewish tradition, culture, and ceremonies. Many embrace what they can and perhaps find some significance that has to do with their faith in Jesus. But Hashivenu advocates much more than that. They have made it a matter of foundational theology. Hashivenu's postulation of a "binitarian" theology of the Church does not leave it an open matter; in their view, Jewish believers *must* identify first and foremost with the Jewish community, and therefore *must* accord legitimacy to the past 2,000 years of the development of Judaism. "Legitimacy," however, is a slippery word. It remains to be seen whether Hashivenu wants to accord the entire history of Jewish tradition and teaching the status of "truth," or whether they only intend to find value in it as they can. For instance, it is unclear whether Hashivenu will move to the point of accepting the authority of rabbinic tradition for determining how we are to live our lives today.

CONCLUSION

In a way, the position being delineated by the Hashivenu group is comfortable. If there are two separate tracks for Jewish and Gentile believers in Jesus, then many of the

tough practical questions that have come up in the
Messianic movement are no longer problematic. If
evangelism is thought of as not urgent, and accepting Jesus
something that just gives an "extra" to one's existing
relationship with God, then conflict with the larger Jewish
community effectively disappears.

The leaders of Hashivenu are intelligent and they articulate their
views well. They model a level of thinking to which most
Messianic congregations would do well to aspire. Many in the
Messianic movement would also do well to heed Hashivenu's call
for leaders to be well educated, and for the title "rabbi" to stop
being used by those who are untrained. And many Jewish
believers might do well to think about the best ways for them to
identify with their Jewish people. And so far the Hashivenu group
has affirmed the cardinal doctrines of God's tri-unity and the deity
of Y'shua. (See chapter 2.1 for the Jewishness of these doctrines.)

But in relation to ecclesiology, evangelism and theology, it is
reasonable to be concerned that Hashivenu is distancing itself
from the rest of the body of Messiah (though in their view
they are doing exactly what God wants for Jewish believers).
This runs contrary to the unity between Jew and Gentile that
is available to us in Jesus and to which we are called.

Furthermore, Kinzer speaks of Messianic Judaism as one
form of Judaism, other forms of which are also "valid" (a
word that can mean many things). Whatever "valid" or
"legitimate" might mean, it seems to include the perspective
that modern Judaism is as "OK" as the gospel. Kinzer has yet
to spell out the full implications of this for his thinking, but
his book (forthcoming at this time of writing) may unpack
things further.[27] The biggest cause for concern here is that
in Hashivenu's quest for acceptance within the Jewish
community, they "will be tempted to give back recognition
and approval."[28]

FURTHER READING

Kinzer, Mark S., *The Nature of Messianic Judaism: Judaism as Genus, Messianic as Species.* West Harford, CT: Hashivenu Archives, no date. Summarizes Mark Kinzer and Hashivenu's viewpoint.

Kinzer, Mark S., *Postmissionary Messianic Judaism: Redefining Christian Engagement with the Jewish People.* Brazos Press. Forthcoming, November 2005.

Robinson, Rich and Ruth Rosen, "The Challenge of Our Messianic Movement, Part One," *Havurah* 6:2 (May 2003), at http://www.jewsforjesus.org/publications/havurah/6_2/challenge1

Robinson, Rich and Ruth Rosen, "The Challenge Of Our Messianic Movement, Part 2" *Havurah* 6:3 (August 2003), at http://www.jewsforjesus.org/publications/havurah/6_3/challenge2

Nash, Ronald, *Is Jesus the Only Savior?* Grand Rapids: Zondervan, 1994.

Richard, Ramesh, *The Population of Heaven: A Biblical Response to the Inclusivist Position on Who Will Be Saved.* Chicago: Moody Press, 1994.

Notes
1. http://www.hashivenu.org
2. Cohn-Sherbok, Dan, *Messianic Judaism.* Cassell, 2000.
3. Prager, Dennis, "A new approach to Jews for Jesus." *Moment,* Jun 30, 2000 (Vol 25, No 3), pp. 28-29.
4. Klinghoffer, David, "The Disputation: Are We Being Fair to Messianic Jews?" http://www.forward.com/articles/3280, dated June 10, 2005.

5. Eaton, Tony, "A Case for Jewish Leadership," in *Voices of Messianic Judaism*, Dan Cohn-Sherbok, Ed. Baltimore: Lederer/Messianic Jewish Publishers, 2001, p. 121.

6. Kinzer, Mark. S., *The Nature of Messianic Judaism: Judaism as Genus, Messianic as Species* (West Harford, CT: Hashivenu Archives, no date), p. 17.

7. http://www.hashivenu.org/core_values.htm

8. Kinzer, p. 38.

9. Ibid., p. 39.

10. "The Real Identity of the One New Man" at: http://rabbenu.blogspot.com

11. Rich Nichol, as quoted in "Defining Messianic Judaism," UMJC Theology Committee, Summer 2002, Commentary by Russ Resnik available at:
http://www.umjc.org/main/faq/definition/ResnikCommentary.pdf

12. http://www.jewsforjesus.org/publications/havurah/7_1/letters

13. Ibid.

14. Blog of Sean Emslie, who attends Stuart Dauermann's congregation:
http://towardblog.blogspot.com/2005_02_01_towardblog_archive.html, posting for February 9, 2005, entitled, "2 Religions—1 Messiah." His extensive blog has a number of posts distancing "Messianic Judaism" from "Jews for Jesus" and "mission" groups.

15. As cited by Gabriela Karabelnik in "Competing Trends in Messianic Judaism: The Debate over Evangelicalism," unpublished senior thesis, Department of Religious Studies, Yale University, 2002, note 203, "Kinzer interview."

16. Ibid., note 212.

17. Ibid., note 204, "Eaton interview."

18. *Havurah* 7:1 (February, 2004) available at:
http://www.jewsforjesus.org/publications/havurah/7_1/letters

19. http://rabbenu.blogspot.com, post "Toward an Expansive Biblicism," January 23, 2005.

20. Ibid. "This is a revolutionary truth . . . however, the Church has generally been blind to this."

21. Ibid., "Toward a New Paradigm of Messianic Jewish Outreach," January 2, 2005.

22. Pardo-Kaplan, Deborah, "Jacob vs. Jacob: Jewish Believers in Jesus Quarrel over Both Style and Substance," in *Christianity Today*, February 2005. Accessed online at: http://www.christianitytoday.com/ct/2005/002/31.76.html. Does Kinzer mean missions to Jews only? He is quoted as saying: "I think they should be dismantled," Kinzer says. "I think that whatever constructive role they may have played in the past, times have changed. For the present situation and the future, I see missions as primarily an obstacle."

23. Niebuhr, H. Richard, *Christ and Culture*. HarperSanFrancisco, 1956.

24. It is not clear what Hashivenu will have to say about the rabbinic oral law, without which there is little guidance in Judaism in how to observe the 613 commandments in modern times.

25. Primarily in the "birkat ha-minim," the "blessing on the heretics," which was recited in the late first-century synagogue to exclude various groups, including Jews who believed in Jesus. Also following the Bar Kochba war of A.D. 132-135—which was fought under the platform that Rabbi Akiva was the Messiah—something Jewish believers in Jesus could not accept.

26. http://www.hashivenu.org. "HaShem" is an Orthodox Jewish way of referring to God, literally, "the Name."

27. Kinzer, Mark S., *Postmissionary Messianic Judaism: Redefining Christian Engagement with the Jewish People*, Brazos Press. Announced date, November 2005.

28. Klett, Fred, "The Centrality of Messiah and the Theological Direction of the Messianic Movement," Proc. of LCJE-NA Conference, 2002, Orlando. (http://www.lcje.net/papers/2002.html). Also Gabriela Karabelnik, "Competing Trends": "One of the central challenges of the UMJC involves balancing how much to strive for recognition and acceptance from the Jewish community versus how much to give back—if too much is given; its own existence becomes relativized," section "Conclusion: Some Challenges Ahead."

Appendices

Appendix A
A Word or Two about Nazarene Judaism

Mention should also be made of "Nazarene Judaism," a movement that in the United States is most closely identified with a man named James Scott Trimm. This is not to be confused with the Protestant denomination known as the Church of the Nazarene.

Nazarene Judaism believes Jesus to be the Messiah—but the available statements of faith are not in any way recognizably evangelical when it comes to the person of Christ or the Trinity. Trimm's website explains the nature of God in this way: "We believe that YHWH reveals Himself in many ways, characteristics and sefirot, including those of Father, Word (Memra), and the Ruach HaKodesh (Holy Spirit)."[1]

The statement that God "reveals" Himself in many ways is entirely different than the evangelical doctrine that God exists in three persons. The term "sefirot" is in fact borrowed from Kabbalah (Jewish mysticism), which teaches that God exists in ten emanations called *sefirot*. Another Nazarene Judaism website specifically identifies the Trinity as a pagan doctrine.[2]

In other areas of doctrine, Nazarene Judaism:

- believes in the necessity to observe the Torah. It is a kind of "restorationist" movement:"Today we are seeking to put Y'shua back into the context of first century Judaism. Nazarene Judaism is a spiritual renaissance, a revival, a return to the pure faith of first century Nazarenes."[3]
- believes in an original non-Greek New Testament. As a corollary,Trimm does not believe in the doctrine of inerrancy: "In addition to grammatical errors in the Greek New Testament, there are also a number of 'blunders' in the text

which prove that the present Greek text is not inerrant."[4]
• does not believe the New Covenant is for today: "The truth is that the New Covenant is not the Good News (Gospel) but is a covenant which HaShem will make with '*the House of Israel and the House of Judah*' when He establishes the Kingdom. There is nothing in the Scriptures to indicate that there is more than one New Covenant."[5]

Further insight into Nazarene Judaism's theological orientation can be gained from looking at their teaching institute, which they call a yeshiva. Under a listing of theology courses offered, we find:

> Advanced Systematic Theology—Jewish Mysticism I– This course will cover Jewish mysticism, especially in relationship to understanding the Godhead. Textbook: MYSTERY OF THE GODHEAD; BASIC CONCEPTS OF KABBALAH available from SANJ.[6]

The Kabbalah, however, is radically unbiblical, teaching concepts such as reincarnation, the existence of God in ten emanations or *sefirot*, and an explanation of evil and redemption remarkably at variance with the Bible's story.[7] Another Nazarene Judaism website (in which the movement is called Netzarim Judaism— Netzarim being Hebrew for Nazarene) garnishes its front page with a chart of the ten kabbalistic sefirot and a list of Kabbalistic books on the side. Nothing could be further from biblical teaching and certainly should not be called "Messianic Jewish."

Yet, adherents to Nazarene Judaism identify as Jewish and appear to be content to be called "Messianic Jews":

> *SHOULD NAZARENES DENY BEING "MESSIANIC JEWS"?*
> Absolutely not! Although the term is scripturally inaccurate, we are Jews who believe in Messiah. In fact any Jew who believes

in the concept of "Messiah" (even if that "Messiah" is not Yeshua) might reasonably be termed a "Messianic Jew." So we need not deny that we are "Messianic Jews" to those who ask.[8]

It is not clear whether Trimm was born Jewish; according to his website, he "began practicing normative Rabbinic Judaism at the age of fourteen. At the age of eighteen, James concluded that Yeshua of Nazareth had been the Messiah of Judaism."[9] He does not spell out in detail what he came to believe about Jesus. He claims to have received a doctoral degree from Saint John Chrysostom Theological Seminary, which claims to be affiliated with the Catholic Apostolic Church of North America. (For more on Trimm's qualifications, see the Further Reading section.)

Besides teaching Kabbalah, it is instructive that a course called "Answering Christendom" is taught alongside courses in "Answering Islam" and "Answering Mormonism."

Nazarene groups are sometimes listed under a "Messianic" heading in online search engines. Theologically, though, Nazarene Judaism is well outside the pale of the Messianic movement.

FURTHER READING
On James Trimm:
> Doctor James Scott Trimm
> http://www.seekgod.ca/trimmdoc.htm

> Saint John Chrysostom Theological Seminary
> http://www.seekgod.ca/saintjohn.htm

> James Trimm as Rabbi Yosef
> http://www.seekgod.ca/rabbiyosef.htm

On the Kabbalah:
> "Kabbalah: Fact or Fiction," *ISSUES* 12:2
> http://www.jewsforjesus.org/publications/issues/12_2/kabbalah

"A History of the Kabbalah," *ISSUES* 12:2
http://www.jewsforjesus.org/publications/issues/12_2/
kabbalahhistory

Notes

1. http://www.nazarene.net/Statement.htm
2. http://www.nazarite.net/answer-18.html
3. Trimm, James Scott, "What is Nazarene Judaism?" Online at:
http://www.unjs.org/what_is_nazarene_judaism.htm
4. Trimm, *Nazarene Jewish Manifesto*, p. 58, available as a PDF
download at: http://www.unjs.org/NazareneJudaismManifesto.pdf
5. http://www.nazarene.net/newcovenant.htm
6. http://www.nazarene.net/yeshiva/course_descriptions.htm
(emphasis in the original)
7. In one popular form of the Kabbalah, original "shells" broke,
emptying divine "sparks" to earth. To achieve redemption, man must
work according to Torah and "raise the sparks" back to heaven.
8. Trimm, *Manifesto*, p. 7.
9. http://www.trimmfamily.com/JamesSTrimm.html

Appendix B
More Recommended Reading

For your convenience, we have listed all the URLs cited in this book at: http://www.jewsforjesus.org/publications/fieldguide

History and Theology: Jewish Believers in Jesus and Missions

Ariel, Yaacov, *Evangelizing the Chosen People: Missions to the Jews in America, 1880-2000*, Chapel Hill, NC: University of North Carolina Press, 2000. A comprehensive and unusually sympathetic survey of the history of modern Jewish evangelism in the U.S. written by a non-Jesus-believing Jew.

Cohn-Sherbok, Dan, *Messianic Judaism*. New York: Cassell, 2000. A non-Jesus-believing rabbi describes the history and beliefs of the modern Messianic movement, arguing for the authenticity of Messianic Judaism as a legitimate branch of Judaism within a pluralist model.

Fruchtenbaum, Arnold, *Hebrew Christianity: Its Theology, History and Philosophy*. Tustin, CA: Ariel Ministries Press, 1983. Gives a theological basis for Hebrew Christianity and practical suggestions for Hebrew-Christian (now more commonly called Messianic Jewish) identity and practice.

Gundry, Stanley N. & Louis Goldberg, eds. *How Jewish is Christianity: Two Views on the Messianic Movement*. Grand Rapids: Zondervan, 2003. A discussion of the rationale, biblical basis and practice of Messianic faith and Messianic Judaism.

Harris-Shapiro, Carol, *Messianic Judaism: A Rabbi's Journey Through Religious Change in America*. Beacon Press, 1999. A Reconstructionist rabbi offers insight, history and observation.

Maoz, Baruch, *Judaism is Not Jewish: A Friendly Critique of the Messianic Movement*. UK: Mentor: Christian Focus Publications and Christian Witness to Israel, 2003. A critical survey of the theology and practice of the Messianic movement in Israel and the U.S.

Pritz, Ray, *Nazarene Jewish Christianity: From the End of the New Testament Period Until Its Disappearance in the Fourth Century*, Leiden: E.J. Brill, 1988. A historical study of Jewish Christians in the early centuries.

Sevener, Harold A., *A Rabbi's Vision: A Century of Proclaiming Messiah, A History of Chosen People Ministries*, Charlotte, NC: Chosen People Ministries, 1994. A history of one of the older U.S. Jewish missions.

Stern, David H., *Messianic Jewish Manifesto*. Jerusalem: Jewish New Testament Publications, 1988. One approach to the theological development of Messianic Judaism.

Tucker, Ruth A., *Not Ashamed: The Story of Jews for Jesus*. Sisters, OR: Multnomah Publishers, 1999. A missiologist and historian provides background and analysis of the people and methods used in the first 25 years of this Jewish mission.

"Jewish Evangelism: A Call to the Church," Lausanne Occasional Paper No. 60, produced by the Issue Group on this topic at the 2004 Forum for World Evangelization, hosted by the Lausanne Committee for World Evangelization in Pattaya, Thailand, September 29 to October 5, 2004
Available at:
http://community.gospelcom.net/lcwe/assets/LOP60_IG31.pdf

Resources for Jewish Ministry
Brown, Michael L., *Answering Jewish Objections to Jesus*. Grand Rapids: Baker Books, 2000, 2003. In three volumes. The

most comprehensive books of Jewish apologetics since the early twentieth century. A fourth volume is planned.

Cohen, Steve, *Beginning from Jerusalem*, St. Louis: Apple of His Eye Mission Society, 2001. A Jewish believer in Jesus and mission leader offers insights about Jewish evangelism, especially for American Lutherans.

Goldberg, Louis, *Our Jewish Friends*. Neptune, NJ: Loizeaux Brothers, 1977. Advice on Jewish evangelism from a scholarly Jewish believer in Jesus, who once headed the Jewish Studies program at Moody Bible Institute, Chicago.

Rosen, Moishe and Ceil, *Witnessing to Jews*, San Francisco: Purple Pomegranate Productions, 1998. A practical handbook of creative lessons on Jewish evangelism written for Christians by a modern missionary pioneer and his wife.

Wan, Enoch and Tuvya Zaretsky, *Jewish-Gentile Couples: Trends, Challenges and Hopes*, Pasadena: William Carey Library, 2004. Research into the difficulties encountered by Jewish-Gentile couples with insight and some practical strategies for ministry to them.

Periodicals
Mishkan: A Forum on the Gospel and the Jewish People, Jerusalem: Caspari Center for Biblical and Jewish Studies. A journal dedicated to biblical and theological thinking on issues related to Jewish evangelism, Hebrew-Christian/Messianic-Jewish identity, and Jewish-Christian relations.

Kesher, Albuquerque, NM: Union of Messianic Jewish Congregations. A journal of Messianic Judaism which provides a forum to address the issues that face contemporary Messianic Judaism.

The Messianic Times. International Messianic newspaper published six times a year.

Messianic Jewish Life (archives only).

Boundaries (archives only).

ISSUES: A Messianic Jewish Perspective. A bimonthly mini-magazine for Jewish believers and seekers.

Havurah (formerly *Mishpochah Message*). A quarterly publication for the Jewish believing community.

Messianic Good News. Prophecy and other Scripture articles are contained in this newsletter.

Israel, My Glory. Articles on Israel and prophecy, published bimonthly.

Appendix C
LCJE Member Organizations

Celebrate Messiah, Australia

Jews for Jesus, Canada

Den Danske Israelsmission, Denmark

Israelsmissionens Unge, Denmark

The Faroese Israel Mission, Faroe Islands

Finnish Evangelical Lutheran Mission, Finland

Finnish Lutheran Mission, Finland

Patmos, Finland

Evangeliumsdienst für Israel, Germany

Beit Sar Shalom, Germany

Caspari Center, Israel

LCJE Japan

Den Evangeliske Lutherske Frikirkes Israelsmisjon, Norway

Norwegian Church Ministry to Israel, Norway

AMZI, Switzerland

Board for Israel of the NRC, The Netherlands

Church's Ministry among Jewish People (CMJ), United Kingdom

Christian Witness to Israel (CWI), United Kingdom

Ariel Ministries, USA

CJF Ministries, USA

International Messianic Jewish Alliance, USA

Hope of David, USA

Messiah Now Ministries, USA

Jews for Jesus, USA

Tikkun Ministries, Inc., USA

Not included is a list of individual members who represent other organizations, as such a list would be too long.

Appendix D
Judaism 101

THE THREE MAIN BRANCHES OF JUDAISM

The three divisions mentioned in this chart are not denominations. They are more like associations, with classifications according to cultural and doctrinal formulas. Within each branch you will find adherents with varying degrees of observance. Many Jewish people formulate their own informal version of Judaism, and do not fit strictly into any one of these categories. Nevertheless, the information in the chart below should be helpful.

CATEGORY	Orthodox	Conservative	Reform
History	Orthodoxy dates back to the days of the Talmud (2nd to 5th centuries A.D.). Orthodoxy today seeks to preserve classical or traditional Judaism.	Conservative Judaism emerged in the 19th Century Germany as a reaction to the assimilationist tendencies of Reform Judaism. It tried to be a middle ground, attempting to maintain basic traditions while adapting to modern life.	Reform Judaism emerged following the emancipation from ghetto life in the late 18th century. It sought to modernize Judaism and thus stem the tide of assimilation threatening German Jewry.
Other Terms	Traditional or Torah Judaism	Historical Judaism	Liberal or Progressive Judaism

CATEGORY	Orthodox	Conservative	Reform
View of Scripture	Torah is truth, and we must have faith in its essential, revealed character. A true Jew believes in revelation and the divine origin of the oral and written Torah.	The Bible is the word of God and man. It is not inspired in the traditional sense, but rather dynamically inspired. Revelation is an ongoing process in the evolutionary sense.	Revelation is a continuous process. Torah is a human document preserving the history, culture, legends and hope of a people. It is valuable for deriving moral and ethical insights
View of God	God is spirit rather than form. He is a personal God: omnipotent, omniscient, omnipresent, eternal and compassionate.	The concept of God is non-dogmatic and flexible. There is less atheism in Conservative Judaism than in Reform, but most often God is considered impersonal and ineffable.	Reform Judaism allows a varied interpretation of the "God concept" with wide latitude for naturalists, mystics, supernaturalists or religious humanists. It holds that "the truth is that we do not know the truth."
View of Man	People are morally neutral, with good and	This group tends toward the Reform view,	Human nature is basically good. Through

CATEGORY	Orthodox	Conservative	Reform
View of Man (cont.)	evil inclinations. They can overcome their evil bents and be perfected by their own efforts in observation of the Law.	though it is not as likely to espouse humanism. Perfectibility can come through enlightenment. Humanity is "in partnership" with God.	education, encouragement and evolution humans can actualize the potential already existing within them. Humankind may be God.
View of Sin	Orthodox Jews do not believe in "original sin." Rather, one commits sin by breaking the commandments of the Law.	Conservative Jews do not believe in "original sin." The individual can sin in moral or social actions.	Reform Jews do not believe in "original sin." Sin is reinterpreted as the ills of society.
View of Salvation	Repentance (belief in God's mercy), prayer and obedience to the Law are necessary for salvation.	Conservative Jews tend toward the Reform view, but include the necessity of maintaining Jewish identity.	Salvation is obtained through the betterment of self and society.
View of the Tradition of the Law	The Law is the essence of Judaism. It is authoritative and	Adaptation to contemporary situations is inevitable. The	The law is an evolving ever-dynamic religious code that adapts

CATEGORY	Orthodox	Conservative	Reform
View of the Tradition of the Law (cont.)	gives structure and meaning to life. The life of total dedication to Halakhah (Jewish Law) leads to a nearness to God.	demands of morality are absolute. The specific laws are relative.	to every age. They maintain, "If religious observances clash with the just demands of civilized society, then they must be dropped."
View of Messiah	The Messiah is a personal, super-human being who is not divine. He will restore the Jewish kingdom and extend his righteous rule over the earth. He will execute judgment and right all wrongs.	Conservative Jews hold much the same view as the Reform.	Instead of belief in Messiah as a person or divine being, they favor the concept of a Utopian age toward which mankind is progressing.
View of Life After Death	There will be a physical resurrection. The righteous will exist forever with God in the Garden of Eden. The unrighteous will suffer, but	Conservative Jews tend toward the Reform view, but are less influenced by Eastern thought.	Generally, Reform Judaism has no concept of personal life after death. They say a person lives on in the accomplishments or in the minds of

CATEGORY	Orthodox	Conservative	Reform
View of Life After Death (cont.)	disagreement exists over their ultimate destiny.		others. There is some similarity to Eastern thought, where souls merge into one great impersonal life force.
Distinctives in Synagogue Worship	The synagogue is a house of prayer; study and social aspects are incidental. All prayers are recited in Hebrew. Men and women sit separately. The officiants face the same direction as the congregants.	The synagogue is viewed as the basic institution of Jewish life. Alterations listed under Reform are found to a lesser degree in Conservative worship.	The Synagogue is known as a "Temple." The service has been modernized and abbreviated. English, as well as Hebrew, is used. Men and women sit together. Reform temples use choirs and organs in their worship services.

RECONSTRUCTIONIST JUDAISM

Reconstructionists believe that Judaism is an "evolving religious civilization." In one way, it is *more* liberal than Reform Judaism: the movement does not believe in a personified deity that is active in history and does not believe that God chose the Jewish people. In another way, Reconstructionist Judaism is *less* liberal than Reform Judaism: Reconstructionists observe *halakhah* (Jewish Law) if they *choose* to, not because it is a binding Law from God, but because it is a valuable cultural remnant.

CHASIDISM

This "Ultra-Orthodox" Jewish sect, founded in 18th century Europe by the Ba'al Shem Tov, believes that acts of kindness and prayer can be used to reach God, as opposed to the older view that one could only become a righteous Jew through rigorous learning. The word Chasid describes a person who does *chesed* (good deeds for others). Chasidic Jews dress distinctively, live separately from modern society, and are dedicated to strict observance of Jewish Law. They have also preserved the "mystical" foundations of Jewish theology, such as kabbalah.

SOME COMMON TERMS IN JUDAISM THAT WILL BE HELPFUL TO KNOW AS YOU EXPLORE THE MESSIANIC MOVEMENT:

Ashkenazic Jews (ahsh-ken-AH-zik) or Ashkenazim (ahsh-ken-ah-ZEEM)
Jews from eastern France, Germany and Eastern Europe, and their descendants. Most Jews in America are Ashkenazic.

Kabbalah (kuh-BAH-luh)
Literally, tradition. Jewish mystical tradition.

Mikvah (MIK-vuh)
Lit. gathering. A ritual bath used for spiritual purification. It is used primarily in conversion rituals and after the period of sexual separation during a woman's menstrual cycles, but many Chasidim immerse themselves in the mikvah regularly for general spiritual purification. The Messianic movement sometimes incorporates this tradition in public profession of faith through immersion.

Oral Torah (TOH-ruh) or Mishnah
Jewish teachings explaining and elaborating on the Written Torah, handed down orally until the 2nd century A.D., when they began to be written down in what became the Talmud.

Rabbi (RAB-bye)
A religious teacher and person authorized to make decisions on issues of Jewish law. Also performs many of the same functions as a Protestant minister.

Ruach HaKodesh The Holy Spirit

Sephardic Jews (s'-FAHR-dic) or Sephardim (seh-fahr-DEEM)
Jews from Spain, Portugal, North Africa and the Middle East and their descendants.

Shofar (sho-FAHR)
A ram's horn, blown like a trumpet as a call to repentance.

Shul (SHOOL)
The Yiddish term for a Jewish house of worship. The term is used primarily by Orthodox Jews.

Siddur (SID-r; sid-AWR) Lit. order. Prayer book.

Synagogue (SIN-uh-gahg)
From a Greek root meaning "assembly." The most widely accepted term for a Jewish house of worship. The Jewish equivalent of a church, mosque or temple.

Tallit (TAH-lit; TAH-lis)
A shawl-like garment worn during morning services, with *tzitzit* (long fringes) attached to the corners as a reminder of the commandments. Sometimes called a prayer shawl.

Talmud (TAHL-mud)
The most significant collection of the Jewish oral tradition interpreting the Torah

Tanakh (tuhn-AHKH)
Acronym of Torah (Law), Nevi'im (Prophets) and Ketuvim

(Writings). Written Torah; what non-Jews call the Old Testament.

Temple
1) The central place of worship in ancient Jerusalem, where sacrifices were offered, destroyed in A.D. 70

2) The term commonly used for houses of worship within the Reform movement.

Torah (TOH-ruh)
In its narrowest sense, Torah is the first five books of the Bible: Genesis, Exodus, Leviticus, Numbers and Deuteronomy (sometimes called the Pentateuch). In its broadest sense, Torah is the entire body of Jewish teachings.

Yarmulke (YAH-mi-kuh)
From Tartar "skullcap," or from Aramaic "Yirei Malka" (fear of the King). The skullcap head covering worn by Jews during services, and by some Jews at all times.

Y'shua (sometimes spelled Yeshua) Jesus

Zionism (ZYE-uhn-ism)
A political movement to create and maintain a Jewish state. The word is derived from Zion, another name for Jerusalem.

Appendix E
A Rationale for Jewish Evangelism

What happens when the most loving thing you can do is tell someone something they do not want to hear? How do you tell someone something that is crucial to their welfare, when they think they know what you are going to say and they have already decided it does not apply to them? Is there ever a right time to say something that may cause offense?

These questions are not just hypothetical. Caring people face such questions in relating to family and friends. Because we care, we tell them the truth as lovingly as we can, even if their response may cause us pain.

That is exactly what is at issue with Jewish evangelism. Our Jewish people do not want to hear the gospel; many think they know what we are going to say and have already decided it does not apply to them. The most loving thing we can do is to tell them, as carefully as possible, what Jesus has done for them. Yet many Christians are finding it difficult to believe that Jews really do need Jesus. Why?

The Jewish people have walked a long road of persecution. Sadly, Church history has been a major intersection on that road. Christians are becoming increasingly aware of that history, and of the fact that some who claimed to represent Jesus used His name to commit atrocities against the Jewish people. Many Christians are now deeply sensitized to anything that smacks of anti-Semitism. As Jews for Jesus, we are grateful for that sensitivity, especially when it leads people to be extra tactful and loving in sharing the gospel.

At the same time, some Christian friends have taken their sensitivity in a different direction. They have concluded that Jewish people do not need Jesus, and that it is unkind and arrogant—even anti-Semitic—to suggest that they do. In many cases, these conclusions are drawn from discussions with Jewish friends whose opinions these Christians greatly value. After all, when you respect and care for friends it is only natural to take them at their word about such things, especially when they speak with strong conviction. And yet, Jesus also spoke with conviction when He announced: "I am the way, the truth, and the life. No one comes to the Father except through me" (John 14:6). We believe that accepting Christ's claims means accepting the privilege and the burden of communicating His claims to others, even if they are insulted by the prospect.

The apostle Paul holds a key to the question of why we continue reaching out to those who insist they do not need or want the gospel. In Romans 11, he spoke of a partial hardening, a spiritual blindness that has come to the people of Israel.

If the Bible is not God's truth for us, such talk about blindness and hardening is demeaning. Certainly, if it were a matter of Paul's personal opinion it would be. But if the Bible is true, the reality is that Jewish people as a whole are committed to disbelieving the gospel because they cannot, at this point in history, see the truth. Paul says this "partial blindness" is not complete, nor is it permanent. Most people know that Jesus' first followers were Jewish, and that the first Christian missionaries were "converted Jews" preaching the gospel to Gentiles. Yet, in a sense, they were not converted Jews—they were converted sinners who happened to be Jewish. And they remained Jewish, never renouncing their heritage or the faith of their ancestors. They were part of a believing remnant of Jews whom God is calling to follow

Jesus. We Jews for Jesus are part of that believing remnant, and our efforts to make the gospel an unavoidable issue to the rest of our people are adding to that remnant.

As Jews who believe in Jesus, we sympathize with those who feel offended by the gospel, yet we do not accept the notion that it is offensive to tell Jewish people about Jesus. Many of us were offended the first time someone tried to share their faith with us. We know that there is some choice involved in being offended, and we also know that a negative reaction is not necessarily the end of the story—we have been there! We Jews who have found faith and everlasting life in Jesus recall how we once felt. Most of us considered anyone who confronted us with the gospel a minor annoyance at best, if not a major aggravation. Now we thank God for those who cared enough to tell us what we did not wish to hear. Can we do less than was done for us?

It's been said that most people are looking for God about as much as someone playing hooky is looking for a truant officer. That applies even more to Jewish people looking for Jesus! It's no wonder that our desire to make Him an unavoidable issue is considered intrusive by many. Yet our mission is not to intrude. It is simply to call attention to the Savior in ways that Jewish people cannot dismiss as being for someone else. We believe it is possible to draw attention to Jesus in respectful, loving and good natured ways. But it is always a battle to go against popular opinion, which tells us to keep the gospel to ourselves.

We are grateful for the many Christians who stand with us and are willing to face discomfort for the sake of Christ, and for their concern to see Jewish friends heavenbound. Still, the controversial nature of our cause makes it difficult for us to gain the friendship and support of many Christians who feel it's not

quite polite to tell people who have their own religion that they
need Jesus. We can only hope those Christians will think through
the implications of that line of thinking. What if the Apostles Peter
and Paul had decided it was impolite or disrespectful to tell
Gentiles (who also had their own religions) about Jesus? There
would be very few Christians in the world today!

It is not our task to buttonhole or force people to converse
with us. Once we present people with an invitation to
interact with our message—be it a gospel tract, a billboard, a
gospel ad or even a phone call—they can choose to avoid,
embrace, or seek further information about Jesus. If it's either
of the latter two, we want to help.

HOW DOES THE JEWISH COMMUNITY RESPOND TO FORTHRIGHT EVANGELISM?

We have organized opposition which, oddly enough,
encourages us. Our opposition points to the fact that more
and more Jews are coming to faith in Jesus. We are honored
to be "blamed," but God deserves the credit. We lift up Jesus,
but He alone can draw Jews and Gentiles to Himself.

Rabbis and Jewish community leaders cannot allow
themselves to believe that it is legitimate for a Jew to believe
in Jesus, so many attempt to delegitimize us. Some allege that
we are a cult or an exotic new religion, but most will say we
are dishonest and disingenuous. (The latter accusations refer
to our refusal to give up our Jewish identity as dishonest,
since they believe that anyone who believes in Jesus cannot
be Jewish.) In part, their attempts to undermine our credibility
are meant to keep Jewish seekers away from us. However,
our opposition also understands that we depend upon the
friendship and support of our brothers and sisters in Christ.
Statements undermining the integrity of Jewish evangelism
drive a wedge between us and many members of Christ's Body.

HOW SUCCESSFUL IS THE OPPOSITION?

When it comes to keeping Jewish people from hearing us, our opposition mostly affects those who are not prepared to "go against the flow." Frankly, any Jewish people who would seriously consider Jesus are already questioning religious authorities and realizing they must investigate certain issues for themselves.

Ironically, our opposition seems to have more success within the Church. It has become increasingly popular among liberal and even among some not-so-liberal Christians to say that Jews have salvation apart from Christ. Therefore, they say that evangelizing Jewish people is an unnecessary, even unchristian, endeavor. *This is what happens when Christians view the Great Commission through the eyes of unbelieving friends and colleagues.*

Whereas empathy for the sensitivities of Jewish people is appreciated, it becomes tragic when allowed to take the place of a Bible-based philosophy of missions. How can one surmise from Scripture that it is insulting to speak to Jews of the love of Jesus, who came as a Jew? How can it be insulting to tell of the great sacrifice He made for all people? How can it be insulting to offer the abundant life He gives?

Unbelieving Jewish people who are willing to go against the flow to explore the gospel have a sense of what is at stake—their own salvation. Unfortunately, too many Christians do not have that urgent sense of what is at stake. For some, the friendship or respect of unsaved Jewish people seems to determine their view of Jewish evangelism. Saying that Jesus is the only way to salvation would mean risking rejection. As Jews who are for Jesus, we have no choice but to make that statement and take the heat. If we were not convinced that Jesus is the only way of salvation, we would not have given up the respect and acceptance of the

Jewish community. Since we are convinced that the salvation of our people is at stake, we *have* to reach out and take the risk.

Appendix F
The Willowbank Declaration

"The Gospel is the power of God for salvation, to everyone who believes, to the Jew first and also to the Greek." (Romans 1:16)

"Brethren, my heart's desire and prayer to God for Israel is that they may be saved." (Romans 10:1)

THE WILLOWBANK DECLARATION ON THE CHRISTIAN GOSPEL AND THE JEWISH PEOPLE

PREAMBLE

Every Christian must acknowledge an immense debt of gratitude to the Jewish people. The Gospel is the good news that Jesus is the Christ, the long-promised Jewish Messiah, who by his life, death and resurrection saves from sin and all its consequences. Those who worship Jesus as their Divine Lord and Saviour have thus received God's most precious gift through the Jewish people. Therefore they have compelling reason to show love to that people in every possible way.

Concerned about humanity everywhere, we are resolved to uphold the right of Jewish people to a just and peaceful existence everywhere, both in the land of Israel and in their communities throughout the world. We repudiate past persecutions of Jews by those identified as Christians, and we pledge ourselves to resist every form of anti-Semitism. As the supreme way of demonstrating love, we seek to encourage the Jewish people, along with all other peoples, to receive God's gift of life through Jesus the Messiah, and accordingly the growing number of Jewish Christians brings us great joy.

In making this Declaration we stand in a long and revered Christian tradition, which in 1980 was highlighted by a landmark statement, "Christian Witness to the Jewish People," issued by the Lausanne Committee for World Evangelization. Now, at this Willowbank Consultation on the Gospel and the Jewish People, sponsored by the World Evangelical Fellowship and supported by the Lausanne Committee, we reaffirm our commitment to the Jewish people and our desire to share the Gospel with them.

This Declaration is made in response to growing doubts and widespread confusion among Christians about the need for, and the propriety of, endeavors to share faith in Jesus Christ with Jewish people. Several factors unite to produce the uncertain state of mind that the Declaration seeks to resolve.

The Holocaust, perpetrated as it was by leaders and citizens of a supposedly Christian nation, has led to a sense in some quarters that Christian credibility among Jews has been totally destroyed. Accordingly, some have shrunk back from addressing the Jewish people with the Gospel.

Some who see the creation of the state of Israel as a direct fulfillment of biblical prophecy have concluded that the Christian task at this time is to "comfort Israel" by supporting this new political entity, rather than to challenge Jews by direct evangelism.

Some church leaders have retreated from embracing the task of evangelizing Jews as a responsibility of Christian mission. Rather, a new theology is being embraced which holds that God's covenant with Israel through Abraham establishes all Jews in God's favor for all times, and so makes faith in Jesus Christ for salvation needless so far as they are concerned.

On this basis, it is argued that dialogue with Jews in order to understand each other better, and cooperation in the quest for socio-economic shalom, is all that Christian mission requires in relation to the Jewish people. Continued attempts to do what the Church has done from the first, in seeking to win Jews to Jesus as Messiah, are widely opposed and decried, by Christian as well as Jewish leaders.

Attempts to bring Jews to faith in Jesus are frequently denounced as proselytizing. This term is often used to imply dishonest and coercive modes of inducement, appeal to unworthy motives, and disregard of the question of truth even though it is truth that is being disseminated. In recent years, "Messianic" Jewish believers in Jesus, who as Christians celebrate and maximize their Jewish identity, have emerged as active evangelists to the Jewish community. Jewish leaders often accused them of deception on the grounds that one cannot be both a Jew and a Christian. While these criticisms may reflect Judaism's current effort to define itself as a distinct religion in opposition to Christianity, they have led to much bewilderment and some misunderstanding and mistrust.

The Declaration responds to this complex situation and seeks to set directions for the future according to the Scriptures.

I. THE DEMAND OF THE GOSPEL
Article I.1
WE AFFIRM THAT the redeeming love of God has been fully and finally revealed in Jesus Christ.

WE DENY THAT those without faith in Christ know the full reality of God's love and of the gift that he gives.

Article I.2
WE AFFIRM THAT the God-given types, prophecies and visions of

salvation and shalom in the Hebrew Scriptures find their present and future fulfillment in and through Jesus Christ, the Son of God, who by incarnation became a Jew and was shown to be the Son of God and Messiah by his resurrection.

WE DENY THAT it is right to look for a Messiah who has not yet appeared in world history.

Article I.3

WE AFFIRM THAT Jesus Christ is the second person of the one God, who became a man, lived a perfect life, shed his blood on the cross as an atoning sacrifice for human sins, rose bodily from the dead, now reigns as Lord, and will return visibly to this earth, all to fulfill the purpose of bringing sinners to share eternally in his fellowship and glory.

WE DENY THAT those who think of Jesus Christ in lesser terms than these have faith in him in any adequate sense.

Article I.4

WE AFFIRM THAT all human beings are sinful by nature and practice, and stand condemned, helpless and hopeless, before God, until the grace of Christ touches their lives and brings them to God's pardon and peace.

WE DENY THAT any Jew or Gentile finds true peace with God through performing works of law.

Article I.5

WE AFFIRM THAT God's forgiveness of the penitent rests on the satisfaction rendered to his justice by the substitutionary sacrifice of Jesus Christ on the cross.

WE DENY THAT any person can enjoy God's favor apart from the mediation of Jesus Christ, the sin-bearer.

Article I.6

WE AFFIRM THAT those who turn to Jesus Christ find him to be a sufficient Saviour and Deliverer from all the evil of sin: from its guilt, shame, power, and perversity; from blind defiance of God, debasement of moral character, and the dehumanizing and destructive self-assertion that sin breeds.

WE DENY THAT the salvation found in Christ may be supplemented in any way.

Article I.7

WE AFFIRM THAT faith in Jesus Christ is humanity's only way to come to know the Creator as Father, according to Christ's own Word: "I am the Way and the Truth and the Life; no one comes to the Father except through me" (John 14:6).

WE DENY THAT any non-Christian faith, as such, will mediate eternal life with God.

II. THE CHURCH OF JEWS AND GENTILES

Article II.8

WE AFFIRM THAT through the mediation of Jesus Christ, God has made a new covenant with Jewish and Gentile believers, pardoning their sins, writing his law on their hearts by his Spirit, so that they obey him, giving the Holy Spirit to indwell them, and bringing each one to know him by faith in a relationship of trustful gratitude for salvation.

WE DENY THAT the blessings of the New Covenant belong to any except believers in Jesus Christ.

Article II.9

WE AFFIRM THAT the profession of continuing Jewish identity, for which Hebrew Christians have in the past suffered at the hands of both their fellow-Jews and Gentile church leaders, was consistent with the Christian Scriptures and with the nature of the church as one body in Jesus Christ in which Jews and non-Jews are united. WE DENY THAT it is necessary for Jewish Christians to repudiate their Jewish heritage.

Article II.10
WE AFFIRM THAT Gentile believers, who at present constitute the great bulk of the Christian church, are included in the historically continuous community of believing people on earth which Paul pictures as God's olive tree (Romans 11:13-24).

WE DENY THAT Christian faith is necessarily non-Jewish, and that Gentiles who believe in Christ may ignore their solidarity with believing Jews, or formulate their new identity in Christ without reference to Jewishness, or decline to receive the Hebrew Scriptures as part of their own instruction from God, or refuse to see themselves as having their roots in Jewish history.

Article II.11
WE AFFIRM THAT Jewish people who come to faith in Messiah have liberty before God to observe or not observe traditional Jewish customs and ceremonies that are consistent with the Christian Scriptures and do not hinder fellowship with the rest of the Body of Christ.

WE DENY THAT any inconsistency or deception is involved by Jewish Christians representing themselves as "Messianic" or "completed" or "fulfilled" Jews.

III. GOD'S PLAN FOR THE JEWISH PEOPLE
Article III.12
WE AFFIRM THAT Jewish people have an ongoing part in God's plan.

WE DENY THAT indifference to the future of the Jewish people on the part of Christians can ever be justified.

Article III.13
WE AFFIRM THAT prior to the coming of Christ it was Israel's unique privilege to enjoy a corporate covenantal relationship with God, following upon the national redemption from slavery, and involving God's gift of the law and of a theocratic culture; God's promise of blessing to faithful obedience; and God's provision of atonement for transgression.

WE AFFIRM THAT within this covenant relationship, God's pardon and acceptance of the penitent which was linked to the offering of prescribed sacrifices rested upon the fore-ordained sacrifice of Jesus Christ.

WE DENY THAT covenantal privilege alone can ever bring salvation to impenitent unbelievers.

Article III.14
WE AFFIRM THAT much of Judaism, in its various forms, throughout contemporary Israel and today's Diaspora, is a development out of, rather than as an authentic embodiment of, the faith, love and hope that the Hebrew Scriptures teach.

WE DENY THAT modern Judaism with its explicit negation of the divine person, work, and Messiahship of Jesus Christ contains within itself true knowledge of God's salvation.

Article III.15
WE AFFIRM THAT the biblical hope for Jewish people centers on their being restored through faith in Christ to their proper place as branches of God's olive tree from which they are at present broken off.

WE DENY THAT the historical status of the Jews as God's people brings salvation to any Jew who does not accept the claims of Jesus Christ.

Article III.16
WE AFFIRM THAT the Bible promises that large numbers of Jews will turn to Christ through God's sovereign grace.

WE DENY THAT this prospect renders needless the active proclamation of the gospel to Jewish people in this and every age.

Article III.17
WE AFFIRM THAT anti-Semitism on the part of professed Christians has always been wicked and shameful and that the church has in the past been much to blame for tolerating and encouraging it and for condoning anti-Jewish actions on the part of individuals and governments.

WE DENY THAT these past failures, for which offending Gentile believers must ask forgiveness from both God and the Jewish community, rob Christians of the right or lessen their responsibility to share the Gospel with Jews today and for the future.

Article III.18
WE AFFIRM THAT it was the sins of the whole human race that sent Christ to the cross.

WE DENY THAT it is right to single out the Jewish people for putting Jesus to death.

IV. EVANGELISM AND THE JEWISH PEOPLE
Article IV.19
WE AFFIRM THAT sharing the Good News of Jesus Christ

with lost humanity is a matter of prime obligation for Christian people, both because the Messiah commands the making of disciples and because love of neighbor requires effort to meet our neighbor's deepest need.

WE DENY THAT any other form of witness and service to others can excuse Christians from laboring to bring them to faith in Christ.

Article IV.20
WE AFFIRM THAT the church's obligation to share saving knowledge of Christ with the whole human race includes the evangelizing of Jewish people as a priority: "To the Jew first" (Romans 1:16).

WE DENY THAT dialogue with Jewish people that aims at nothing more than mutual understanding constitutes fulfillment of this obligation.

Article IV.21
WE AFFIRM THAT the concern to point Jewish people to faith in Jesus Christ which the Christian church has historically felt and shown was right.

WE DENY THAT there is any truth in the widespread notion that evangelizing Jews is needless because they are already in covenant with God through Abraham and Moses and so are already saved despite their rejection of Jesus Christ as Lord and Saviour.

Article IV.22
WE AFFIRM THAT all endeavours to persuade others to become Christians should express love to them by respecting their dignity and integrity at every point, including parents' responsibility in the case of their children.

WE DENY THAT coercive or deceptive proselytizing, which violates dignity and integrity on both sides, can ever be justified.

Article IV.23

WE AFFIRM THAT it is unchristian, unloving, and discriminatory to propose a moratorium on the evangelizing of any part of the human race, and that failure to preach the gospel to the Jewish people would be a form of anti-Semitism, depriving this particular community of its right to hear the gospel.

WE DENY THAT we have sufficient warrant to assume or anticipate the salvation of anyone who is not a believer in Jesus Christ.

Article IV.24

WE AFFIRM THAT the existence of separate churchly organizations for evangelizing Jews, as for evangelizing any other particular human group, can be justified pragmatically, as an appropriate means of fulfilling the church's mandate to take the Gospel to the whole human race.

WE DENY THAT the depth of human spiritual need varies from group to group so that Jewish people may be thought to need Christ either more or less than others.

V. JEWISH-CHRISTIAN RELATIONS
Article V.25

WE AFFIRM THAT dialogue with other faiths that seeks to transcend stereotypes of them based on ignorance, and to find common ground and to share common concerns, is an expression of Christian love that should be encouraged.

WE DENY THAT dialogue that explains the Christian faith without seeking to persuade the dialogue partners of its truth and claims is a sufficient expression of Christian love.

Article V.26
WE AFFIRM THAT for Christians and non-Christian Jews to make common cause in social witness and action, contending together for freedom of speech and religion, the value of the individual, and the moral standards of God's law is right and good.

WE DENY THAT such limited cooperation involves any compromise of the distinctive views of either community or imposes any restraint upon Christians in seeking to share the Gospel with the Jews with whom they cooperate.

Article V.27
WE AFFIRM THAT the Jewish quest for a homeland with secure borders and a just peace has our support.

WE DENY THAT any biblical link between the Jewish people and the land of Israel justifies actions that contradict biblical ethics and constitute oppression of people-groups or individuals.

SPONSOR: WORLD EVANGELICAL FELLOWSHIP
INTERNATIONAL HEADQUARTERS
1, Sophia Road #07-09
Peace Centre
SINGAPORE 0922

WEF North American Headquarters
P. O. Box WEF
Wheaton, IL 60189

This Declaration was developed and adopted on April 29, 1989 by all those present at the Consultation on the Gospel and the Jewish People after several days of intense consultation, undergirded by prayer. Together the participants commend this document to the churches with a call to prayerfully consider and act upon these very serious matters as touching the Christian Gospel and the Jewish People.

Dr. Vernon Grounds (Chairman) U.S.A.; Dr. Tokunboh Adeyemo, KENYA; Dr. Henri Blocher, FRANCE; Dr. Tormod Engelsviken, NORWAY; Dr. Arthur Glasser, U.S.A.; Dr. Robert Godfrey, U.S.A.; Mrs. Gretchen Gaebelein Hull, U.S.A.; Dr. Kenneth Kantzer, U.S.A.; Rev. Ole Chr. Kvarme, NORWAY; Dr. David Lim, PHILIPPINES; Rev. Murdo MacLeod, ENGLAND; Dr. J. I. Packer, CANADA; Dr. Bong Ro R.O.C.; Dr. Sunand Sumithra, INDIA; Dr. David Wells, U.S.A.; Tuvya Zaretsky, U.S.A.

Appendix G
A Final Word from David Brickner, Executive Director of Jews for Jesus

AN OPEN LETTER TO THE FAMILY OF JEWISH BELIEVERS IN JESUS

In the first century, Jewish believers in Jesus were the Church's leaders, worldwide. The apostles and those they mentored set an example for this far-flung and diverse community of faith. They provided instruction, primarily in letter form. Those "epistles" that were uniquely inspired by the Holy Spirit became sacred Scripture. One such epistle, Hebrews, addressed perplexing matters of crucial concern primarily to first-century Jewish believers.

Many Jewish followers of Jesus face the same crucial concerns today. This open letter to Jewish followers of Jesus directs us back to the wisdom of the book of Hebrews and seven challenges to my Messianic family:

1. Love Y'shua
2. Love His Body
3. Resist the lure of triumphalism
4. Resist the lure of rabbinic Judaism
5. Resist the lure of assimilation
6. Proclaim the gospel
7. Proclaim the return of Messiah

We live in a world of deafening noises and competing demands for our attention and our affections. When the world shouts out obvious temptations to ungodliness we have a clear choice to avoid sin or fall prey to it. The choice is not always so clear when urgent and earnest voices tempt us in high-minded and spiritual-sounding terminology. The way to recognize these other temptations is the same as it was in the first century: fall deeply in love with Jesus. *Veyahaftah et Adonai Y'shua elohecha, vechol levavcha.* (And you shall love the Lord Jesus your God with all your heart.)

The author of Hebrews spent considerable time emphasizing the glories of Messiah Jesus. Jewish believers understood the dangers of idolatry, but many were confused concerning the very proper and biblical adoration of the God/man, Y'shua HaMashiach. Accordingly, the first three verses of the book of Hebrews present a beautiful clarification of Christ's deity.

> God, who at various times and in various ways spoke in time past to the fathers by the prophets, has in these last days spoken to us by His Son, (1) whom He has appointed heir of all things, (2) through whom also He made the worlds; (3) who being the brightness of His glory (4) and the express image of His person, and (5) upholding all things by the word of His power, (6) when He had by Himself purged our sins, (7) sat down at the right hand of the Majesty on high. (Hebrews 1:1-3)

Using a rabbinical device known as "stringing pearls," the author of Hebrews proclaims a seven-fold majesty of Messiah Jesus (indicated by the numbers in parentheses that I have inserted into the text). Y'shua's deity is never in question. His glory is equal to that of the Father.

As Jewish believers, we should be leading the exaltation of our Messiah Jesus. Yet certain claims seen in the above passage are de-emphasized among some (repeat, *some*) of the Messianic brothers and sisters. Of course, this would make sense if traditional Judaism were our model—since it is not traditional for Jews to believe in Jesus and the rabbis insist that believers in Him are no longer Jewish. If the rabbis were right and we could not be Jewish and believe what the New Testament says about Jesus, I hope we would be willing to choose our Jesus over our Jewish identity.

Fortunately, the rabbis are absolutely wrong. The most Jewish thing any of us could do is believe in and lovingly follow Jesus our Messiah. We need to express our love for Jesus in ways that are both theologically rich and devotionally warmhearted. Our "Jesusness" is more important than our Jewishness— because we can be reconciled to God whether or not we are Jewish, whereas we cannot be reconciled to Him without faith in Jesus. And our destiny as human beings rests on whether or not we are reconciled to God. That is not to trivialize our Jewish identity, which is a precious gift from God. But the gift cannot be elevated above the Giver.

Our love for Jesus will also help us to love one another more fully. I don't know if there has been a time in recent history when Jewish believers in Jesus have been more divided from one another than we are at present. A host of issues seems to come between us. But if we truly love Jesus with our whole hearts, we will love one another as He loves us. Our differences and disputes will pale in the light of our passionate adoration for the Messiah, who truly makes us one in Him.

Indeed, if we fall in love again with Jesus, we will more fully love His Body (the Church) in all of its diversity. Y'shua's love for the Church is described as the love of a husband for his wife: "Husbands, love your wives, *just as Christ also loved the church* and gave Himself for her" (Ephesians 5:25). How can anyone fully love Messiah without having a proper appreciation for His beloved Church?

We are all very sensitive to the terror and tragedy of past Christian anti-Semitism, particularly in Europe. This has been a

stain on the reputation of Christianity—a mark that we
Messianic Jews do not wish to bear. Some Jewish believers
draw away from the Church to avoid guilt-by-association—
even though the majority of the Church (which includes all of
Jesus' disciples to this day) had no part in that guilt. Ironically,
the majority of Jesus-followers in the world today are from
African, Latin and Asian parts of the world. Neither they nor
their ancestors had any part in the terrible chapters of church-
related anti-Semitism. Our unbelieving Jewish people may
paint the Church with a broad stroke of the brush, but we
who know Jesus and know His people have no business
laying responsibility for anti-Semitism at the feet of those who
had nothing to do with it. If we allow the past to control our
present attitude toward the Church, we will be guilty of
holding in contempt what God loves.

When the God of Israel looks on His Church today, He sees a
colorful mosaic of people from every tribe and tongue and
nation. We Jewish believers have an important part in that
mosaic. There has been an emphasis on recovering the Jewish
roots of faith in Jesus and I applaud this. But we must beware
of "cultural imperialism." Christians are enriched through
understanding the Jewish backgrounds of the Christian faith,
but we cannot reincarnate today's Church to be a first century
Jewish expression of faith in Christ. We should not berate our
non-Jewish brethren for their own cultural expressions of faith
in Christ as though it were some kind of paganism.

Despite the problems of history, God's people have been
exceedingly good to us Jewish believers in Jesus. They have loved
us. They have welcomed us as family when our own families
rejected us for our faith in Messiah. They have been patient with
our immaturities. They have encouraged our attempts to express
our Jewish identity alongside our faith in Christ. They have
generously supported our efforts to make Messiah known among
our own people. We cannot ask for much more than that.

God never intended the Church to be entirely Jewish. He established a richness of cultural diversity in the worship of Israel's Messiah for all time and eternity. Let us celebrate that diversity and humbly take guidance from the future vision of John the Apostle: "After these things I looked, and behold, a great multitude which no one could number, of all nations, tribes, peoples, and tongues, standing before the throne and before the Lamb, clothed with white robes, with palm branches in their hands, and crying out with a loud voice, saying, 'Salvation belongs to our God who sits on the throne, and to the Lamb!'" (Revelation 7:9-10).

If we as Jewish believers want to be as we were in the first century, an example to the rest of the Church, let it begin with two emphases. Let us love Messiah Jesus completely and passionately and let us love His Body, the Church, fully and without reservation.

RESIST THE LURE OF TRIUMPHALISM

When Jewish people become followers of Jesus we face several problems. Most commonly, there is stress and in some cases estrangement from unbelieving family members. But there are other problems that are far less obvious. For example, there's the pedestal problem: the new Jewish believer is immediately given a place of prominence in the local church simply because he or she happens to have been born Jewish. Suddenly, this baby believer is sought out as an expert in the Old Testament. Many well-meaning Christians mistakenly think that all Jews are thoroughly conversant with the Hebrew Bible. Most Jewish believers know that this is not the case and many are keenly aware of their own lack of biblical knowledge. Yet it can be very embarrassing to admit that lack. It can also be difficult for a new and spiritually immature believer to resist the flattery of Christian friends. Some of us have been tempted to think higher of ourselves than we ought to, despite the clear admonition of the Scriptures (Romans 12:3).

This danger applies not only to new Jewish believers, but also to some that have been in the faith long enough to know better. God has placed a special love for Jewish people in the hearts of many Christians and, as a result, we Messianic Jews are at times treated to a place of honor in the Body of Christ. Some have begun to believe that we actually deserve it. In fact, there are those who are calling for the restoration of Jewish believers to a place of leadership over the Church, just as it was in the first century. This is wrongheaded triumphalism and some Christians have added their endorsement to it.

God has been doing something wonderful in bringing greater numbers of Jewish people to Jesus in modern times, and the Church should give glory to God by acknowledging and affirming this work of grace. However, the Church needs leaders who, by piety and strength of godly conviction, show the way forward for the rest of Christ's followers. Whether one is Jewish or Gentile has no bearing on that piety and godly conviction.

Ours is a small and relatively immature movement within the Body of Christ, one that has not yet led the way in growth or unity. And while some in our ranks are unusually bright and gifted, as a whole we are not particularly exemplary in scholarship or sanctification. The fact is, we haven't been doing such a good job leading ourselves, let alone anyone else. And though I'm embarrassed to admit it, there may be a subtle racism in the notion that Jewish believers should be given prominence within the Body of Christ.

Unless or until we Messianic Jews are qualified to lead, we should not expect or accept leadership or prominence in the

Church—and we certainly should not seek it on the basis of our ethnicity or even historic precedent (Proverbs 27:2).

RESIST THE LURE OF RABBINIC JUDAISM

The demographics of the Messianic movement reflect those of the wider Jewish community, which means most were raised in fairly secular Jewish homes. Many Jewish believers learn more about what it means to be Jewish after coming to faith in Jesus—which leads to an altogether appropriate appreciation for their Jewish heritage. However, some want to make up for lost time by becoming "more Jewish," and that is when Jewish believers become vulnerable to a different kind of temptation.

The mature Jewish believer recognizes that Jewish religious leaders, particularly rabbis, are going to deny our identity as Jews unless we deny certain things about Jesus, or agree to keep silent about them. That recognition serves as a warning not to seek their affirmation because it comes at a cost we can't pay. Yet some in our Messianic movement remain uncertain about the relationship of Jewish believers to rabbinic Judaism.

It is understandable that Jewish believers want to be "authentically" Jewish while still following Jesus. But what does that actually mean? Who is to say what it means to be authentic in one's Jewish identity? The rabbis have pronounced themselves the trustees and guardians of what is authentically Jewish. It stands to reason that anyone who is working out his or her Jewish identity will be drawn to rabbinic teaching. Some of the teaching and tradition is good and wise. However, the rabbis are inherently opposed to our faith in Jesus and hostile to our desire to tell other Jews about Him. Do we really want to look to their standards to validate whether or not we are authentically Jewish?

Validation can be a big problem for Jewish believers. Where do we look for it? It is easy to fall prey to our own pride and desire for acceptance from our fellow Jews—and often we don't see those things for what they are. Pride is especially hard to pinpoint when it is hiding behind more noble qualities such as piety or zeal for God.

Some Messianic Jews are teaching that it is incumbent on all Jewish believers to observe the Law of Moses and to worship exclusively in Messianic congregations. They would agree that we are saved by grace through faith in Messiah Jesus. However, they would add that Jewish believers who want to fulfill their destiny as Messianic Jews must continue to be a part of the Jewish community, which means living a "Torah-observant" lifestyle, a lifestyle that can only really be lived out in the context of a community of Messianic Jews. I have heard of instances where, failing to find a Messianic congregation in the area, some Jewish believers have chosen to attend a synagogue rather than a church. This is a form of neo-Galatianism, pure and simple (Galatians 3:2-3).

There is nothing wrong with celebrating the biblical feasts or following certain rabbinical traditions, but we can do so only to the extent that we do not contradict the clear teaching of the Scriptures, both Old and New Testaments. And part of that New Testament teaching is that, in Messiah, we are fully free to practice these things or not as a matter of choice and conscience.

To declare rabbinical teachings and traditions obligatory in any way for the follower of Jesus, or to seek acceptance as Jews at the expense of our forthright identification with Christ, puts us on a slippery slope towards spiritual disaster. It has caused many people to separate from brothers and sisters in the Church, and eventually from Christ Himself.

The Messianic Jews of the first century faced similar temptations under more dire circumstances. They were subject to Roman prosecution for refusing to pay homage to Caesar. They had only to return to the synagogue to be granted immunity for not participating in this forced idolatry. However, they would only be accepted in the synagogue if they did not speak of their faith in Jesus.

The author of Hebrews admonished them: "Therefore Jesus also, that He might sanctify the people with His own blood, suffered outside the gate. Therefore let us go forth to Him, outside the camp, bearing His reproach" (Hebrews 13:12-13).

To bear the reproach of the Messiah is a badge of honor, not of shame. Are we willing to bear that reproach, even if it means going "outside the camp" of what the rabbis consider authentically Jewish?

Jesus is our rabbi as well as our Savior and Lord. He freely interacted with the teaching of the rabbis. Where He was in agreement with them, He said so. But when He was at odds with the rabbis, He clearly spoke out. The crowds recognized that Jesus taught with authority and not as the scribes (the rabbis) of the first century (Matthew 7:29). Shouldn't those of us who claim Jesus as our authority give Him the honor and obedience He so rightly deserves?

RESIST THE LURE OF ASSIMILATION
"Why don't you just call yourself a Christian?" I can't count the number of times I have been asked this "question," which often sounds more like an accusation.

When it comes from unbelieving Jewish people, I take it to mean, "If you want to believe in Jesus that is your business. But calling yourself a Jew makes it my business. Just call yourself a Christian so I can go on believing that Jesus is not for Jews and therefore not for me."

When Christians ask the question, it usually indicates a misunderstanding about our Jewish identity. Is it a matter of ethnic pride, and an effort to disassociate from the rest of the Body of Christ? Is it a desire to return to works salvation?

The easiest thing *would* be to "just call ourselves Christians," (identify *only* as Christians and forsake our Jewish identity). Many Jewish believers in Jesus have chosen to do just that. But the trend to assimilate, or to blend into the larger culture, is not unique to those Jewish believers. Many Jews who don't believe in Jesus have chosen to walk away from their Jewish identity, making assimilation a top concern among Jewish leaders worldwide.

Nevertheless, the lure to assimilate can be even more powerful for Jewish believers in Jesus. The Jewish community insists that it is deceptive for us to call ourselves Jews, and many in the Christian community appear confused or even hurt when we maintain our identity. Caught between the two, many Jewish believers in Jesus feel uncertain about how Jewishness and Jesus go together. Assimilation beckons with the promise to end the uncertainty and the accompanying angst.

I want to challenge Jewish believers to resist that lure. We need to remember that God still has a plan for the Jewish people. "God has not cast away His people whom He foreknew" (Romans 11:2a). The first and most compelling evidence of that ongoing plan is the presence of Jewish believers in Jesus: "Even so then, at this present time there is a remnant according to the election of grace" (Romans 11:5).

Identifying as a Jew is not a rejection of God's grace. Rather, that remnant of Jewish believers stands as a testimony to

God's grace. Moreover, there is no such thing as an invisible remnant or an undetectable testimony.

The Apostle Paul believed that his Jewish identity was evidence of God's gracious choice. Ethnic pride or a "middle wall of partition" had nothing to do with it, nor should it for us. None of us can claim any credit for having been born Jewish—we had no choice in the matter. God made us that way and the Scriptures teach us: "Let each one remain in the same calling in which he was called" (1 Corinthians 7:20).

Each individual must work out what that means and how they choose to remain a visible part of this remnant. For many, their Jewish identity will remain similar to what it was before they received Christ. That might mean a mostly cultural expression—with little felt need to express Jewishness through special observances. Other people prefer a more active approach to Jewish identity, such as Shabbat dinners, festival celebrations or participation in a Messianic fellowship or congregation. These choices are especially important when it comes to succeeding generations. However, by maintaining our Jewish identity in some form or other, we bear witness to the grace of God and His continuing purposes for the Jewish people.

PROCLAIM THE GOSPEL AND THE RETURN OF MESSIAH

Which brings me to this: Our calling as Jews is never more fulfilled than when we are proclaiming the good news of Messiah Jesus. My colleague Avi Snyder has pointed out that our people were created to proclaim. We were chosen to be a "light to the nations," and that is not a passive role.

Ultimately, God fulfilled His far-reaching intention through Israel's greater Son, the Messiah Jesus. Through His blood He purchased our salvation and the salvation of all who trust in Him. That is why Jewish believers in Jesus are never more fulfilled in our destiny than when we are fully engaged in proclaiming His Messiahship and His salvation. It is His light and His message that can give hope to a lost and dying world. Yet many Jewish believers when challenged to proclaim the gospel (especially to our fellow Jews), behave like Jonah when God called him to Nineveh—and there are many ships headed to Tarshish. What kind of giant fish will it take to turn us toward our true destiny?

It need not be a crisis—a renewed confidence in Messiah's return can also help us on our way. And that is my final point. We need to believe and actively proclaim that the coming of the Lord draws near.

The belief that Y'shua (Jesus) could return at any moment is not wishful thinking. It is our "blessed hope" (Titus 2:13). God intends that hope to compel us to holy, unashamed and unreserved gospel proclamation. The risen Lord of glory might step through the portals of heaven at any moment! This should be at the forefront of our minds and hearts, motivating us to be a light to the nations, now and until He comes again.

James, the leader of the Messianic movement in Jerusalem, admonished the remnant of Jewish believers under his care, "You also be patient. Establish your hearts, for the coming of the Lord is at hand" (James 5:8). The author of Hebrews encouraged those early Jewish believers to continue in active fellowship, ". . . exhorting one another, and so much the more as you see the Day approaching" (Hebrews 10:25). Along with this we must remember with confidence the promises of God concerning His future purpose for our "countrymen according to the flesh" (Romans 9:3).

I am persuaded that as Jewish believers bear witness to our faith among our own people, we are sowing seeds for a harvest that is yet to come. In the same way that those first century Messianic Jews set the pace for the rest of the Body of Christ, so we Jewish believers in Jesus today ought to be an example of faith and hope in the soon coming of our Lord.

We share a glorious destiny with our brothers and sisters in Christ from every tribe and tongue and nation. That destiny is most beautifully depicted in the architecture of the New Jerusalem, bearing the names of the 12 tribes of Israel on its gates and the 12 apostles on its foundations (Revelation 21:12,14). God's people will ultimately be joined together in Messiah for all time and eternity. What a glorious future we have. Let's embrace that future here and now.